MW01107300

Assignment

ROWDY ROOKSY

The

This book is a work of fiction. Names, characters, places, and incidents are either products of the author's imagination or are used fictitiously. Any resemblance to actual events, locales or persons, living or dead, is entirely coincidental.

© Rowdy Rooksy

*This book is dedicated to all the romance lovers out there.
To all those amazing bookish folks who support us Indie
Authors and help spread the word through Book Reviews
and all those amazingly artistic social media posts.
Thank You!!*

PLAYLIST

"Butterflies" - Micheal Jackson
"The Closer I Get To You" – Luther Vandross ft. Beyonce'
"Damage" – H.E.R.
"Unfold" – Alina Baraz & Galimatias
"Take You Down" – Chris Brown
"Put In Work" – Jaquees & Chris Brown
"Only Fan" – Kiana Lede' & Jacquees
"Comfortable" – H.E.R.
"Dream" – Queen Naija
"Don't Judge Me" – Chris Brown
"Do It" – Chloe x Halle
"A & B" - Jhene Aiko
"Blue Dream" – Jhene Aiko

CHAPTER ONE

NATHAN

Nathan Black frowned as he stared at his computer screen. He was on *TheRag.com,* one of the country's premier gossip sites. They were known for having the scoop on celebrity love lives and they particularly liked reporting on his.

Retired Soccer Star and Playboy Extraordinaire
Scores Again

That was the headline. Below it was a picture of him with his latest fling, underwear model Jazelle Banks, locked in a steamy kiss outside the W Hotel. Nathan had no idea how those photographers knew exactly where he'd be. Not that he really cared. He did what he wanted and made no apologies, but that didn't mean he wanted all his business in the streets as his Grandmother put it.

Nathan's cell phone buzzed but he didn't bother to look at it. He already knew who it was. Another scandalous headline meant a call from his cousin Jax who would give him plenty of shit about it.

Nathan hit ignore on his phone and stared back at his computer screen. He had to admit the photo was hot. He and Jazelle's bodies were pressed together intimately, he had one arm wrapped around her waist while his other hand had a fist full of her hair in a light tug as he tipped her head back and devoured her mouth.

A shiver of remembrance skidded through Nathan and he grinned. Jazelle Banks was a firecracker. They'd done all sorts of nasty things in that hotel room.

Nathan's cell phone sounded again this time indicating a new text message had come in. Nathan sighed and looked at it.

Jax: *Answer the phone jackass! We've got important business to discuss. I'm serious.*

His cell phone buzzed again. Another message from Jax.

Jax: *Yes, I saw the article but I'm not even trippin' on that. I won't even mention it. Answer the phone!*

Nathan just shook his head and set his cell phone back on his desk. His cousin was full of shit. The minute he answered Jax's call, dude was going to go full throttle fucking with him about today's headline.

No thanks, I'll pass, Nathan thought.

Just then the phone on his desk buzzed and he hit the speaker button. "Yes, Leanne."

"I have Jax on the line for you, sir."

"Tell him I'm busy."

There was a slight pause then, "Umm he said you would say that and to tell you that he knows you're... umm," Leanne paused nervously.

"He knows what, Leanne? Go ahead and say it," Nathan coaxed.

"He said he knows you're full of shit and that he's not hanging up until he gets you on the line," Leanne said, her voice quiet.

Nathan laughed and shook his head. "My cousin's an idiot, Leanne. I'm sorry you have to deal with his nonsense. Go ahead and put him through."

"Yes, sir," she said then the line went silent.

While he waited the few seconds for his cousin to come on the line, Nathan braced himself for the ribbing he was about to get.

"Goal!" Jax yelled into the phone as soon as he was patched through. "I see you scored again, cuz. Looks like you bagged a keeper this time."

"You're an idiot, man. You know that?"

"What?" Jax asked, feigning innocence.

"First of all, stop harassing my assistant and making her say crazy shit," Nathan said.

"Oh, come on. Leanne loves me and I wouldn't have to do that if you would answer my calls to your cell or respond to my text messages."

"I didn't answer because I'm busy," Nathan said.

"Yeah, right. Busy bangin' Jazelle Banks, who you forgot to mention that you were even seeing. Nathan, bro, Jazelle Banks is the hottest thing smokin' right now. How could you not tell me you were hittin' that?"

"Because it's not a big deal," Nathan replied smoothly.

"Not a big deal? Nathan, this is Jazelle Banks we're

talking about. Beautiful brown skin, full, pouty mouth, perfect tits, legs for days. This might be one you wanna keep."

"Eh," came Nathan's flippant reply but Jax was right, Jazelle was gorgeous and he loved fucking her. He liked the way she wrapped her long legs around his body when he took her against the wall and the way her lush lips wrapped around his dick when she took him in her mouth. Yes, they had great sexual chemistry but that's as far as it went. Outside of sex, they had nothing at all in common. Jazelle loved the gossip rags, wasn't much into sports and was a bit of a brat if she didn't get her way. Nathan on the other hand hated the tabloids, lived for sports and really liked a low-key sort of lifestyle. One that he thought he would surely have now that he was retired. Boy was he wrong. The tabloids followed his every move. Especially when it came to the women he dated. And he dated a lot of women. He just didn't understand the public's interest in his love life, scratch that, his sex life. Love had nothing to do with the women he dated. Nathan was a self-proclaimed bachelor and he planned to keep it that way. There were too many beautiful women in the world for him not to enjoy as many of them as he could. Although, he did try to keep his trysts on the low but somehow his exploits kept getting out.

"So just another conquest for the gossip rags, huh?" Jax smirked.

Nathan could hear the smile in his cousin's voice. He shook his head and chuckled. "Shut up, man. Why are you such a fool?"

"Me a fool? But you're always the one in the papers caught up with some woman," Jax replied.

"Bro, I have no idea how these photographers keep

finding out where I be at. Shit, I prefer to keep my sex life private but they won't let me live, man."

"Hey, that's what happens when you're the world's best soccer player who stays plastered on the cover of magazines. Everybody wants to know everything about you. Where you live, what you eat, how many times a day you shit, who you fuck..."

"I'm retired," Nathan cut him off.

"Yeah, for like two seconds. You just retired six months ago, Nate."

"So what! I'm still retired. Which means I'm out of the spotlight."

"Hardly," Jax laughed. "They're even more interested in what you're doing now that you have all this free time on your hands. And they're especially interested in who you're bangin'."

Nathan rolled his eyes. "Yeah, well I'll be glad when they all lose interest and I can quietly blend in with the rest of the common folk."

"That's never gonna happen, cuz. Retired or not you're still Nathan Black, multi-millionaire, two time MVP of the USA Men's Soccer Team, three times on the cover of *Sports Illustrated*, Calvin Klein underwear model and bagger of many bitches, like the beautiful Jazelle Banks. By the way, how is she in the sack?"

"G-code, man. G-code. You know I don't kiss and tell, Jax," Nathan said.

"I had to try," Jax said, his voice light, playful. "I mean c'mon, it's Jazelle Banks."

Nathan laughed. His cousin was a mess.

Jaxson Black aka Jax, his cousin and best friend, was always teasing him when it came to the ladies and all the wild tabloid headlines. Nathan never really paid him any mind seeing how Jax's reputation with the ladies was just as notorious as his, only Jax seemed to be able to keep his numerous exploits out of the papers. But not Nathan, he couldn't even say hello to a woman without some scandalous headline showing up about how he'd *scored* again. It was annoying and quite frankly Nathan was tired of the use of the word score in every headline. Yes, he was an athlete. Yes, he scored many goals but the play on the word was getting old. At least to him anyway.

"Now for the real reason I called," Jax said.

"Oh, so you weren't calling just to give me shit about the latest headline?" Nathan said, his voice dripping with sarcasm.

"That was one of the reasons but not the only one. I want to talk about your memoir."

"What about it?" Nathan asked, a hint of agitation lacing his voice.

His agent had pitched the idea of him doing a memoir a few months ago and Nathan hadn't been too keen on it especially with all the gossip and interest in his personal life but his agent thought it would be perfect. He claimed it would give the people a real glimpse into his life and who he really was. Then maybe the tabloids would back off a little with all the wild headlines but Nathan was skeptical and besides he wasn't a writer. In fact, he didn't have a creative bone in his body.

"Chris called me," Jax said.

"He called you?" Nathan fumed. The nerve of his agent calling his cousin behind his back.

"Yeah, he asked me to help out with the memoir. He thinks it's a really great next move and so do I, so I agreed to help," Jax said.

Nathan could picture the smug smile on his cousin's

face. "Well, I don't need your help because I'm not doing it."

"Nathan, don't be such a punk man. This memoir thing is a good idea. And don't give me that shit about you not being a writer. We're all clear on that which is why I found you the perfect ghost writer."

"You found me a what?" Nathan asked, his brow furrowing in confusion.

"A ghost writer. I found you the perfect ghost writer."

"What the fuck is a ghost writer?" Nathan asked.

Jax let out a hearty laugh then said, "A ghost writer is someone who writes the book for you-"

"Oh hell no! Someone else is going to write my story. No way! Fuck that! That's the same thing the tabloids do to me every week and half the time they get it wrong. Nah, no thanks."

"Calm down, Drama Queen. She won't just write whatever she wants. You'll work closely with her, tell her stories about your life, how you grew up and she'll put them into beautifully written words. Words that you'll get to approve."

"She?"

"Yeah, the person I have in mind is a woman," Jax said matter-of-factly. "Is that a problem?"

"Depends," Nathan responded.

"On what?"

"On how fine she is."

"I'm not sure why that matters, Nathan, but yes, Remington English is a beautiful woman."

"Then she can't be my ghost writer," Nathan said plainly.

"Why not?"

"Because you know me around beautiful women. I

like to fuck beautiful women. So, if you send her my way you know what's gonna happen."

"Oh, hell no, man. You cannot fuck Remington. She's a good girl. She's smart and funny and happens to be one of my most promising up and coming writers. She's perfect for this memoir but you cannot fuck her. I mean it, Nathan."

"Then you better not send her to me," Nathan said, then hung up the phone.

CHAPTER TWO

REMINGTON

Remington English checked herself out in the mirror for the fourth time. She looked cute and casual in a pair of black skinny jeans and a t-shirt. Her normally curly, jet black hair was blown straight, parted down the middle and hung like a silk curtain around her shoulders. She had applied a light coat of mascara and eyeliner to her light brown eyes making the tiny gold specs within noticeable and added some clear Mac lip gloss to her full lips. As far as Remington was concerned, she looked fine but still she tugged at the fitted black tee wondering if she should change into something more professional like a suit or maybe a nice blouse and skirt.

Remington didn't normally fret over what she wore to work. She was a writer after all and fashion was not really at the top of her agenda. She spent most of her time huddled over her pc reading, writing and doing research, so dressing to the nines on a daily basis was just not a thing. But today was different. Today was the first day of her new gig as ghost writer for retired soccer sensation, Nathan Black, and she was nervous as hell. Not only because this was her first official writing job but also because of who she would be working with.

Nathan Black was *the* most eligible bachelor in the city. Hell, probably the country. He was worth millions and had just retired from a very successful career as a soccer player and had recently started his own sports agency. The man was large and not to mention, sexy as hell.

Remington walked over to her desk and stared at the headline blasted across her computer screen.

Retired Soccer Star and Playboy Extraordinaire
Scores Again

She'd read that headline at least four times already today. So, for the fifth time, she stared at the picture of the man and woman below the caption. Nathan Black and Jazelle Banks. They were practically making love outside the W Hotel. The way their bodies were intertwined. The way Nathan fisted a handful of Jazelle's hair. The way he devoured her mouth and the way Jazelle's neck arched so her head fell back as she surrendered to Nathan's kiss. It was total possession and Remington could only imagine what it must be like to be possessed by Nathan Black. The feel of his hands caressing her body, the taste of his lips on her tongue. Remington's nipples beaded at the thought.

Remington's cell phone buzzed, playing the text-tone for her best friend, Natalie Gutiérrez. The familiar tone infiltrated her mind snapping her out of her fantasy. She turned away from the computer screen and picked up her cell phone and opened the message.

Natalie: *Morning doll! It's your big day!! I know you're super excited. I cannot believe that you're going to be working with Nathan Black! He's so...ugh...I can't even. Jealously party of one over here. lol! Anyway good luck. I know you'll do fantastic. P.S. feel free to give my number to Nathan. I'd love to be his next headline. Ha! Ha! Hit me up later. I want to know everything that happens today.*

Remington: *Thanks bestie! I needed the extra boost of confidence. I'm so nervous. And OMG! He's so hot. I can't believe that I'll be working with him either. And just maybe I'll slip him your number if you make me some of those bomb ass lemon drop cookies of yours. TTYL.*

Remington slipped her cell phone in her back pocket, took one more glance in the mirror then grabbed her bag and headed out the door.

It was a beautiful morning in Burbank, California. The sky was clear, the sun was high and there was a gentle breeze blowing. Remington made her way from the parking garage and into the fifteenth-floor building that housed the offices of N. Black Sports Agency. She was surprised to see Jaxson Black, owner of Black Publishing, where she interned for the last year, standing outside the building.

He waived as she approached. "Good Morning, Remington," Jax greeted her.

"Good Morning, Mr. Black. I didn't expect to see you here," Remington said with a smile.

"I figured I'd do formal introductions between you and my cousin since I'm the one who set this up and you've never met him."

"That's really nice of you," Remington said, shifting from one foot to the other.

"You nervous?" Jax asked, watching her closely.

Remington's stomach churned with anxiety and nerves but she stamped it down, lifted her chin and said, "Nope, I'm good."

Jax eyed her skeptically but didn't press the issue. "Let's go inside," he said then opened the door and allowed her to enter first.

Remington followed Jax to the security desk where she was given a badge and access card for the building.

"His offices are on the fifteenth floor," Jax said as they headed towards the elevator. The door slid open just as they walked up. "After you," Jax said, extending his arm out for Remington to step inside.

"Thanks," she smiled and stepped into the elevator.

Jax followed her inside and hit the button for the fifteenth floor. "Thanks again for agreeing to do this. I really appreciate it."

"Are you kidding? This is a dream job. I'm writing the memoir of one of *the* most prolific athletes of our generation and it's a paid gig so I'm the one who's appreciative. Thank you, Mr. Black, for thinking of me for this opportunity."

Jax smiled and nodded. Remington really was a sweet

and very talented young woman. In fact, she was the best writer amongst his latest crop of interns. He hoped he wasn't sending her into the viper's pit with his cousin.

The elevator dinged and Remington followed Jax out of the elevator car and into the main reception area of N. Black Sports Agency.

Remington was a bit overwhelmed with all of the activity going on. Young men and women in suits passed through the reception area with air pods hanging out of their ears as they negotiated deals with big brands, a young man passed by with a cart full of breakfast items to which people shouted out what they wanted, and the phone at the reception desk was ringing nonstop.

Remington followed Jax to the reception desk where a beautiful, young Asian woman with long dark hair framing a delicate heart shaped face was manning the phones. She had creamy porcelain skin and when she looked up and saw Jax her faintly rosy mouth split into a sensual smile. She quickly put whoever she was on the phone with on hold.

"Jaxson Black," she said, his name rolling easily off her tongue. "It's been a while."

The reception desk was one of those really tall counter style desks where the receptionist sat up high and could see everything and everyone but you couldn't see behind the desk.

Jax being as tall as he was folded his arms, leaned in and rested them on top of the desk. "I know," was all he said.

The woman's lips pursed into a playful pout. "You said you'd call. You never called."

"Things have been really busy at the publishing house and I've been tied up. But I'll make it up to you."

"You promise?" the young woman asked, her voice light and almost child-like.

"Now, you know I don't make promises but I will call you soon," Jax said and hit her with a devastating smile.

The woman giggled and a deep rose color flushed her porcelain cheeks.

Remington watched the exchange in awe. Here was this beautiful woman, who could probably have any man she wanted, getting all googly-eyed after Jaxson Black who obviously wasn't serious about her. He couldn't even commit to calling her. And it wasn't lost on Remington that Jax didn't even attempt to apologize for not calling her the first time.

Jaxson Black was a great boss and phenomenal publisher but he was clearly shit when it came to women.

"Ready to meet my cousin and your new employer?" Jax asked, turning his attention to Remington.

"Yep," Remington said, with a nod.

"This way," Jax said, holding his hand out to the side allowing Remington to pass in front of him.

"Bye, Jax," the beautiful young woman behind the reception desk called out.

Jax didn't even bother to turn around. He just threw his hand in the air and waved.

Remington shook her head in disbelief. One thing she would never be was one of those women who pined after a guy who couldn't even be bothered to turn around and say goodbye.

Remington walked stiffly next to Jax as they made their way down the hall.

He must have noticed the change in her demeanor because he eyed her curiously and asked, "You alright?"

"I'm fine," Remington lied, her reply short and stiff. It

really wasn't her business but she was low-key annoyed with Jax's dismissive attitude towards the receptionist.

Jax stopped walking and stared down at Remington who, at five foot six was not short by any means but Jax being six foot three towered over her. "I know what that looked like but I'm not a total dick. I promise you."

"It's really none of my business," Remington said.

"True, it's not, but since you witnessed that little exchange back there I have a feeling you're judging me right now."

Remington shook her head. "Nope, not judging you at all."

"Well in case you are, you should know that that woman back there just happens to be dating three other guys so she's really not all that sad about me not calling her."

Remington's eyes rounded in shock.

"See, I was right. You thought *I* was the jerk in that situation."

Remington's cheeks heated. "I'm sorry. It's just that guys usually are so…"

Jax laughed. "C'mon, English let's go," he said then continued walking down the hall.

Remington couldn't help but laugh. She knew better than to judge a situation without knowing all the facts.

Remington moved quickly down the hall and fell into step with Jax. They walked a few feet then turned left down a very long, very quiet hallway. There were no well-dressed men talking into air pods, no dessert cart boy and no offices aligning the hallway. But, at the far end of the hall was an opening that fed into an average sized reception area where a lone woman stood behind one of those new age ergonomically correct desks that rose up and down and allowed you to work standing up or sitting down.

The woman was standing as she clicked away on her keyboard. She looked up as they approached. Her grey eyes lit with recognition and she smiled. "Hello Jax. We were not expecting you this morning." She turned to Remington. "You must be Ms. English."

"Remington. Please call me, Remington."

"Alright, Remington. I'm Leanne Smith, Nathan Black's executive assistant. *You,* he's been expecting." she threw a side eye at Jax. "I'll let him know you're here as well."

"No need," Jax jumped in. "We'll announce ourselves," he said and walked towards the massive double doors behind Leanne's desk.

"Jax, wait," Leanne called after him but it was too late. He had already thrust the doors open.

"Cuz! What up?" Jax sang as he waltzed into the office.

"Somehow, I knew you'd show up today," Nathan grumbled. He had heard Jax outside the door and was leaning against the front of his desk waiting for him to make his grand entrance.

"I'm sorry, Mr. Black. He barged in before I could stop him." Leanne said, a worried look on her face.

"It's alright, Leanne. We both know my cousin is a Neanderthal."

Leanne smiled but her brow still held a few lines of worry as she looked at the men. "I'll just be at my desk," she said then quickly left.

"Why do you always do that to her?" Nathan asked.

"Do what? Leanne loves me," Jax said, laughing.

"Whatever. What are you doing here?" Nathan asked. His voice was level but held just the tiniest hint of annoyance.

Jax didn't seem to notice. "I thought I'd personally bring your new ghost writer over and do introductions. After all, I'm the one who recommended her."

"Well, where is she?" Nathan asked, his words gruff, cool.

"She's right here," Jax said, pointing over his shoulder.

Remington had hung back in the doorway and was standing directly behind Jax so during the cousin's entire exchange Nathan didn't even see her.

Jax stepped to the side opening a direct line between Remington and Nathan.

All of the breath, wind and whatever else kept her body functioning left Remington the moment she laid eyes on Nathan Black. He was leaning on the edge of his desk looking like a model straight out of *GQ Magazine* with his perfectly cut blue suite sans tie. The collar of his crisp white shirt was open revealing a hint of smooth, dark brown skin that Remington would love to see more of. He was tall, even leaning on the desk she could tell he was tall. About the same height as Jax probably. And God his body was perfection. Long, lean, and muscular. And that face - ruggedly handsome with the sexiest shadow of a beard, mesmerizing light brown eyes, and a generous mouth.

Nathan looked past Jax right at her and Remington almost creamed herself right then and there.

"Hello," Nathan said.

His voice sounded different now that he was speaking directly to her. It was deeper, velvet edged and was like luxuriating in a steamy hot, silky milk bath. For a second Remington lost all her senses and rational thought as she stood there staring at him.

"Is she mute?" she heard Nathan ask Jax.

Remington wasn't mute but she was definitely mortified. She needed a minute. A redo. She had to get out of there. "Bathroom," was the only thing she could think to say.

"Through there," Nathan said, pointing to a door over his shoulder.

"Thank you," Remington mumbled and nearly raced to the bathroom. "What was that?" she chastised herself as soon as she closed the bathroom door.

Remington pulled her cell phone out of her back pocket.

Remington: *Natalie! Girl! OMG! I literally just made the worst first impression in life.*

Natalie: *OMG! What happened?*

Remington: *Nathan Black said hello and I said bathroom.*

Natalie: *What?!?!*

Remington: *Yes!!!! I'm fucking mortified right now.*

Natalie: *Where are you?*

Remington: *IN THE BATHROOM*

Natalie: *OMG! NO! LOL! Girl, get yo shit together and get your ass back out there.*

Remington stared at herself in the mirror. "Great job, English," she reprimanded. "Nice first impression. Ugh!"

Her cell phone buzzed.

Natalie: *NOW ENGLISH!!!*

Remington: *ALRIGHT!! I'M GOING!*

Natalie: *Luv you, bitch! Text me later.*

CHAPTER THREE

NATHAN

Nathan watched through hooded eyes as Remington scurried to the bathroom. His cousin was right. The woman was fine, beautiful actually. And not in an over the top, social media, put a filter on everything sort of way. Her beauty was soft, natural. Her light brown skin had a glowy tint, her lips were full with a perfect cupid's bow and her brown eyes popped underneath heavily lashed lids. And that tight little body of hers didn't go unnoticed. Even in the simple jeans and t-shirt she wore, Nathan could tell she was hiding some killer curves. But, it really didn't matter how hot she was, he still wasn't on board with this memoir bullshit and he was not about to give Jax an inch regarding it.

Nathan looked pointedly at his cousin. "So, that's who you want to write my memoir?" He asked.

"That's her," Jax said, proudly.

Nathan stared at his cousin for a few seconds then shook his head. "She seems a little odd."

"What? No," Jax said, waving him off.

"Man, I said hello and she ran to the bathroom."

"I guess she had to pee," Jax said with a shrug.

"Whatever. Why are you really here, Jax?" Nathan asked, raising up from the desk and folding his arms across his chest.

"I told you, I came to make introductions. It's only right. I'm the one putting you two together after all," Jax smirked.

Nathan cocked his head at his cousin and frowned knowing full well that Jax was full of shit. He wasn't there to make introductions. He was there to make sure Nathan didn't act an ass and scare the woman off, which he had every intention of doing seeing how he didn't want to do this stupid memoir thing.

"Well, you can take your introductions and little miss skittish right back out the door. Is she even a good writer?"

"Good enough to get into the English program at Columbia and good enough to get an internship at your cousin's publishing house," Remington said from behind him. Her tone was cold as ice and she spaced each word evenly making sure he felt the sting of every one of them.

Shit. She wasn't supposed to hear that but fuck it. She did hear it and maybe it would be just the thing to get rid of her and dead this memoir bullshit before it even got started.

Nathan was about to say something smart-ass back to

Remington but Jax spoke before he could get it out.

"She's absolutely right, Nathan. She was top of her class at Columbia and she's the best writer of all my interns. I'm lucky to have her and you are too," Jax said with a smug smile.

Nathan's jaw clenched and the tiny pulse at his temple thundered. His cousin was on his last nerve.

"Now let me do what I came here for," Jax paused looking at Nathan then at Remington. "Remington English meet Nathan Black."

Nathan watched her as she stared at him. Those lovely whiskey eyes of hers were hard and her lips were pressed in a firm line. She was clearly not pleased with him but Nathan didn't give a rat's ass. "Hello... again," he said and hit her with a smirk that showcased the dimple in his right cheek.

"Hello," Remington replied, her voice cool, professional.

Despite the look of death she was giving him, she didn't seem too rattled. Nathan was slightly impressed by her resilience.

"Now was that so hard?" Jax asked, his tone playful.

Nathan rolled his eyes. "Don't you have somewhere to be?"

Jax looked down at his very expensive Rolex. "Shit, you're right. I gotta jet. I have a very important meeting in twenty minutes." He looked at Nathan. "Play nice," he said then turned to Remington and whispered, "Don't let him bully you."

Remington smiled and nodded.

"Later kids," Jax said then strode out the office.

Nathan stared at Remington. God, she was gorgeous and fuckable. Very, very fuckable. Perhaps that was the route he should go here. Seduce her, bed her and keep her so pre-occupied with sex that she wouldn't have time to write his little memoir.

Nathan shook his head and chuckled. Although it was an entertaining thought, Jax would kill him. And despite how much his cousin got on his nerves he was family and he'd never do anything that would fuck over his family.

"Care to let me in on the joke," Remington said, a suggestion of annoyance hovering in her eyes.

Since seduction was off the table, Nathan decided the only way to go was to be so over the top rude that'd she'd refuse to work with him.

"Nope," he said and crossed his arms over his massive chest causing the sleeves on his suit jacket to pull taut against his biceps. He watched as Remington's whiskey eyes lit with interest as she stared at his arms. Normally, this would be the moment he turned up the charm. All it ever took was a charming smile and some flirty quip and he had women eating out of his hands. And if the circumstances were different he'd have Remington English doing the same. But, his goal here was to be a world class ass so he hardened his eyes as he stared at her. "So, are you going to just stand there staring at me?" Nathan asked, his deep voice gruff.

A lovely flush covered Remington's pretty face making it glow a bit. Nathan bit his lip as he stared at her. *Damn, she's beautiful,* he thought. He could only imagine how she'd looked all flush and naked writhing beneath him.

Remington cleared her throat. "Right, we should get started."

Nathan quickly shed thoughts of Remington sprawled naked beneath him and slipped into his bad guy demeanor. "Sit," he said, pointing to the chair in front of his desk.

If looks could kill Nathan would be dead. Remington glared at him with burning reproachful eyes but she said nothing. He knew she wanted to, but she didn't. Instead, she quietly sat down in the seat in front of him.

"So, how do we do this memoir thing?" Nathan asked, sitting down behind his desk knowing full well that he couldn't care less about understanding the process.

"Well," Remington began but Nathan quickly tuned her out and grabbed one of the folders on his desk, opened it and started reading the documents inside. It was a profile on D'Mariyon Taylor, superstar running back for Texas A&M. The kid was the top ranked running back in the country. He was a senior and was being heavily scouted by numerous NFL teams. Every sports agency in the country wanted to sign this kid, including him. Nathan needed to get a meeting with him ASAP.

Nathan thumbed through the file. There was a highlighted note in his profile about losing his mother at an early age and being raised by his grandmother. Nathan could totally relate seeing how he also lost his mother at an early age and was raised by his own grandmother.

Nathan tapped the paper. This was his in. He reached over and pressed the speed dial button for Leanne.

"How can I help you, Mr. Black?" Leanne asked.

"Get me Thompson on the phone."

"Now?" Leanne asked.

"Yes, now. Why would you ask me that?"

There was silence and then, "Umm, aren't you still meeting with Ms. English?"

Nathan frowned and looked up to find Remington shooting daggers at him, her eyes black with rage. He'd completely forgot she was there. "Right... Just give him a call and see if he's good to meet me at Jake's Bar in an hour. I need some info on a kid I'm trying to sign and I need him to jump on it immediately."

"Yes, sir," Leanne said, then hung up.

Nathan closed the folder and set it on his desk. He leaned back and looked at Remington. She was passed pissed. He could see it all over her pretty face. That lush mouth of hers was set in a hard line and her eyes were resentful.

"I'm sorry, what were you saying?" Nathan asked, amusement playing at the corners of his eyes.

Remington was anything but amused. "Oh, do I have your attention now?" She fumed.

Nathan grinned. She was cute when she was mad. "Sure," he replied.

"Good," she said then reached into her bag and pulled out a notebook and pen. "I was thinking the best way to go about this is for me to first understand why you want to do this memoir."

"I don't," Nathan said plainly.

Remington's brows lifted in shock. "You don't?"

"Nope. This was my agent's idea."

"Then why are you doing it?"

"Because my agent thinks it's a good idea and he schemed with my backstabbing cousin and now you're here."

Remington bit down hard on her lower lip and Nathan guessed she was trying really hard to keep her cool. He decided to goad her even more.

"Look, lady, I know my cousin hired you to write this memoir but it ain't happenin'. I don't want my private life out there for everybody to read about and make judgements. My private life is for me and me alone."

"Really?" She spat back. Her brown eyes growing darker and insolent as she stared at him.

"Yes, really," Nathan ground the words out between clenched teeth. She was bating him and he didn't like it.

"Well, today's article on The Rag would say otherwise. In fact, if I recall, your *private life*," she said making air quotes with her fingers, "has made the home page of The Rag's website at least once a week. And let's not mention how many times you've been in the gossip magazines," she finished with a smug smile.

Nathan's jaw clinched and his eyes narrowed. Even through his aggravation he noticed the perfect cupid's bow in her top lip. He inwardly cursed himself. *Really? You're focusing on her mouth? Get your head in the game, Nathan. You're supposed to be scaring her off.*

Nathan squared his shoulders and turned up his jerk meter. "It's no wonder that this if your first paid gig seeing how unprofessional you are. Spouting nonsense they put in gossip rags," he spat. "I should call my cousin and tell him to fire you. I mean he sent me an intern for God's sake."

Nathan watched as her mouth thinned into a hard line and her chin gave the slightest quiver. A soft mist clouded her eyes and he knew she was on the verge of crying.

Oh, hell. He wasn't trying to make the woman cry. Maybe he took his little rant too far. "Remington," he said, his voice softening.

"I should go," she said, shoving her notepad and pen back into her bag.

Yes! Looks like this thing is officially over. "If you think that's best."

"I do. We didn't get off to the best start today. We should try again tomorrow. Have a do-over."

Nathan was floored. He did not expect her to say that. He was hoping she'd hightail it out there and never return. She was a tough one. He'd give her that.

"Does nine o'clock work for you?" she continued.

"Uh...I guess," Nathan replied, staring at her in disbelief.

"Fine, I'll see you tomorrow at nine," Remington said and nearly ran out of his office.

Nathan stared curiously after her as she disappeared out the door. He was half confused and half impressed. He had really laid on the asshole bit pretty thick yet she was coming back tomorrow. He didn't get it.

A light tap on his door pulled Nathan out of his thoughts. "Come in," he called.

The door opened and Leanne peeked her head inside. "Is everything all right, Mr. Black?" she asked, a concerned looked on her face.

"Yes, why do you ask?"

"Well...Remington looked upset. She practically ran out of here."

Nathan frowned. "Everything's fine, Leanne. Did you get Thompson on the phone?" He asked, trying to change the subject.

"Yes, sir, I did. He'll meet you at Jake's this afternoon at two. That's the soonest he could meet."

"That's fine," Nathan said and opened the folder on his desk and pulled out the papers inside.

Leanne was still standing in the doorway, her eyes radiating sympathy as she looked at him.

Nathan sighed. His executive assistant was like a mother hen. Most of the time he didn't mind it. She always meant well. He just wasn't in the mood right now. "Is there anything else?"

"No, sir," came her quiet response.

"Thank you, Leanne," Nathan said, dismissing her and went back to staring at the papers on his desk.

Nathan knew she was gone when he heard the quiet click of his office door closing.

CHAPTER FOUR

REMINGTON

Remington finally understood what it meant to see red. Her vision was blurred and literally hazed in crimson. "I'm not gonna cry," she repeated over and over as she made her way to her car. She'd dealt with difficult people before but nobody had ever treated her as rudely as Nathan Black had. The man was an ass with a capital A. And to make matters worse she'd allowed him to push her buttons so far that she acted completely out of character.

Remington prided herself on her professionalism so to lose control like she did and take jabs at Nathan's personal life was not like her at all and she was utterly disappointed in her behavior.

"Dammit," she cursed as she yanked open the door

to her vintage Volvo P1800S Coupe. She pulled out her cell phone and texted Natalie as soon as she got into the driver's seat.

Remington: *Nathan Black is the biggest asshole I've ever had the displeasure of meeting and I'm pretty sure I lost this writing gig which sucks because it was a really great opportunity for me get exposure and kick off my writing career.*

Natalie: *???*

Remington: *I lost my shit and read him for filth about his sexual escapades in the tabloids.*

Natalie: *No way! Why? What exactly happened?*

Remington: *Long story short, he's rude and condescending and is just an ass.*

Natalie: *How is that even possible? He has women falling all over him. He can't be that bad.*

Remington: *IDK. Maybe he's so busy using his mouth to pleasure the many women he screws that he never actually talks to them and they don't get to see how big a jerk he is.*

Natalie: *WOW! He really pissed you off. That's shitty. He's too pretty to be such a jerk.*

Remington: *Let's just say that Nathan Black's personality doesn't match the pretty package it's wrapped in.*

Natalie: *Sorry things didn't go as planned. Where are you right now?*

Remington: *In my car.*

Natalie: *In your car? Where's Nathan?*

Remington: *Who cares!!! I ended our meeting early. I*

couldn't stand to be in the same room with that man another minute. I'm going home. I'll try again tomorrow.

Natalie: *You know I'm here if you need me.*

Remington: *I know. Luv u!*

Remington closed her eyes and inhaled deeply. She held the air in her lungs for a few seconds then slowly let it pass through her lips. It was a new day and she was mentally preparing for her meeting with Nathan. She was determined not to let him get under her skin today.

After the disastrous first meeting yesterday she had gone home, took a long, hot bath and went to bed early. Not that she got much sleep. To her dismay, Nathan invaded her dreams the minute she closed her eyes. His handsome face. That sexy ass dimple. That hard body. It was like watching a one man freak show every time she closed her eyes.

Remington took one more deep inhale, let it out then opened her eyes. She pulled down the sun visor and flipped open the mirror staring pointedly at herself and making a silent commitment not to let Nathan Black ruffle her feathers today.

"You got this," she said, then grabbed her bag out of the passenger seat and headed for round two with the overwhelmingly sexy and utterly frustrating, Nathan Black.

The lobby at N. Black Sports Agency was just as busy today as it was yesterday. Remington gave a quick wave to the pretty receptionist that was swooning over Jax yesterday and made her way to the elevator. She was shocked to find Nathan standing in the elevator car as the doors slid open.

"Hello, Ms. English," he grinned, stepping out of the elevator.

Remington willed her pulse to stop racing. The man was even more gorgeous today than he was yesterday, if possible. He was wearing another dark suit, no tie; that hung perfectly off his athletic frame. That damn dimple in his right cheek appeared as he smiled, adding a devilish charm to his face. Remington felt a tight knot in the pit of her belly which annoyed her to no end seeing how she was still pissed at him.

"I was just on my way up to see you," she managed to get out.

"We'll, I'm on my way out," Nathan said, moving past her.

He smelled of bergamot, patchouli and vanilla. Remington almost swooned at the delicious combination. The knot in her stomach unfurled and turned into skittish butterflies and her breast peaked.

Nathan Black, without even touching her, aroused her more than any of her past boyfriends ever had. This was *no bueno*.

"We have a meeting this morning," Remington said, casting an accusatory look at him.

Nathan stopped and turned to face her. "Do we?"

Remington pursed her lips and fixed her gazed on him. She studied his chiseled face which was masked in feigned innocence. He knew good and well that they were supposed to meet this morning. He was deliberately goading her.

"Yes, we do. But you knew that, Nathan," Remington said, bracing her hands on her hips and giving him her best, *don't even try it,* look.

Nathan's eyes narrowed as he stared down at her, his pupils darkening as he assessed her.

His look was so intense that for a second Remington wanted to back away but she held her ground, locking eyes with him.

Why did she do that? The moment her brown eyes connected with his dark, indigent ones, she lost herself. And for one endless, excruciating, pulsing moment, they stared at each other, connected by a force as powerful as it was invisible. Looking into his unfathomable eyes, Remington felt a succession of emotions—curiosity, lust and something darker. Her cheeks flamed with enough wattage to light up Atlantic City.

Nathan took a step forward, closing the distance between them. His eyes held hers for a few moments. "You're welcome to come," he offered.

Remington swallowed the dry lump in her throat. Was she imagining things? His invitation for her to tag along sounded more like him sweet talking her thighs open and coaxing her to ecstasy which was crazy because he was Nathan Black. He could have any woman he wanted for one and for two, he didn't seem to care for her all that much. Still, tremors went through her body sending her into a tailspin and she lowered her lids against his gaze.

This cannot happen. She cannot get pulled in by the dazzle of Nathan Black. NO. NO. NO.

Remember how he treated you yesterday? She reminded herself. *Nathan Black is an arrogant ass-bag. Focus, Remington.*

Remington took a step back removing herself from the magnetic aura Nathan had surrounded her in. She closed her eyes and took a beat before speaking. "Where are you going exactly?" She asked surprised at how normal and controlled her voice sounded.

Amusement danced in Nathan's eyes. "Are you okay?" He asked.

"I'm fine," Remington replied, trying her best to keep her cursed hormones in check. This man would be the end of her. She had two emotions around him. Rage and lust. Neither of which were good. "I've decided to tag along with you. Now, where are we going?"

"To meet with a potential client."

Okay, this was good. She'd get to see him in action in his new role as sports agency owner. It would be good for the memoir and with this potential client being there, there would be a buffer between the two of them. Perfect.

"Okay, it will actually be really good to observe you working. It'll give me an idea of what type of business man you are."

"Fine, let's go," Nathan said, then turned and strode towards the exit.

Remington followed behind him trying her best not to stare at his perfectly round and firm ass.

A black sedan was waiting at the curb when they exited the building. The driver, dressed in all black, greeted them and held the back door open.

"After you," Nathan said, motioning for Remington to get into the car first.

She moved past him, making a conscious effort not to touch him but it didn't matter; she didn't have to touch him. His scent surrounded her, clouding her mind as she climbed into the car. She scooted as far to the other side of the backseat as possible.

Nathan climbed in after her, settling against the seat and looking completely in control and at ease which annoyed her.

Neither of them spoke as the driver pulled away from the curb and into traffic.

Remington fixed her gaze out the window, attempting to focus on something other than how close Nathan was to her. Or, how his arousing scent was wreaking havoc on her mind and body. Being irritated and aroused at the same time by this man was really confusing. No guy had ever elicited such emotions in her. Just thinking about it confused her all the more so she decided to focus her attention on the scenery out the window.

The city of Burbank, aka "The Media Capital of the World" whizzed by as they drove. Remington smiled. She loved her city. Being on the outskirts of Tinseltown, it had that suburban feel but with all the glitz and glamour of Hollywood and the exciting thrill of Disneyland.

The car hit Victory Boulevard and Remington frowned. It looked as if they were headed to the Burbank Airport.

"Where exactly is this meeting of yours?" Remington asked, casting a sidelong glance at Nathan.

"Texas," Nathan said, not bothering to look at her.

"Texas!" Remington shrieked. "Your meeting is in Texas?"

"Yep," he said, with a slight nod.

Remington shifted in her seat, turning to face Nathan. "And you didn't think you should mention that your meeting was in another state when you invited me to tag along."

Nathan turned his head, finally looking at her. His expression bored. "You didn't ask."

"Really? You've got to be kidding me. You don't ask a person to come along to a meeting that's out of the state without letting them know that it's out of the state."

"People normally ask questions before hopping into cars with strangers. And we are strangers," Nathan said, leveling his gaze at her.

Fire flashed in Remington's eyes as she looked at Nathan who was staring at her with all the smugness of a professional soccer player who just scored a goal.

"I didn't think we'd be leaving the state," she said through gritted teeth.

"Well, we are," Nathan countered then fixed his attention forward again.

Remington was livid. Nathan had tricked her. Deliberately. He knew very well that his meeting was in Texas and he could have told her so. Instead, he goaded her into going with him knowing she was just stubborn enough to take him up on his offer to come along.

The car pulled into the entrance of the airport and drove past the Departures sign, taking the road around the back to where the private planes were located.

Remington's brow lifted in awe as the car drove on the private jet way and stopped near a Falcon 50Ex Jet.

The pilot, tall and handsome stood next to the flight attendant who was just as tall. Not only that, she was blonde and curvy to boot.

The driver opened the car door for Remington who got out and stood awkwardly next to the car.

Nathan got out and made his way over to the pilot. The two men shook hands and exchanged a few words before Nathan turned and looked in her direction.

"You still coming?" He asked, amusement playing at the corners of his eyes.

Annoyed, Remington narrowed her gaze at him. He was really getting a kick out of this. What she'd really like to do was give him the finger and storm off but she had a feeling that would only play into his little game. Instead, she straightened her shoulders and made her way over to the trio.

Nathan held her gaze for a few seconds, his eyes penetrating as if he was trying to figure out what was going on in her head.

Remington kept her regard neutral, giving him nothing.

Nathan's mouth tipped at the corners and he gave her a slight nod as if to acknowledge her stubbornness.

"Remington English, this is Captain Matthew Helm, our pilot, and this is Amber Farrow, our flight attendant."

"Pleasure to meet you," Captain Matthew said, tipping his pilot hat at her.

"It's very nice to meet you," Remington said with a smile. She looked over at Amber. "Hello."

Amber smiled sweetly at her. "Hello, Ms. English. I'm happy to serve you on this flight to Texas. If there's anything I can do to make your flight more enjoyable, just let me know."

Remington smiled appreciatively at Amber. "Thank you."

"Shall we go?" Nathan said, looking at the Captain.

"Let's do it," Captain Matthew said, opening his arm and inviting Nathan and Remington to board the plane.

"After you," Nathan said, tilting his chin toward the small flight of stairs leading to the entrance of the plane.

Remington climbed the stairs tentatively, glancing over her shoulder at Nathan who was right behind her. Why was he so close? She was already having the damnedest time keeping her hormones in check around him. Eager for some distance, she jogged the rest of the way up the stairs and disappeared inside the plane.

Remington's eyes bugged out as soon as she stepped inside. The interior of the plane was spacious and luxurious with large, plush leather seats.

Remington took a seat in the middle of the plane and to her dismay, Nathan took the seat across from her. There was a small table situated between them but she could still smell him and feel his heat.

Captain Matthew's voice floated over the loudspeaker, "Welcome aboard! Buckle up and settle in for this four hour, forty-five minute flight to College Station, Texas. We're working with clear skies and high visibility today so it should be smooth sailing all the way there."

A five hour flight? Remington was not prepared for this. She was going to be stuck on a plane with Nathan Black for five hours. A lot could happen in that amount of time. They could quite literally kill each other or even worse they could end up in the back of the plane with her on her back and Nathan planted firmly between her thighs. She'd read a few stories about some salacious things that went down on private planes. Images of her and Nathan doing all kinds of dirty things flashed across her mind. Remington's body warmed and her cheeks flushed.

"You good?" Nathan asked, studying her.

Remington brushed her fingertips along the back of her neck. "I'm fine. It's just a little warm in here," she lied.

Nathan's dark eyes smoldered as he perused her face, his eyes roaming over her cheeks, down to her mouth where they lingered, then back up to her eyes where they settled. And then it was there again—that connection that showed itself earlier. Remington's heart thundered in her chest.

They stared at each other for several seconds before Nathan spoke, breaking the connection.

"I'll have Amber turn up the air," he said, his voice low.

"No, it's okay. I'm good," Remington replied, looking away. She focused her attention out the window where the ground crew were doing whatever it was a ground crew did before takeoff.

They were in the air cruising at an altitude of 35,000 feet in no time.

Amber appeared from the rear of the plane. "Can I get you two anything to eat or drink?" She asked.

"I'll have a ginger ale," Remington said.

"Whisky on ice," Nathan said.

Remington narrowed her gaze at him. It was barely 10a.m. and the man was already drinking.

"It's for my nerves," Nathan explained. "I never did get used to flying."

"You don't have to explain to me. It's none of my business," Remington shrugged.

"But isn't it? You are writing my memoir and the last thing I want you doing is painting a narrative that I'm some kind of alcoholic."

"I wouldn't do that." Offense to his words played clearly on Remington's face.

"Why not?" Nathan asked, the intensity in his dark gaze going up a notch.

"Because alcoholism is a sickness, a disease. And, I would never exploit that," Remington replied, her tone dead serious. She tilted her chin and stared back at Nathan with as much intensity as he was staring at her. She could swear she saw a hint of approval in those dark eyes of his.

"How old are you, Remington?" Nathan asked.

"Twenty-five. How old are you?"

Nathan chuckled, unleashing that damn dimple on her again. "I'm thirty-five."

"You're still really young," Remington commented.

Nathan was still in his prime and extremely physically fit. The entire world had been shocked when he retired at the height of his soccer career and he never explained why he did it.

Nathan chuckled. "Yeah..."

"Can I ask you something?"

"That depends," Nathan said, leveling his gaze at her.

"On what?"

"Is this on the record or off the record?" He asked.

"I'm writing your memoir. Everything is on the record."

The look he gave Remington was loaded with annoyance and fire. "This is why I don't talk to the press," Nathan said, his voice quiet.

"I'm not the press. I'm a writer, yes, but not some tabloid reporter writing for The Rag. What I write for your memoir will be the truth," Remington countered.

"Fine. Ask your question," Nathan sighed.

"Why did you retire?"

"It was time," Nathan said simply.

"That's it?" Remington asked not believing that a man at the height of his career would just quit because "it was time."

Nathan shrugged. "I accomplished everything I wanted to and more. Why keep going? I was at the top of my game which meant the only way for me was down and there's nothing the press or the public loves more than watching a man fall."

Remington considered him for a moment. Nathan Black was a confident man. Anyone could see that. He was used to being the best and clearly wanted people to only see him that way. It was understandable. And he was right. For some reason, people liked to watch other people fall. They reveled in it, really. Especially in this day and age of insta-famous and going viral.

"Is that the only reason?" Remington asked.

"Do I need any other?" Nathan asked, lifting his brow.

"I don't know. It's just that I didn't peg you as someone who cares what people think."

Nathan leaned forward in his seat. "Don't we all in some form or fashion?"

"I guess. It's just that you're a little difficult to read. The media is always posting about you and your love life. Doesn't that bother you?"

"It doesn't bother me, per se. Most of that shit they print is not the full truth anyway."

Remington didn't miss the hard edge in his voice when he spoke. He may not let it bother him but he clearly didn't like it.

Amber appeared with their drinks, sitting Remington's ginger ale on the table then handing Nathan's whiskey to him.

Remington watched as Nathan lifted his glass and took a sip. His full lips curling over the edge of the glass did something to her. She was doing everything she could to stamp down the lust that Nathan Black incited in her but there was clearly an attraction there . Hell, the man was insanely gorgeous. Who wouldn't be attracted to him? But this brewing attraction annoyed her on so many levels. Not only because as his ghost writer, she needed to remain professional but also because he took every opportunity to get under her skin. Nonetheless, her body warmed and her belly tingled as she watched him sip on his drink.

The remainder of the flight was taken in silence. Nathan finished his whiskey then rested his head against the back of his seat and closed his eyes while Remington pulled out her notebook and jotted down a few notes from the brief conversation they had.

It was clear that Nathan wasn't going to cooperate and allow her to question him about his life in the traditional way she had planned on going about this memoir so she would have to employ a different strategy. She would be casual about it. Tag along with him to meetings and events and observe him, ask questions here and there and hopefully he'll start to let his guard down and she could get this memoir done quickly and be done with Nathan Black for good.

The plane landed with a gentle thud as they touched down in College Station. Another black sedan with tinted windows waited for them on the tarmac.

"So, who exactly are we going to see?" Remington asked as they got in the car.

"D'Mariyon Taylor, running back for Texas A&M. He's the most sought after running back out right now. The kid's definitely going one or two in the draft."

"And you want to sign him to your agency?" Remington asked.

Nathan nodded. "It would be a huge win for us."

"And a lot of money," Remington added.

Nathan shot her a look. "It's not about the money."

"It's not?"

"No, it's not," Nathan replied.

Remington could hear the agitation in his voice. She wasn't trying to offend him with her comment. She knew very little about sports agencies except that they represent highly paid athletes who brought a lot of revenue to the company.

"I didn't mean to offend you, Nathan. I'm not all that familiar with how sports agencies work. I only know what they report about on television and on the internet," Remington said.

"Don't worry about it," Nathan snapped, then turned to stare out the window.

"I've clearly offended you. I'm sorry," Remington offered.

Nathan didn't say anything. He just kept looking out the window.

They rode in silence the short distance from the airport to the college campus. The car dropped them off at coffee shop right outside of A&M's campus.

Remington knew who they were meeting as soon as they walked into the coffee shop. Sitting in the far back corner was a good looking young man with dark brown skin, a perfectly angular jaw and even though he was sitting down, Remington could tell he was a little taller than average and was all muscle and strength. He had his head down studying a playbook when Remington and Nathan approached.

"D'Mariyon! What up man?" Nathan called, his arms outstretched as they approached the table.

The young man looked up, a charming grin on his boyishly handsome face. He stood up. "What's up, Nathan?

Looking good," he said and the two men dapped each other up.

"Thanks, man. I gotta keep my workouts up now that I'm not running up and down a soccer field everyday anymore."

"I hear that," D'Mariyon grinned.

"This is Remington English," Nathan said, looking over at Remington.

"Hello," Remington said, extending her hand to D'Mariyon.

The grin on the young man's face widened as he stared at her. He did that whole lip bite, hand rubbing thing young men do when they see something they like.

"Damn, youngin'! You just gonna stand there drooling or shake the woman's hand?" Nathan said with a chuckle.

"Aw c'mon, man. Don't do me." D'Mariyon dropped his head in mock shame.

"It's cool. I'm very flattered," Remington laughed. "It's good to meet you, D'Mariyon."

"Thanks. "Nice to meet you as well. You guys want something to eat or drink?" D'Mariyon asked looking from Remington to Nathan.

"I could eat a donut or croissant," Remington said, eyeing the glass case by the register that housed an assortment of pastries.

"Cool. You want anything, Nathan?" D'Mariyon asked.

"Just a coffee, black," Nathan said.

"Why don't I grab some pastries and the coffee and you two have a seat and start your meeting," Remington offered, already making her way over to the counter.

By the time Remington returned with two coffees and a plate full of pastries, Nathan and D'Mariyon were deep in conversation.

"It's a lot to think about, D'Mariyon. I was a top athlete in college, highly recruited so I know how it is. Everybody's coming at you from all angles. It can give you a big head and that's cool for a while but you need to be smart about the decisions you make," Nathan said.

"I hear you, man. The shit is crazy. I got agents offering me crazy ridiculous things. I'm talking cars, houses, and women. It's nuts, man," D'Mariyon said, shaking his head.

Nathan nodded. "I know what that's like. It's all glitz and glamour to reel you in. But all that's bullshit. What is it that you really want out of this? What's important to you?"

D'Mariyon's dark brown eyes went glossy as he leaned forward, placing his elbows on the table. "Taking care of my granny. That's what's important to me. She raised me, you know? All I wanna do is pay her back by making sure she's straight."

"I feel that," Nathan said. "I was raised by my grandmother too."

"Oh word," D'Mariyon said, a new look of respect for Nathan framing his face.

"Yeah. My parents died in an accident when I was very young and my grandmother took me in and raised me. She's a special lady. Kept me in line growing up. Made sure I had everything I needed. So I get it. This need you have to take care of your granny."

"Yeah, she's the most important person in the world to me, man."

Remington was touched by the exchange between Nathan and D'Mariyon. And hearing Nathan speak so fondly about his grandmother hit her right in the heart. There was clearly more to the man than scoring goals and bedding women.

Remington set the tray of drinks and goodies on the table. "Here we are, fellas," she said as she slid into the seat next to Nathan.

Remington regretted her seat choice as soon as she sat down. She could feel the heat of Nathan's body and the overwhelming scent of his cologne tickle her nose. She grabbed her coffee and inhaled trying to rid her nostrils of Nathan's dizzying scent. It worked. Sort of. It took care of the smell but there was nothing the coffee could do about the butterflies dancing in her belly from being near him.

"Thanks," Nathan said, casting her a sideways glance before grabbing one of the coffee cups.

"Yeah, thanks Remington," D'Mariyon added, grabbing one of the pastries. He took a huge bite then focused his attention on her. "So, who are you to Nathan?"

Remington started. She didn't expect that question. "Well, I'm a writer and I'm working on Nathan's memoir."

"Oh, shit! That's what's up. See, that's major league status right there. That's how I want my shit to go." He looked at Nathan. "Have a bang-up career, make lots of bread, retire at the top of my game then have a sexy ass writer help me write my memoir."

Remington blushed.

Nathan let out a quiet chuckle. "I can help you do that, D'Mariyon. You focus on your game and I'll focus on the other stuff. I have a lot of connects in the sports industry and the advertising world. I can get you a lot of endorsements. Make you a lot of money so you can take care of your granny the way you want to. Not only that, my cousin owns a publishing house so when you retire, I'll get him to hook you up with a writer for your memoir."

"That sounds good, man. I'm seriously considering going with your agency but can you get me signed to the Cowboys?"

"The Cowboys?" Nathan asked, leaning back in his chair.

"Yep. Granny wants to stay in Texas and I want her to live with me when I go to the league. It'll be a win-win for both of us."

"I know a few folks in the Cowboy's organization," Nathan said.

"Well, I'mma be honest. Whoever can secure that deal has the best chance of signing me," D'Mariyon said then popped the other half of his pastry in his mouth.

"I remember when I was in your shoes. Trying to decide which agency to sign with and what team I wanted to be on. There was a lot to consider but the main thing was making sure I took a deal that my Grandmother would be proud of," Nathan said.

D'Mariyon stopped chewing and cocked his brow. "Really?"

"Yeah, man. My grandmother's opinion was super important to me. It still is."

"I hear that. My granny's had my back since day one. Her opinion is really the only one that matters. She's all the family I got," D'Mariyon said, a whimsical smile on his face.

"She sounds like an amazing woman. I'll have to meet her," Nathan said.

"If you're trying to sign me, you'll definitely meet her," D'Mariyon smirked. "She gets the final say on who I sign with."

"Understood," Nathan said, lifting his coffee cup in salute.

Remington sat quietly watching the two guys. She admired D'Mariyon's unabashed love and respect for his grandmother. The kid was set on his desire to stay in Texas for her and from the determined set of Nathan's brow he seemed to already be thinking about how to make that happen.

Remington fixed her gazed on Nathan. He was a natural at this sports agent thing. He was completely at ease talking with D'Mariyon and the interest he took in the young man's grandmother was touching. It really wasn't all about the money for him. He seemed to really want what was best for the boy. No wonder he got touchy when she mentioned money. The man sitting here at the table was nothing like the ass who dissed her writing skills and completely ignored her during their first meeting. The man sitting here was considerate and cared about doing the right thing.

Remington could feel a sense of admiration bubbling in her chest which unnerved her. She was already trying to fight this growing attraction for Nathan which was hard enough seeing how hot he was. At this point, the only thing keeping her lust at bay was the fact that he could be a real dick to her at times. That and the fact that she needed this memoir to happen. It was a first step in establishing her career as a writer. She had to remain professional. She couldn't afford to be a notch on Nathan Black's belt. She knew that. But, seeing this softer side of him made her want to throw caution to the wind. It made her want to know the feel of his hands on her body, the pressure of his lips against hers, and the heavy length of his manhood between her thighs.

Remington shot up from the table, causing it to wobble a little.

Nathan and D'Mariyon looked over at her.

"You good?" D'Mariyon asked, the space between his brow puckering.

"Ummm, yeah. I'm fine. I just have to use the ladies room. Excuse me," Remington said and hurried away from the table. Away from Nathan.

CHAPTER FIVE

NATHAN

Nathan traced his finger across his bottom lip as he stared out the small window of his private plane. They were headed back to California and he was running through his mental rolodex ticking off the names of his contacts at the Dallas Cowboys organization. Two of his boys from college were actually coaches. He would reach out to them as soon as he got back home.

The meeting with D'Mariyon went really well but the young man was clear that not securing him a spot on a team in Texas, namely the Cowboys, and failing to impress his grandmother were deal breakers.

Impressing the grandmother would be a piece of cake for Nathan. He would handle her the way he handled his own grandmother - respectfully, genuinely and with care. He would make her see that he had nothing but the best intentions for her grandson. Not only for his football career but personally as well. She'd want to know that whoever he signed with would look out for his well-being and that the relationship wouldn't be all about money.

Nathan reached for his cell phone sitting on the small table in front of him but stopped short. He could feel the burning heat of Remington's gaze on him and he looked up to find her soft, whiskey eyes locked on him.

Nathan studied her face for a moment. Could it be possible that she was becoming more beautiful everytime he looked at her? He was doing his best to be as standoffish and inconsiderate as possible, all to dead this memoir, but he wasn't sure how much longer he could keep it up. Especially when she looked at him like that. There was a dark, hot intensity to her gaze that had everything male in him standing at attention.

He narrowed his eyes at her. "You good?"

She fidgeted and cast her eyes to the side. "Yeah. It's just been a long day. I didn't think I'd be spending the day traveling. You know?"

Nathan sat back in his seat and studied her. "Really? Is that what's bothering you? The traveling?"

He was provoking her. He knew it was more than that. Women watched him all the time with that same hot look in thier eyes.

Nathan watched as Remington wet her lips, her pink tongue slipping between her full lips and running along her bottom lip before disappearing back into her mouth. Sexy as fuck was all he could think.

"What else would it be?" Remington asked, the rapid

beat of the pulse at the base of her throat belied her even tone.

Nathan leaned back in his seat. He brought his hand to his chin and rubbed the faint stubble that was starting to come in as he considered how to respond. He could let it go and say never mind or he could pursue his line of questioning and figure out if what he was reading in her gaze was what he thought. That she was attracted to him. He certainly was attracted to her. Hell, who wouldn't be. She was bright, beautiful and that tight little body would have any man hard with the slightest brush.

He should probably drop it. But of course he didn't. "I don't know. You were looking at me like..."

"Like what?" Remington asked stiffening in her seat. She looked nervous and a light color filled her cheeks, flushing them.

Nathan grinned. The condescending, rude black man routine wasn't scaring her away. Maybe he should reconsider the seduction route. Jax would be pissed but hey, they were family. He'd forgive him. Nathan decided to test the waters.

"You're staring at me like I'm a piece of meat," Nathan said.

Remington's eyes rounded in horror. "What? No I'm not," she protested.

"Really? Maybe I misunderstood that hot look of lust in your eyes. I'm usually pretty astute when it comes to women. They throw themselves at me quite frequently so I've grown accustomed to the look."

Her pretty face contorted in outrage. "You really are a pompous ass you know that?"

Nathan pulled his bottom lip between his teeth in an effort to suppress his smile. She was a feisty one and man was she cute when she got mad.

"Not every woman is attracted to the great Nathan Black," Remington spat.

Nathan held up his hand in surrender. "I guess I misread things. I rarely get this wrong but I suppose there's a first time for everything."

"Like you said, you're used to women throwing themselves at you so I suppose it was an honest mistake."

"I suppose…"

Remington narrowed her eyes at him. "Do you enjoy it?" She asked.

"Enjoy what?"

"Having women fall at your feet all the time."

Nathan considered her question. Certainly, when he was younger he enjoyed all the attention he got from women. He'd been a star athlete in high school and college and ran through girls with the ease of a Casanova. And he'd enjoyed every minute of it.

When he joined the professional soccer league the attention he garnered from women became even more egregious. They would wait for him outside the stadium, in hotel lobbies and a few even managed to get into his hotel room.

He liked the attention a lot back then. Giggling young women eyeing him and swooning when he graced them with a smile.

Back then him and his buddies kept count of their endless conquests. And there were many. He was never all that picky about the women he slept with. They just had to be pretty. Brains, class, and ambition, none of that mattered back in the day. But as he got older, he found that he liked a challenged. He wanted some depth to the women he got involved with. The women he slept with now were not only gorgeous, they were smart. They were entrepreneurs, business women, doctors, lawyers, movie stars, models. Granted, the movie stars and models could be a bit shallow but damn they were beautiful. And he hadn't met a woman more ambitious than an actress.

Nathan stared down at the table, wet his lips then looked back at Remington. "I used to."

"And you don't anymore?" She asked, a skeptical look in her eyes.

"Not really. I enjoyed the shit out of it when I was young. But what young man wouldn't? Now that I'm older it's not as exciting as it used to be."

"But you sleep with so many women."

Nathan chuckled at her candor. "I do enjoy myself. I don't see anything wrong with that. I'm grown. I'm single."

"What about settling down? Being with one woman? You ever thought about that?"

Candidly, the thought never occurred to Nathan. He considered himself an eternal bachelor. In fact, he and Jax had a bet going about that. The first one to marry had to be the permanent escort for their grandmother to her annual garden party. A party that both he and Jax hated attending. The fact that they'd both slept with most of the granddaughters of the women who attended may have something to do with it.

"Nope," Nathan replied, his face serious.

"So, you're just going to spend the rest of your life hopping from woman to woman making no real connection. You'll end up old and alone doing that."

Her comment made him think of a line in one of Drake's songs where he says his mother tells him that nobody wants to be seventy and alone. The thought of that was a bit cringe worthy but marriage just wasn't on his agenda.

"You clearly have a strong opinion about it," Nathan said.

"I just know that I don't want to end up an old woman with a bunch of cats as my only companions."

Nathan laughed. He doubted she would end up as the crazy, old cat lady. She was too pretty and way too smart for that. "I don't think you'll have a problem there," he said.

"Why do you say that?" She asked, cocking her head to the side.

He shrugged as if it was obvious. "You're beautiful, smart and determined. You'd make a good catch for any man."

Remington shifted in her seat. Hers lips parted as if she wanted to say something but she pressed them back together. There was a slight flush to her face.

"Do my compliments embarrass you?" Nathan asked, locking eyes with her. He could hear the hard swallow that Remington choked down as she stared back at him.

"No, it's just...I didn't expect it," she said, her voice low.

"Why not?" Nathan's brow furrowed as he looked at her.

"I don't know. I'm not nearly as glamorous as the women you date and..." her voice trailed off.

"And what?"

"You don't really like me. I mean, you put up with me because I keep showing up but you're not particularly nice to me."

There was an insecurity to her as she said those words. A timidness in her eyes that was not normally present when they interacted. She was usually very confident and steadfast. Or, at least she appeared to be.

Nathan sighed. "It's not that I don't like you, Remington. I barely you know you."

"Then why do you act like such a jerk?" Her eyes were piercing and her lips pressed together forming an angry pout.

Nathan tried not to focus on her lips instead training his gaze on her eyes. "Like I told you, I don't want to do this memoir. And like you said, you just keep showing up. It's irritating."

Remington's mouth quirked at the corners and she shook her head. "I *can* be persistent. My father says I'm like a hound dog when I get my eye on something."

"Well, Daddy's right," Nathan grinned.

Remington let out a small chuckle as she looked at him. "So, what are we going to do?"

"Do about what?"

"About you, me, this memoir?"

Nathan shrugged. "Got any suggestions?"

Remington lowered her lids and pulled her bottom lip between her teeth.

Unable to help himself, Nathan zoned in on her mouth. He'd love to pull that same lip between his teeth and nibble on it. He could only imagine the sounds that would escape her pretty little mouth.

"Maybe if you get to know me, I wouldn't be so irritating," Remington said.

"What?" Nathan asked, letting go of thoughts of her mouth.

"I said that perhaps if you got to know me I wouldn't be as irritating," she repeated.

"Maybe but it still won't make me want to do the

memoir."

"One thing at a time, Casanova," Remington smirked.

"Casanova? Really?" Nathan grinned and shook his head.

Remington smiled, flashing an even row of bright, white teeth at him. "See, you're getting to know my sense of humor already. There's a lot about me that's quite likable."

Nathan's eyes roamed over her face. She was right about that. Her beauty being one of them.

"I'll tell you whatever you want to know. Where should I start?" She asked looking at him like an eager Girl Scout hawking cookies in front of a grocery store.

"I don't know. Tell me whatever you'd like," he replied.

"Ok. Let's start with the basics. I grew up in Anaheim, no brothers or sisters, my parents are both retired professors, I graduated from Columbia with a Masters in English, I want to be a successful writer one day, my best friend Natalie lives in San Francisco, I love fast cars and Italian food and I hate peas," she finished with a smile.

"You hate peas?" Nathan asked, his mouth quirking at the corners.

"That's what you got from all of that?" Remington frowned.

"I love peas," Nathan shrugged.

"Okay," Remington acquiesced. "Tell me something about the great Nathan Black. Something not in the tabloids."

Nathan ran his fingers across his chin as he thought about what exactly to share with her. Building his sports agency was the most important thing in his life right now. He'd start with that. "For starters, the sports agency

I opened is a big deal for me. Being a famous athlete is hard. There's so many people out there trying to get a piece of you and you need a solid team on your side. A team that really has your back and doesn't just give lip service. And that's what I'm building at N. Black Sports Agency. I want my clients to feel like family. To know that we're going to take care of them like we would our blood. You know?"

"That's beautiful, Nathan. I know I've only been privy to one meeting with one potential client but I think that any young athlete would be lucky to sign with your agency," Remington said, her smile warm and open as she looked at him.

Nathan's heart thumped. Like literally thumped in his chest and he wasn't sure what to do with that. He'd been on the receiving end of many a beautiful smile but none ever did that to him. He didn't understand it and he didn't like it.

"Thanks," Nathan said, the word coming out much gruffer then he meant it to.

Remington flinched and pressed back into her seat as if she was trying to put distance between them.

The air around them thinned and just like that there easy banter had been broken and replaced with the heavy tension that normally existed between them.

Captain Matthew's voice drifted into the cabin. "We're about two hours out from Burbank Airport. We've got clear skies ahead so sit back and enjoy the rest of the flight."

"You mentioned you were tired. Why don't you try and get some sleep. I'll wake you when we land," Nathan offered.

"Good idea," Remington said.

She looked disappointed as she stared back at him. A part of him wanted to ask her about it but he thought it better to just let it ride. She was different than every other woman he'd ever met or dealt with. Remington had a different affect on him and he had to be careful. His little test had backfired. He wanted to flirt a little. Get under her skin and see how she reacted instead he found himself being drawn in by her mouth and her kind words. She was chipping away at his resolve and he couldn't have that.

He decided to go back to jackass mode. It was easier to not get caught up in her when he was focusing on pushing her away.

CHAPTER SIX

REMINGTON

Remington rushed through the doors of Black Publishing House and raced down the hall. Jax was holding a staff meeting in the large conference room at eight and she was two minutes late already.

The entire staff was already seated and listening to Jax when she slipped into the room and posted up against the wall by the door.

"I'm excited to announce that we're in talks with Elleory Davis to sign with Black Publishing. This could be a huge get for us. She's one of *the* best-selling indie authors out there. Candidly, she doesn't need a publishing house to put her books out. She's already built a huge readership through her social media and sells plenty of books on her own. I'm working on showing her why she needs us and how much further we can take her career."

Remington smiled. Signing Elleory Davis would be huge. Several of the large publishing houses wanted to sign her. She made no bones about being wholly opposed to large publishing houses. She ranted on social media often how they basically keep most of the profits after the writer has poured their blood, sweat and tears into their work. Remington wondered how Jax managed to get her to even meet with him. Knowing Jax he'd charmed her into it.

Remington couldn't help but smile. Her boss could be very persuasive.

The staff meeting lasted about thirty minutes with Jax going over the upcoming release schedule and ended with him giving shout outs to various staff members.

Remington was heading out with the rest of the staff when Jax called out to her.

"Hey English, hang back," he called.

Remington moved to the side letting everyone else out of the conference room then made her way over to Jax. "Hey, Mr. Black. What's up?"

"I keep telling you to call me Jax, English," he said with a frown.

"I know. It's just that you're my boss and I feel like I should address you as Mr. Black out of respect. You know?"

"I get it but as your boss I'm telling you to call me Jax."

"Fine, Jax," Remington said, a sarcastic edge to her voice.

"That's better. Now how's my cousin? Is he behaving?" Jax asked, a skeptical look on his face.

"Well, I'm sure you already know that he's not happy about the memoir so he's not being very forthcoming and cooperative with me at all. And honestly after you left his office after doing your introductions, things didn't go so well."

"I'm sorry to hear that. What did my jackass cousin do?"

"Let's see. He ignored me for the first part of our meeting then accused me of being unprofessional and said he should have you fire me."

Jax frowned. "Geezus, Nathan. Remington, on behalf of my cousin, I apologize. The man can be a Neanderthal at times but I promise underneath all of that assholery, he's a good guy."

"You don't have to apologize. It's not your fault. And don't worry. I'm a pretty tough chic. I don't scare easily."

"Well, that's good to hear because I have a feeling my cousin is only going to amp up the antics." Jax said, leaning against the conference room table.

"Oh, he already has."

Jax folded his arms across his chest and leveled his gaze at her. "What did he do?"

"He tricked me into going to Texas the other day."

"What?" Jax exclaimed and shook his head.

"Yeah, that cousin of yours is something else. But it's cool. I handled it and I got some really good insight for the memoir."

"Well I guess that's something," Jax reasoned.

"Yeah and it got me thinking. Nathan really doesn't want to cooperate with me on this thing so instead of going the traditional route of doing formal meetings and Q&As, I figure I'd keep it casual. Shadow him throughout his day. You know, just observe him and take notes. And as he warms up to me I'll just chat with him. Keep it totally casual so he doesn't feel pressured."

Jax's mouth spread into a sly grin and he rubbed his chin. "I like that. And I know the perfect place for you to start."

Remington turned her car down a long road lined with large, beautiful trees that eventually fed into a paved circular driveway. A driveway that was the foreground to a very lovely, very large, two story home with a well-manicured lawn and a gorgeous rose garden off to the side.

Remington guided her car into the spot next to a shiny, black Lamborghini Veneno Roadster. She eyed the sexy beast of a car and couldn't help but smile. It was a thing of beauty. She loved fast cars. Was practically obsessed with them actually and her father was to blame for that. He was a total car man. He especially loved fast ones. He had a hobby of buying vintage speed demons and fixing them up and as a child Remington would sit in the garage and watch her father work on cars. As she got older she started helping him. She probably worked on more than ten cars with her father. In fact, she spent more time in the garage learning about cars then she did in the house. Maybe that's why she hated cleaning and could barely boil water.

Remington checked herself in the mirror. Her nerves were all over the place. Jax had the bright idea of inviting her to Sunday dinner at him and Nathan's grandmother, Della Black's house. He said that it was a family tradition that Nathan never missed and it would be perfect for her to get to know Nathan on a more personal level.

It sounded like a great idea when Jax pitched it to her

but now that she was here, Remington felt uneasy. Like she was crashing on a private family tradition, which she was.

Maybe she should leave. Remington was sure that Nathan would be none too pleased with her showing up at his grandmother's house. Yes, she would leave.

Remington was just about to turn the key in the ignition when a sleek black MV Agusta motorcycle pulled up next to her. She stared awestruck at the bike. It was one of the fastest motorcycles out there. Her eyes travelled along its sleek lines and powerful frame. It was a thing of beauty.

She watched as the rider hopped off the bike and was relieved to see Jax when he pulled off the helmet.

Jax grinned and waved as he looked over at her.

There was no way she could retreat now.

Remington smiled at Jax and got out of the car.

"Nice ride, English," Jax said, smiling appreciatively at her car.

"Thanks. Nice bike," she nodded towards his motorcycle.

"Just one of my toys," Jax grinned. "You ready for this?"

"I think so," Remington replied, butterflies already flittering around in the pit of her stomach. "I'm a little worried about how Nathan will take me being here though."

"Don't worry about him. He'll behave, trust me."

Remington wasn't so sure about that. Nathan hadn't behaved since she'd met him.

"Let's go inside," Jax said, heading for the house.

Remington followed behind him then stopped. "Wait! I have a pie in the car." She jogged back to her car and grabbed the pie off the front seat.

"You baked? Impressive," Jax said.

"I bought," Remington corrected him, her mouth splitting into a sly smile.

Jax chuckled. "Very funny. What kind of pie is it?"

"Pecan. It's one of those Patti Labelle pies. My best friend swears by them."

"My grandmother loves Patti Labelle so I'm sure it'll be a hit," Jax said, then continued on to the house.

Remington followed Jax inside. The smell of home cooking floated through the house and invaded her nostrils. It was like going home for the holidays. Her mother would be in the kitchen whipping up soul food magic and she and her father would be in the living room watching the football game. The familiarity of it had her nerves settling just a bit.

"This way," Jax said over his shoulder.

He led her through the foyer and down the hall into a large, open kitchen. An older woman stood over the stove humming as she lifted lids off pots and added various seasonings to them.

Jax moved quietly behind her, opened his arms, wrapped them around her and planted a kiss on her cheek.

The older woman let out a small yelp as she turned around but her mouth quickly split into a warm smile at seeing her grandson. "What I tell you about sneaking up on me, boy," she said, her eyes crinkling at the corners. "Get over here," she ordered and wrapped Jax in a tight embrace.

Jax laughed and hugged her back just as tight. "Hey Momma D."

"Don't hey me, boy," she said releasing Jax and stepping back to eye him up and down before patting his stomach. "You been eating? You looking a little thin since the last time I seen you."

Jax swatted her hand away playfully. "You just saw me last Sunday, Momma D."

"Yeah and you look like you haven't ate a thing since then."

"Aw, don't start. I eat a lot. I just work out even more."

"Mmmhmm," she mumbled.

Jax shook his head and placed a wet kiss on her cheek. "Momma D, I brought a guest to Sunday dinner," Jax said directing her attention to Remington.

Anxiety spurted through Remington and her grip tightened on the pie she was holding. She was intruding on a family moment and she felt awkward as hell. "Hello," she said, her voice thin and barely audible.

Della Black was older, probably in her sixties but she didn't look a day over forty-five. Her dark brown skin wasn't marred with age lines but instead was smooth and vibrant. Her light brown eyes were bright, alert and welcoming. She smiled warmly at Remington.

"Hello, darlin'", she sang as she made her way over to Remington. "You brought a pie."

"Yes, it's one of those Patti Labelle pies. Pecan," Remington smiled as she held the pie out towards Momma D.

"Chile, I love me some Patti Labelle and those pies of hers are delicious," she said, taking the pie from Remington and handing it to Jax. "I'm Momma D."

"Remington English," Remington said, holding her hand out for the older woman to shake.

Momma D swatted Remington's hand away. "Girl, if you don't get over here and give me a hug." She pulled Remington in, hugging her tight to her bosom.

Remington had no choice but to hug the woman back. Besides, who could resist with all the love and warmth radiating from her. All the nerves and anxiety Remington was feeling seemed to melt away in Momma D's loving embrace until she heard footsteps enter the kitchen. Remington didn't need to turn around to know who it was. Even the strong smell of collard greens and roasted chicken couldn't cover up the heady scent of bergamot she was coming to associate with Nathan.

"What's going on here?" Nathan asked as he entered the kitchen.

Remington stiffened, bracing herself for what Nathan's reaction would be to seeing her in his grandmother's home.

Momma D pulled back, releasing Remington. She smiled at Nathan. "Jax brought a friend to Sunday dinner," she said, wiggling her eyebrows.

Remington turned, lifted her chin and looked at Nathan.

Nathan's jaw stiffened and his eyes went black as he stared back at her.

It took everything inside Remington to stay put when she really wanted to shrink back and hightail it the hell out of there.

The room went dead silent as the two stared at each other.

Momma D looked from Nathan to Remington trying to figure out what was going on.

"What up, cuz? I was wondering when you would turn up. I saw your car outside so I knew you were here somewhere," Jax said, walking over and slapping Nathan on the back.

Nathan's dark expression didn't change as he shifted

his gaze to his cousin. "What is she doing here?"

"I invited her. I figured it would be good for the memoir for her to see you with family. You're not such a jackass when you're with family," Jax smirked.

"Oh, I can be," Nathan spat through clenched teeth.

"Hey, I'm just trying to help," Jax shrugged.

"I think you've helped enough already."

Nathan looked as if he could choke Jax. And he might have if Momma D hadn't stepped between the two men.

"Alright boys. What are you two going on about now?" She turned to Remington. "These two have been cuttin 'up since they was knee high. Jaxson was the little instigator then and I'm sure that whatever is going on now is his doing."

"C'mon, Momma D. Why am I always the bad guy?" Jax said, feigning hurt.

"Cuz you're always up to no good," Momma D chastised in that loving way only a grandmother could. "Now what's going on, boys?" She looked from Jaxson to Nathan.

"Jax is sticking his nose where it doesn't belong, as usual," Nathan replied.

"No!" Jax held up a finger in protest. "I'm helping. Nathan's doing a memoir which will be good for his image. It'll counter all the salacious press he's gotten his entire career and folks can start focusing on the positive things he's doing in athlete management. And since we all know Nathan can't write to save his life, I loaned him my best up and coming writer to write it for him."

"Oh, well that's nice. Nathan you should be grateful not ornery." Momma D shook her head disapprovingly.

Jax's mouth split into a smug smile.

Nathan rolled his eyes, his face still holding the same

dark expression.

Remington watched the exchange with amusement, almost forgetting the nerves rattling around in her stomach. Jax, Nathan and their grandmother were clearly a tight trio. Jax loved razzing his cousin, Nathan was easily annoyed by it and Momma D was right there to keeping the guys in line.

Momma D turned to Remington. "So, Remington, you're actually here for Nathan, not Jax."

"I suppose but I don't want to intrude. This is a family dinner. Maybe I should go."

"Good idea," Nathan quickly chimed in.

"Nonsense." Momma D said, shooting Nathan a stern look before turning back to Remington with a kind smile. "You're staying and having Sunday dinner with us and we're more than happy to have you. Right boys."

"Absolutely," Jax said, a humorous twinkle in his eyes.

"Yeah, of course," Nathan added, his dry tone belying his words.

"Nathan, why don't you show Remington around. Jax, you help me set the table," Momma D said.

"I can set the table," Nathan offered.

Momma D leveled her gaze at him giving him that don't play with me look that elders give children when they know they're about to misbehave.

Nathan clearly knew not to put up a fight. He sighed and looked at Remington. "This way," he said, gesturing towards the hallway.

"This is the hallway," Nathan said dryly, walking a few paces in front of her.

Remington stared after him unable to stop herself from taking in the magnificent view that made up his backside. His gait was relaxed, slightly bowed and sexy as hell. He was dressed casually in a pair of jeans and a fitted white tee that hugged his sculpted arms and stretched taunt across his back and thick shoulders. An intricate work of tattoos crawled from under his short sleeves and weaved its way down his forearms. Remington was a bit of a sucker for guys with tattoos and she had to stop herself from staring.

"God lord! Why does he have to be so damn sexy," she thought, tearing her eyes away from him and focusing on her shoes instead. Big mistake. Not looking caused her to crash right into him.

Nathan whipped around and caught her by the arms, steadying her.

This was the first time he'd actually touched her since they met and the feel of his hands on her body was like being singed with a hot flame. There was nothing she could do to stop the shortness of breath or the tingling between her thighs.

The space between their bodies seemed nonexistent as Remington stared up at Nathan who looked down at her with eyes hard and dark but there was something else there too. Something that made Remington's throat go dry and made her heart take on an erratic pace. She'd felt this before. Yes, outside the elevator at his office. The Nathan Black dazzle. The dazzle she swore she would not allow herself to fall under but was currently in the clutch of.

"So in addition to not liking peas, you're also clumsy?" Nathan asked, his voice low.

"Not normally," Remington replied, the words coming out on a breathy note.

Nathan leaned in studying her closely. "You good?"

"Why do you keep asking me that?" Remington

frowned. The words held a frustrated edge to them.

"Because you get flushed often. Like the other day on the plane and like now. Your breaths coming in short and your cheeks are turning red."

Remington swallowed. Maybe if he wasn't all up in her space she could breath and not feel so warm. And the fact that he was still bracing her by the arms didn't help. Her hormones were revved up on ten at this point. She needed some space.

"I'm fine," she said, leaning back.

Nathan didn't remove his hands from her arms and his dark eyes moved down to her mouth and lingered. His lips parted just slightly.

For a second Remington thought he would kiss her. Her heart beat loudly in her ears drowning out everything so that the only thing was her and Nathan. She waited, not breathing, for him to make a move but he pulled back setting her away from him.

He blinked, the dark sultry look in his eyes receded then he straightened to his full height. The pull between them was gone and he was standoffish again.

"We should probably finish the tour. I'm sure dinner will be ready soon and the rest of the gang will be showing up any minute now," he said.

Disappointment filtered through Remington's body even though she knew him pulling back was for the best. Whatever was boiling between the two of them couldn't happen. It needed to be stamped down. They had to remain professional. SHE had to remain professional.

"The rest of the gang?" Remington asked trying to sound unaffected by just having Nathan all in her grill.

Nathan shoved his hands in his pants pockets and Remington relaxed a bit.

"That's a good place for them", she thought.

"Yeah, my Aunt and Uncle, Jax's parents, they come to Sunday dinner as well."

"Oh," Remington said curiously.

"What?" Nathan asked.

"It's just that I thought you were both raised by Momma D."

"Momma D had a hand in raising us both. Trust me. It's just that I came to live with her after my parents died and Jax was here all the time. I think it was to keep me company but really he was just a pain in the ass. He still is."

Remington let out a soft laugh. "Still, it must have been nice having him around."

"Yeah, he gets on my nerves but he's my best friend." Nathan grinned. "Shall we?" He asked, gesturing towards the entrance to the living room.

Remington nodded and walked ahead of him.

The living room was traditional with a homey, southern feel. The entire room was white on white with a touch of woodgrain. There was a large book case built into one of the walls that housed more family pictures than books.

Remington made her way over and checked them out. There were tons of pictures of two young boys with bright eyes and crooked smiles.

"You and Jax," Remington questioned, turning to Nathan.

"Yeah. Momma D stayed taking pictures of us when we were kids."

"Well, you both looked very happy."

"Why wouldn't we? What? Were we supposed to be sad and troubled because my parents died?" Nathan asked bitterly.

Remington turned to face him fully. "No, not at all. Why are you getting so defensive? I just made an honest observation."

"An observation of what? That despite losing my parents at an early age I still managed to have a happy childhood. That's a perfect line for your memoir, right?"

"First of all it's *your* memoir and what's wrong with that? You did lose your parents at a young age and you could have let that derail your life but you clearly didn't. You obviously had a strong family unit that took care of you and I think that's amazing."

Nathan scrubbed his hand down his face. "Okay, look, I know what you're doing here and I'm not cool with it."

"What am I doing, Nathan?"

"You're here fishing for information for that damn memoir. I'm not stupid. I know what you and Jax are up to and no doubt this was my jackass cousin's idea inviting you here."

"It was but don't be mad at Jax. He really is trying to help. Nathan, you've had an amazing life. This memoir is your chance to tell *your* story from *your* perspective. You get to control the narrative. You want everyone to focus on the sports agency you're building, not your love life. If done right, this memoir can allow people to get to know the real you. They'll learn what you're really about beyond the glitz and glamour. Beyond the sports, the money and the women. Don't you want that?"

Nathan stared at her, his eyes considering, and for a moment Remington thought she got through to him but just as quickly he stiffened, his eyes went black and that hard wall of his re-erected itself.

"Tours over. You can find your own way to the dining room. It's just through the kitchen," he said then strode out of the living room.

CHAPTER SEVEN

NATHAN

Nathan let out a low curse as he left the living room and made his way upstairs to his old bedroom. Goddamn! Remington was really getting under his skin. He felt like a teenage boy in puberty. Annoyed one minute, horny the next. He wished she would just give up on writing his memoir and go away. She was too much of a distraction and he really needed to focus on signing D'Mariyon Taylor. He was building a brand at N. Black Sports Agency and that's what he should be focusing on. Not some memoir and not some annoyingly determined, sexy as fuck writer. And damn did she look good today in her tight jeans and fitted sweater. Her hair was curly today, hanging wild and free about her head and shoulders making her look like a sexy, Nubian Goddess. The corkscrew curls looked so soft. He wanted to run his fingers through it and massage her scalp while she pleasured him with her mouth.

Nathan groaned, closed his eyes and tilted his head back. That's an image he didn't need stuck in his mind at dinner with his family.

Nathan leaned against the desk in his old bedroom and stared around the space. It was exactly the same as he left it. The same posters of his soccer idols adorned the walls and his medals and trophies still sat on the book-shelf. The room was cleaner then he left it but other than that Momma D hadn't changed a thing.

He moved over to the dresser where a picture of him and his parents sat. He was very young, around five years old. He was sandwiched between his parents who were staring into the camera with big smiles while he stared up at them with a huge toothy grin of his own.

Nathan remembered that day like it was yesterday. His soccer team had just won the championship game and he'd scored the winning goal. His parents were so proud of him. Momma D too. She was the one who took the picture.

His father had told him later that day that he was spe-cial. That he had a gift. A talent for playing soccer and that he should work at that gift. Work to improve on it. Work to be the best at it. Nathan promised him he would. His parents died in a car accident the very next day.

It was a hard time for him. He was lucky to have Momma D, his aunt and uncle and Jax. They really ral-lied around him. They gave him so much love growing up that he never felt like losing his parents left him alone. He was grateful for that. And maybe that's why he wanted to sign D'Mariyon Taylor so bad. He'd had his private investigator, Thompson, look into D'Mariyon's family and found out that the kid's mother died of a drug overdose and he never knew his father. His grandmother had raised him with a lovingly, stern hand and strong values. Nathan wanted D'Mariyon to carry what his grandmother instilled in him into the football league. The young man was about to enter into a world where money ruled and all people cared about was how much you could make them. The industry could ruin a person. He didn't want that for D'Mariyon. The kid had too much talent to be taken advantage of and used up. He needed to sign him to N. Black Sports Agency to really guide him so he made decisions that were best for him and his future not some money hungry sports agent.

See, this is what he should be focusing on, signing D'Mariyon. Not obessing over some woman.

The bedroom door opened and Nathan turned to see Jax standing in the doorway.

"Momma D sent me to find you. Mom and Pops are here and dinner is ready."

"A'ight, I'll be down in a sec," Nathan said.

Jax turned to leave but stopped and looked back at Nathan. "You cool, cuz?"

"Fo 'sho'. I'm good. I'll be right down."

"A'ight," Jax said, then left.

Nathan took one last look around his old room then headed downstairs.

Everyone was already seated at the table when Nathan entered the dining room. His grandmother was in her seat at the head of the table, his Uncle Raymond was seated at the other end, Jax and his Aunt Tilda were seated on one side and Remington was seated on the other side next to an empty chair. Of course they would be seated next to each other.

Nathan forced a smile on his face as he took his seat.

Remington's delicious scent of vanilla and lavender slapped him across the face as soon as he sat down and he leaned away from her trying not to get caught up in her scent. Having her around a few days during the week shadowing him in his business dealings was bad enough but having her invade his personal space was a bit much.

"Nathan, honey, you look well," his Aunt Tilda said, her soft hazel eyes crinkling at the corners.

His Aunt Tilda was one of Nathan's favorite people. She was kind and witty and treated him like a son.

"Thanks Auntie. And you look gorgeous as always. Not a day over thirty."

"Oh stop, boy. You know I don't look a day over twenty-five."

Laugher erupted around the table.

"That's right, baby," his Uncle Raymond said, eyeing his wife.

"Alright, alright! Enough of that nonsense. Let's say grace so we can grub," Momma D said, reaching for Nathan and Jax's hands.

Nathan took his grandmother's hand then looked over at Remington. She was flushed again and that damn pulse at her neck was beating wildly. He wanted to lean over and place his lips to it just to feel the thumping of it against his mouth.

Nathan watched as she swallowed then laid her hand on the table palm up. An invitation for him to take it. He stared at her hand for a few seconds. Her slender fingers twitched slightly.

"Nathan, take Remington's hand so your Uncle can say grace," Momma D urged.

Nathan closed his eyes then placed his hand on top of Remington's. If he thought touching her arms earlier when he grabbed them to steady her was a shock to his system, he knew nothing at all.

They say the hands are one of the most sensitive areas on the body. It has more sensory neurons than most other parts and Nathan was never more aware of that than he was now. Sparks were flying like the fourth of July. An electric current had charged and was burning fire from Remington's palm to his. He'd never felt anything like it.

Maybe Remington felt it too because his Uncle had barely finished saying grace when she yanked her hand from beneath his and placed it in her lap.

Nathan placed his own hand under the table and flexed his fingers trying to rid them of the electrifying pins and needles marring his hand.

"Well, dig in, ya'll," Momma D said, scooping food onto her plate.

Everyone followed suit piling the aromatic soul food onto their plates.

"Ray, did the boys tell you that Remington here is writing Nathan's memoir?" Momma D asked, beaming with pride.

"They did not but that's exciting." He looked over at Remington. "My nephew had quite the soccer career and now he's retired and building that sports agency which I know will be a success. The boy's always been an over-achiever. Once he puts his mind to something it's a sure fire success."

"I can imagine. I'm just getting to know Nathan but I've read some articles about his time in college and then in the league. He had a lot of success on the soccer field,"

Remington said.

Nathan shot her a look but Remington ignored him.

"It only makes sense. I'm sure he was just as determined as a child," she finished.

"Oh yeah, that's our Nathan. I remember taking the boys fishing one weekend. It was Nathan's first time and he was having a hard time casting his line out. That boy must have flicked that line out a hundred times before he finally got it perfect. He wouldn't stop until he got it right. And not only did he get it right, he ended up catching the most fish out of all of us," Ray laughed.

"He sure did," Momma D smiled. "We had us a big fish fry too."

"Do you still fish?" Remington asked, looking at Nathan.

"Yep," Nathan nodded.

"Nathan has a cabin up in Lake Almanor which is a great fishing spot," Jax offered.

Nathan shook his head at his cousin. The guy just wouldn't quit. He narrowed his eyes at Jax, willing him to shut it.

Jax just grinned and kept talking. "He's up there at least once a month. It's his little private getaway. When he was still playing soccer he would disappear up there every bye week-"

"Thanks Jax. I think Remington gets the idea," Nathan said, cutting him off.

"I think it's great that you have a place you can go to get away from everything. Everyone needs that. Especially someone like you," Remington said.

Nathan set his fork down and cast a sideways glance at Remington. "Someone like me?" He asked, his jaw clenched, his eyes slightly narrowed.

Remington cleared her throat, "I just meant that you're in the spotlight a lot so it must be nice to have a place where you can go and be alone."

"As if I can't handle the spotlight?" Nathan pressed.

"No. That's not what I meant at all," Remington defended.

"Son, I think all Remington is trying to say is that we all need a break every once in a while," Momma D said, placing her hand over Nathan's.

"Exactly," Remington agreed.

The atmosphere around the table had gotten a bit heavy and Nathan knew he was the cause. It's just that Remington was able to push his buttons like no other. And he knew whatever information she gathered here today with his family would be used in the memoir. He didn't want folks thinking he escaped to his cabin because he couldn't handle pressure.

"I'm this close to signing a great author. She's extremely talented and highly sought after and she's agreed to meet with me," Jax said, breaking into the tense silence and shifting the focus away from Nathan.

"That's wonderful, Jax," Tilda smiled and squeezed her son's shoulder.

"Look at my grandsons out here just excelling. Ya'll make me so proud," Momma D said, beaming at Jax and Nathan.

Nathan couldn't help but smile at his grandmother. Win or lose she was always proud of them no matter what.

They spent the rest of meal talking about Jax and the author he was trying to sign. Nathan was grateful for that because the spotlight was off him and Remington wasn't able to get anymore intel.

"Dinner was great as usual," Nathan said, pushing back from the table.

"Where are you going?" Jax asked.

"I have a thing I need to get to," Nathan replied.

"You can't leave yet."

"Why?" Nathan asked, the skin between his brow puckering.

"Remington brought dessert," Jax beamed smugly.

"That's right. She brought one of those Pattie Labelle pecan pies," Momma D said getting up from the table. "I'll just go grab it."

Nathan's jaw tightened as he slid back into his seat.

"You're gonna love this pie, cuz. It has the best reviews," Jax said, amusement dancing in his eyes.

Nathan frowned at his cousin. Jax was such a fucking instigator. He knew Nathan was itching to get out of there. To get away from Remington. Jax was lucky his aunt and uncle were there or he'd cuss his ass out.

Momma D returned with the pie and a stack of dessert plates.

Nathan watched as she sliced into the pie and passed plates around to everyone. He had to admit the pie looked delicious. Now whether it lived up to Jax's rave reviews, he didn't know because he wolfed that pie down in two bites then got up and took his dishes to the kitchen.

Nathan was loading dishes into the dishwasher when Jax came into the kitchen. He turned on his cousin immediately.

"What the fuck, man! You really like annoying me, don't you?"

"I have no idea what you're talking about," Jax said innocently.

"The hell you don't! You invited her here to Sunday dinner," Nathan accused.

"I did but only because I thought it would be good for her to see you around family. You're always so chill and easy going when we're at Momma D's. Not so much today but normally you are."

"That's because normally it's just family. No outsiders and definitely not some thirsty ass writer," Nathan spat.

"Whoa! That's harsh, man. Your asshole meter is on ten right now. "When was the last time you got laid, bruh?"

"Fuck you, Jax!" Nathan spat.

"Don't get mad at me. You're wound tight as shit, dude. Like you ain't had none in a minute. Maybe you should get you some and then you'll chill the fuck out."

Nathan scrubbed his hand down his face. Jax was right. He was more on edge today than he'd ever been. And honestly he hadn't gotten laid since he started working with Remington. For some reason he'd lost interest in other women. Maybe a night of wild sex would do him good.

Nathan pulled out his phone and texted Jazelle.

Nathan: *Meet me for a nightcap at the W Hotel at 10pm?*

Jazelle: *I'll be there sexy. Can't wait to see you.*

"Are you really texting in the middle of our conversation?" Jax frowned.

"Making plans to see Jazelle Banks later tonight."

"My man! Glad to see you're finally taking my advice," Jax grinned and patted Nathan on the shoulder.

Remington cleared her throat as she entered the kitchen. "Sorry to interrupt. I'm gonna head out and I just wanted to say thank you for having me."

"You're leaving already?" Jax asked. "We play spades every Sunday after dinner. You should stay. Nathan and Momma D always partner up against me and my Dad but it might be fun to have a new partner. Mix things up, you know."

"I'm not much of a card player and besides I should really get home. But thank you for the offer."

"Of course. And you're welcome here anytime," Jax said.

"Thank you," Remington smiled.

"I'll finish cleaning up in here. Nathan, why don't you walk Remington out," Jax suggested.

His cousin just couldn't resist pulling at the last thread of patience he had. Nathan tried to keep a neutral disposition as he looked at Remington. "After you," he said, gesturing towards the exit.

They walked to the front door in silence, the air between them thicker than a London fog.

Nathan followed Remington out the door and over to a sweet Volvo Coupe. "This your car?"

"Yeah," she replied without looking at him.

Nathan let out a low whistle. "She's a beauty."

"Thank you. I'm kind of a nut for classic cars. Especially fast ones." She looked over at the Lamborghini Veneno Roadster. "That one yours?"

"Yeah. She's one of my favorites," Nathan said, admiring the car.

"She's beautiful. I've never driven one but I know how fast those Veneno Roadsters are. She must be a motherfucker to drive. All that power," Remington said wistfully.

Nathan looked at Remington who was completely besotted by his car. She was looking at it as if she couldn't wait to feel the vibrations of the engine quake her thighs. Just the thought of it made Nathan's dick twitch.

"You weren't kidding. You really like fast cars," he said.

"I'm obsessed. There's nothing like blazing down an open road with 750 horsepower beneath you. It's intoxicating."

He knew they were talking cars but the way she was damn near salivating over his roadster had him imagining what it would be like being beneath her while she rode *him* hard and fast.

"Maybe I'll let you take her for a spin one day," Nathan spoke, his voice husky.

Remington looked over at him. Once again her skin was flushed over and her chest was heaving. She looked ripe for plunking and it took everything Nathan had in him to not grab her, bend her across the hood of his car and fuck her raw. What the hell was this woman doing to him? Maybe Jax was right. Maybe he did need to get laid.

"Maybe I'll take you up on that sometime," Remington said, her own voice low and uneven. "See you tomorrow, Nathan."

Nathan watched as she climbed in her car and drove away. He stared after her hoping that after he spent the night with Jazelle, Remington English would be no more than the pesky woman his cousin assigned to write his memoir.

Nathan made it to the W Hotel just after ten. Jazelle was waiting for him at the bar looking like she just left a photoshoot. Her pretty face was done up dramatically highlighting her high cheekbones and light colored eyes and the dress she wore clung to her like a second skin. The soft swell of her breasts spilled seductively over the top of the dress and the hem was cut short displaying her toned, caramel colored thighs.

A naughty smile split her full mouth as Nathan approached.

"Hello handsome," she said, handing him her glass of brandy.

Nathan took it and downed the sweet, brown liquid. "You look amazing as always," he said, sitting the glass on the counter.

Jazelle ignored his compliment. "I'm glad you called. It's been a few days. I thought you'd forgotten about me," she pouted.

"I doubt anyone could forget you," Nathan said, playing to her ego.

Jazelle smile sweetly and leaned in close. "How 'bout we go upstairs," she suggested sliding a room key across the bar at him.

Nathan took the key, grabbed Jazelle by the hand and led her out of the bar.

Jazelle was on him as soon as they stepped into the elevator, rubbing her hands up his chest and placing kisses along his neck and ear. She always was aggressive when it came to sex and Nathan liked that about her. She knew what she wanted and went for it.

Nathan was just as aggressive and intense. He guessed that's why they were so great together in bed. Neither minded taking things to the limit.

Nathan grabbed a handful of Jazelle's hair pulling her head back and nibbling and sucking at the tender skin of her throat while placing his other hand underneath her dress and rubbing his fingers between her legs. The lace panties she wore soaked instantly.

Nathan and Jazelle stumbled out of the elevator and down the hall to their room. They were barely inside before Jazelle was pulling at Nathan's shirt and unbuckling his pants.

Nathan helped her along by pulling off his shirt and pushing his pants down and stepping out of them. He rid Jazelle of the scrap of a dress she was wearing and tossed it aside. Her heavy breasts tumbled free and sat like beautiful brown orbs on her chest. Nathan licked his lips. The woman had one hell of a rack. Nathan palmed and kneaded them before pulling one into his mouth.

Jazelle moaned and ground her pussy into his crotch. "I wanna taste you," she said then dropped to her knees. She stared up at him as she reached inside his briefs and released his dick which bounced heavy in the air.

Nathan watched through slitted eyes as Jazelle licked her lips and dove right in, wrapping her mouth around the tip of his dick and tickling it lightly with her tongue before sliding the entire length of him into her mouth.

Nathan groaned, grabbed the back of her head and guided her mouth back and forth on his shaft.

Jazelle gave head like a champ, licking, sucking and applying just the right amount of pressure. Nathan watched as she took the entire length of him into her mouth, sucking and squeezing him. The shit felt good. Nathan tilted his head back and closed his eyes intent on enjoying the feel of her mouth on him but as soon as his eyes closed the unthinkable happened. Remington's sweet smiling face flashed in his mind. Her hair was wild and free like she'd worn it at dinner. Her skin was flush and her heavy lidded eyes called to him.

What the fuck! Nathan thought and jerked his eyes

open. This woman was infiltrating every part of his life and he'd be damned if he'd let her worm her way into what was going on right now.

"Come here," Nathan growled, pulling Jazelle from her knees. He yanked her panties down and bent her over the edge of the bed before moving hurriedly to his pants and grabbing a condom. He put the rubber on quickly as he moved back to the bed.

Jazelle watched him over her shoulder, a sexy catlike grin on her face. She wiggled her tight brown ass at him inviting him to hurry and plunge the very depths of her. Her pink slit was glistening. She was more than ready for him.

Nathan impaled her, burying himself balls deep.

Jazelle screamed out her pleasure and bucked back against him.

Nathan braced her hip with one hand and wrapped the other hand around her hair using it as leverage as he slammed into her over and over again, his face tense with desperation as he tried to fuck the vision of Remington from his mind.

Over and over he slammed into Jazelle and she took each punishing thrust like a champ, screaming, moaning and begging him to fuck her harder.

Jazelle's walls tightened around his dick, squeezing and contracting. Nathan knew she was on the verge of coming and he pounded into her even harder.

Jazelle came hard and fast, her juices drenching him.

Nathan wasn't done with her. He flipped her over, pulled her to the edge of the bed and tossed her long legs over his shoulders then drove back into her. In and out he pounded her closing his eyes only to see Remington before him. His stroke stuttered for a second and he opened his eyes to stare down at Jazelle but it was Remington he saw sprawled before him, moaning, bucking and clawing at the bedspread.

The image of Remington brought out something beastly in him. He wanted to consume her, own her, make her his in every way.

Nathan gripped her hips, sliding her back and forth on his dick. He felt his balls tighten and he knew was about to explode. Nathan closed his eyes and drove into her one final time releasing his seed on a deep moan.

He was somewhat surprised when he opened his eyes to see Jazelle laying beneath him, a satisfied smile on her face.

"That was amazing," she purred.

Nathan said nothing. He pulled out of Jazelle and moved to the bathroom to clean himself up.

Jazelle was still in the same position he'd left her when he came out of the bathroom. Nathan grabbed his clothes from the floor and started putting them on.

Jazelle sat up. "What are you doing?"

"I have an early flight in the morning. I gotta go."

"What the fuck, Nathan? You can't just fuck me silly then leave. What kind of shit is that?"

Nathan sighed. He had no desire to get into it with Jazelle. He thought fucking her would ease the tension he'd been feeling and at the same time take his mind off Remington. That shit didn't work. If anything it only proved how much Remington was really under his skin. He couldn't even get his dick wet without seeing her face. Now he just wanted to get home and get some sleep but he knew he couldn't leave things bad with Jazelle. If there was one thing he was with women, it was careful. He'd dealt with so many of them that he'd learned the importance of leaving things good between he and them.

Nathan walked over to the bed, braced Jazelle by the hips and slid her to edge of the bed. He turned up the charm as he stared down at her. "Don't pout, beautiful. Like I said I have an early flight and I need to get home. If I stay here with you I won't get any sleep at all. I'll call you when I get back to town and we'll do dinner."

Jazelle's mouth was in full pout and her eyes narrowed as she stared up at him considering whether to believe him or not.

Nathan ran his thumb across her bottom lip then slipped it into her mouth. Jazelle sucked on it just like Nathan knew she would. "That's my girl," he cooed, sliding his thumb out of her mouth and dragging it down her lip.

"You're lucky you're so damn sexy and fuck like a rock star, Nathan Black."

Nathan chuckled then leaned down and placed a quick peck on her lips. "Good night, Jazelle," he said then headed for the door.

"You'll call as soon as you get back, right?" Jazelle called after him.

Nathan didn't bother to respond. He simply tossed his hand in the air and left.

Nathan pulled out his cell phone as soon as he got in his car. He searched through his contacts until he got to R and stopped on the name Remington English. He stared down at his phone considering. One little tap is all it would take to dial her up.

It was late. Well after midnight. She would probably be asleep but there was a relentless urge within Nathan to speak with her. The woman had somehow engrained herself into his psyche which was a problem. Hell, just the thought of what happened back in that hotel room rocked him. When he was with a woman, he was with THAT woman. He'd never needed to fantasize about someone else. Seeing Remington's face while fucking Jazelle was a shock and he didn't really know what to make of it. Maybe it was because he was always such an ass to her and his conscious was finally catching up to him. Or, more than likely it was because she fascinated and infuriated him like no other woman. Either way he didn't want thoughts of Remington plaguing him the rest of the night. Maybe hearing her voice would settle him. Maybe he'd even apologize for his behavior toward her. Maybe that would help to purge her from his system.

Nathan let his finger fall lightly on Remington's name and the phone dialed her number. He pressed the speaker button and waited.

After three rings she finally answered.

"Hello," her voice floated over the line, soft and slightly groggy.

"Hey, sorry to call so late. It's Nathan."

"Nathan?"

"Yeah, were you asleep?"

"Umm…I just drifted off. What's going on? Is everything okay?"

"Yeah, everything's fine. I just wanted to apologize for my behavior earlier. I was an ass to you and I'm sorry."

The line went quiet and Nathan figured that she was caught off guard by his apology.

"I know me apologizing is probably a shock but I felt it was necessary. I'm really not a 24-hour asshole."

Remington's soft chuckle floated through the phone.

"Nathan, I know you're not an ass all the time. Only when I'm around." She let out another soft laugh. "But I get it. I'm the one working on the memoir that you don't want to do so it makes sense that you'd take your frustrations out on me. Don't get me wrong. It's not cool but I get it."

"Well you've been a good sport about it and I promise I'll do my best not to be such a jerk anymore."

"Thank you. I appreciate that," she said softly.

The line went quiet with only the sound of their breaths permeating the air.

Finally, Remington spoke, "Is there anything else you wanted?"

Nathan's dick twitched at that question. He imagined her lying in bed wearing next to nothing and his dick went on full rock. So yes, there was definitely something else he wanted.

"Nathan?"

"Uh, yeah. Just to tell you that I'm flying back to Texas in the morning and I figured I'd tell you in advance this time."

"Thanks for letting me know. Last time was a surprise to say the least."

"Yeah, sorry about that. So, will you be coming with me this time?" Nathan asked. "You don't have to," he added.

"No, I want to. I like watching you work."

"Really? Why?"

"You're good at what you do and I can tell that you really care about the well-being of the athletes you represent or are trying sign."

"Thanks. It's important that these young men have someone who's really looking out for their best interest," Nathan said. He cared a lot about his work and it was important for him to represent athletes in their own best interests and not just what they can bring to his bottom line. "You should know it's an overnight trip so pack a bag and I'll see you at eight in the morning."

"Okay, should I just meet you at the airport?"

"No, I'll pick you up. Text me your address," Nathan replied.

"Okay. I'll send it as soon as we hang up."

"Great! Goodnight, Remington."

"Goodnight, Nathan," she replied.

Nathan hung up the phone not feeling any relief from having talked to Remington. If anything he was feeling more eager to see her.

CHAPTER EIGHT

REMINGTON

Remington didn't get much sleep and the oversized luggage gracing her bottom lids were proof of that. After the late night surprise call from Nathan she couldn't seem to get back to sleep. It was the first time they'd actually spoken over the phone and Nathan's deep, velvety voice glided through the receiver and over her body as easily as if he were there in the room with her. Sleep after that phone call was just not gonna happen. Every time she closed her eyes she saw him. His dark eyes, chiseled jaw, full mouth. That perfectly hard and ripped body of his pressed up against her. She'd soaked right through her panties and ended up taking them off. Remington's resolve to not get caught up in Nathan Black's dazzle was completely out the window.

Remington did what she could about the bags under her eyes then quickly dressed in jeans and a fitted t-shirt. She wanted to be comfortable for the plane ride. She was actually grateful that Nathan had a change of heart and decided to let her know about the trip to Texas. This wouldn't be like last time when she was completely caught off guard and unprepared.

Remington pulled her overnight bag out of the closest and threw a pair of jeans, a sweater, and some undies into it then made her way to the bathroom to grab some toiletries.

Her cell phone dinged as she was zipping up the bag.

Nathan: *Be there in ten minutes. Pack something for dinner at a fancy restaurant. We're having dinner with some of my contacts at the Cowboys organization.*

Remington: *kk*

Remington went back to the closet in search of a dress. She wasn't one to wear a lot of dresses and being that she preferred jeans and t-shirts, her choices were limited.

Remington frowned. The section of dresses in her closet was truly dismal. She searched through the rack passing on a floral tie-front mini dress she wore to an alumni luncheon with per parents. She moved even quicker past a purple, satin mini dress Natalie bought for her from *Fashion Nova*. She'd never worn the thing and doubted she ever would. The dress was short with a v-wire front and adjustable spaghetti straps. It was a sexy little dress, it just wasn't Remington's style.

Remington came to the last dress hanging in the back of the closet. It was a black bandage mock-neck fitted dress. It had peek-a-boo slits running down the front of the dress from the base of the neck down to the waist-line. She'd seen it online a few months ago and thought it was super cute. It wasn't over the top. It was just dressy enough to wear some place nice. Perfect for dinner at a fancy restaurant.

Remington grabbed the dress and a pair of black stilettos and placed them in her bag just as the doorbell rang.

She did a quick check of herself in the mirror then hurried to the living room to answer the door.

Remington literally stopped breathing the moment she opened the door and saw Nathan standing there. He was dressed casually in a tan sweater that clung to his thick arms and broad chest and a pair of dark jeans. It must be a sin to look that good every day.

"Hey," Nathan said before tucking his bottom lip between his teeth and looking her up and down.

Every nerve ending in Remington's body took off. She felt hot and cold, nervous and tingly all at the same time. Flashes of last night's salacious dreams invaded her thoughts, hardening her nipples and zinging the tiny bud between her thighs.

"I know you hate it when I ask, but you good? You look...flushed." Nathan said, studying her closely.

Remington's cheeks heated under his gaze. He was right. She didn't like it when he asked her that. It meant he was paying attention. Really seeing her. And clearly she wasn't good at hiding her emotions.

"I'm not a fan of it," Remington said.

Nathan leaned against the door frame as he stared down at her. The move shifted him closer and put him all up in her space.

"Why not?" He asked, his voice low.

Nathan's distinct smell of bergamot attacked Remington's senses and for a second all she could do was stare up at him.

"Remington?" Nathan called to her, pulling her out of her trance.

"Yeah...umm...it's just that I didn't realize I was so easy to read."

"You're not. I just pay close attention," he said with a smirk.

"Really? So what does this face tell you?" Remington challenged pursing her lips and narrowing her eyes at him.

She watched as Nathan's gaze trailed from her eyes to her mouth then back up sending a whole new set of thrills down her spine.

He leaned in close, his face just inches from hers. "Normally when a woman pokes her lips out at me like that it tells me she wants to be kissed."

Remington eyed his lips. She only had to lean a millimeter forward to press her mouth to his and she really wanted to but instead she tilted her head back, looking up at him.

"Well, you're wrong. That's definitely not what that look meant."

"You sure? Because I'm getting some serious pleasure vibes from that mouth of yours," Nathan said, his voice dangerously low and seductive.

Remington swallowed hard. What was happening here? Was Nathan Black outright flirting with her or was she imagining things?

"We both know that pleasure is not something you think about when I'm around. Annoyance maybe but pleasure, doubtful. You can barely stand me."

A soft chuckle bubbled up in Nathan's throat. "You

are a bit of an annoyance at times but I can guarantee you that you have no idea what truly goes on in my head when you're around, Miss English," Nathan said then tucked a stray strand of hair behind her ear. "Now grab your bag. My plane's waiting."

Remington's ear stung where Nathan's fingers had touched. Their eyes held for a few minutes and there it was again, that wild connection pushing and pulling between them.

Remington searched his face trying to figure out what was going on in that head of his but came up blank.

"I'll just grab my bag and we can go," she said finally.

"Cool," Nathan said, not taking his eyes off her.

Remington could feel his gaze on her as she made her way back through her apartment. It was unnerving. Hell, the entire exchange they just shared was unnerving.

Remington had a minor internal freak out as she stepped out of the plane in College Station and saw what was waiting for them on the tarmac. Unlike the car and driver that was waiting for them the last time they travelled to Texas, this time a yellow Aston Martin DBS Superleggera was sitting on the runway.

"Is that for us?" Remington asked, nearly salivating.

The car was a thing of beauty. She'd never seen one in real life but she'd read about them in several car magazines. Constructed out of carbon fiber and paired with a twin turbo charged engine, the Superleggera was one of the most exotic and astonishing cars on the market.

"Yep! If I recall from Sunday dinner, you have a thing for fast cars," Nathan said.

Remington shot him a smile. "I absolutely do."

"Good 'cuz you're driving," Nathan grinned then tossed a set of keys to her.

"Oh my gawd! Are you serious?" Remington squealed and raced around to the driver's side of the car. She snatched opened the door and slid inside. The leather seat was like butter and she sighed in delight at the feel of it.

"Pop the trunk so I can put the bags in," Nathan called.

Remington had no trouble finding the button for the trunk. She'd read so much about the car that she knew it inside and out. One would think she owned one herself.

Nathan tossed their bags in the trunk and hurried to the passenger seat. "We're heading to Texas A&M first to see D'Mariyon then we'll drive to Dallas and check into the hotel. We're not meeting my Cowboys contacts until this evening so we'll have time to relax at the hotel for a bit," Nathan said.

"Sounds good. Let me just plug the address in for the school and we can get going," Remington said, already working her fingers across the navigation screen on the dashboard.

"Ready for a little speed?" Remington asked, looking over at Nathan, her mouth tipped at the corners and her eyes dancing with excitement.

"I've never been scared to go fast. Let's do this."

That's all Remington needed to hear. She pressed her foot to the gas and took off.

Remington was in heaven. The Superleggara was everything she imagined and more. The car handled like a dream and was fast as all get out. She couldn't wait to open her up on the highway.

"You're really enjoying this, aren't you?" Nathan asked, eyeing her with a smile.

"I love it. Me and fast cars are like peanut butter and jelly. We just go together."

"I see that," Nathan said, staring at her.

Remington tightened her grip on the wheel. Not just to keep control of the beast of a machine she was commandeering but to also keep her nerves in check. Nathan's eyes on her was sending her hormones into a tailspin. She really wished he'd look out the window or something.

"Should we play some music?" Remington asked, turning on the radio.

Big mistake. The melodious and sensual voice of Jhene 'Aiko floated through the speakers, spiking the air in the car to scorching.

Remington pressed on the gas taking the Superleggera to almost max speed. She needed to get them to their destination and quick. The tight space in the small two-seater gave her no reprieve from the onslaught of Nathan's scent or the heat his body generated.

She cut her eyes over at Nathan. Unlike her, he was the picture of relaxation. He was situated comfortably in his seat, eyes closed, head resting against the seat and his hands in his lap. Remington watched him for a few seconds taking in the magnificent profile of his face. Even from the side the man was gorgeous. Perfect, skin, perfect nose, perfect everything.

"You a fan?" Nathan asked.

Remington jumped at the sound of his voice. "What?"

Nathan opened his eyes and looked over at her. "Jhene' Aiko? Are you a fan?"

"Oh," Remington sighed in relief. For a second she thought Nathan had caught here staring. "Yeah, I love her music. Her voice is so smooth and soothing."

"Yeah. I feel that. It's relaxing the shit out of me right now which I guess is good since I'm riding with a speed demon."

Remington shot him a look of mock indignation. "I haven't even maxed her out yet, Nathan."

"Well, shit! Everything's a blur out the window. I was sure that you were at max speed."

"Are you scared?" Remington asked, hitting him with a crooked smile.

"Of you?"

Remington raised an eyebrow at him.

Nathan shifted his body and focused his dark gaze on her, studying her. His eyes were intense. Remington could feel her body growing warm.

"I think any man would have a healthy fear of you, Remington."

"Why?"

"So many reasons. You're smart, strong, determined-"

"And that's scary?"

"Only in the sense that a woman like you could make a bachelor change his view on life," Nathan replied then shifted back in his seat and closed his eyes.

Remington wasn't sure what to make of that so she faced the road and focused on the drive.

They made it to Texas A&M in no time and met D'Mariyon at the Aggies practice field. The team had just finished practice and were headed to the locker room. Nathan flagged D'Mariyon down and waved him over.

"What's up Nathan," D'Mariyon greeted when he reached them.

"Sup, man?" Nathan said, dapping him up.

"Shit! Just finished practice. About to go see the trainer to get my quads worked out." He looked over at Remington. "What's up, Remington. Good to see you. Looking beautiful as always."

"You're a terrible flirt. You know that?" Remington said, shaking her head.

"What?" D'Mariyon asked, feigning innocence.

"It's good to see you again, D'Mariyon," Remington laughed. The kid was a riot.

"You two done?" Nathan asked looking from D'Mariyon to Remington.

D'Mariyon snickered and Remington tried hard to keep a straight face as she looked at Nathan.

"I stopped by to tell you that I'm meeting with some of my contacts at the Cowboys tonight," Nathan said.

"Oh word!" That's what's up, Nathan. Put in a good word for me, man."

"Fo' sho! That's the main reason I'm meeting with them. You said you wanted to stay in Texas and I'm trying to make that happen for you."

"I appreciate that, man."

"Already! So, how's everything? Your grandmother good?"

"She's alright. Been a little tired lately. I been trying to get her to go see a doctor but she can be pretty stubborn. I just want to make sure she's good so I'm not worrying about her and I can focus on my game."

"I know what you mean. It's always a task getting my grandmother to a doctor. I nag mine until she's tired of hearing about it and goes just to shut me up."

"I'mma try that," D'Mariyon said.

"Okay. Well, let me know if you need anything. We're going to head out. We're driving to Dallas."

"That's a nice little drive," D'Mariyon said.

"Yeah but I'm rolling with a speed queen here so we'll

probably get there in the half the time," Nathan said pointing at Remington.

"Whatever!" Remington laughed. "You're the one who got us the Superleggera. It's built for speed. What's a girl to do? Driving fast is a requirement."

"Well, be careful," D'Mariyon said. "Imma head inside. Thanks for stopping by and checking in, Nathan. You're different than the other agents."

"How so?"

"Man, when agents come through all they wanna do is talk shop and party. The whole focus is to get me to sign on that dotted line. None of them just stop by to check in and they for sure don't ask about my granny. I appreciate that about you. You be lookin' out."

"Like I told you, my goal is to look out for the well-being of you and your granny. It's not just about signing you for *my* benefit. It's about making sure you and your family are taken care of."

"I hear you. You a good dude, Nathan," D'Mariyon said dapping Nathan up. "I know ya'll trying to get out of here and hit the road and I gotta get in there to see the trainer so I'mma head to this locker room." He turned to Remington. "Later, Remington," he winked then jogged towards the building at the other end of the field.

"He's insufferable," Remington laughed.

"Yeah. The boy flirts with you like crazy. He's a good kid though." Nathan said as he stared after D'Mariyon.

"He really is," Remington agreed.

Nathan turned to Remington. "Ready for this drive to Dallas?"

"You know it," Remington replied, wiggling her eyebrows.

Nathan laughed and shook his head. "This three hour

drive is gonna take us two hours, isn't it?"

Remington just smiled sweetly then started walking towards the parking lot.

They made it to Dallas in just over two hours. Remington hit the gas and didn't let up until she pulled up to the Ritz Carlton Hotel, where Nathan had booked them rooms. Suites actually. Both on the same floor, right across from each other.

"Dinner isn't until seven so we have a few hours to kill. I've got to check on a few things at the office. Let's meet in the lobby at six-thirty. The restaurant is only a few blocks away from here and with your driving it won't take long to get there."

"Ha! Ha! You sure do talk about my driving a lot, Sir. Either you're scared or fascinated." Remington quipped.

"Maybe a little of both," Nathan said with a wink then went into his room.

Remington tapped her keycard on the lock pad and went into her own room. She'd stayed at quite a few hotels but never anything as fancy as the Ritz Carlton. She felt like a celebrity or royalty. The room was amazing. It was super spacious with a beautifully decorated sitting room and a full dining area. The master bedroom was located behind a set of double doors and was just as gorgeous as the rest of the room. A huge feather bed took up the majority of the bedroom and there was an adjoining bathroom constructed mostly of marble. Fancy as fuck!

Remington set her bag down on the bench at the foot of the bed then pulled out her cell phone.

Remington: *Guess where I am?*

Natalie: *Where?*

Remington: *Dallas! Ritz Carlton! Luxury Suite!*

Natalie: *Oh, you fancy!*

Remington: *No, Nathan Black's fancy. We're in Dallas to meet with some of his contacts at the Cowboys organization and he booked us suites at the Ritz. Nat! You should see this room. It's gorge!!!*

Natalie: *OMG! I'm so jelly right now. Nab some of those fancy little hotel shampoos and soaps for me. I know they got the good stuff. Lol!*

Remington: *Girl, you're a mess but I got you.*

Natalie: *Wait! So, you're in Dallas with Nathan? I take it ya'll are good now?*

Remington: *We're definitely better than we were. He called me last night and apologized for being such a dick. Said he'd try to do better.*

Natalie: *Well, that's good.*

Natalie: *Yeah. Hopefully he tries real hard because being an ass seems to come very easy for him. Lol! Anywayz...I'm gonna try and get a nap in before dinner. I'll hit you up later. Luv ya!*

Natalie: *Ditto! TTYL!*

Remington kicked off her shoes and climbed into the oversized bed and immediately sank into the billowy softness of the mattress. She closed her eyes and was asleep in no time.

An hour and a half later Remington woke up feeling well rested and refreshed. Guess that's what a feather bed in a luxury suite at the Ritz will do for you.

Remington grabbed her cell phone and checked the time; five-thirty. She had an hour before she had to meet Nathan in the lobby.

Remington scooted out the bed and made her way over to her overnight bag, pulled out her black dress and hung it in the closet then grabbed her toiletries and headed for the bathroom.

Forget the bed, the shower was amazing. It was like standing under a steaming hot waterfall in the tropics. The water pressure was perfect and the shower head had a setting that gave the most amazing water massage. Remington felt languid and relaxed as she stepped out of the shower.

She quickly oiled her damp skin with a jasmine scented body oil then slipped into a pair of black, lace matching bra and panties. It wasn't often that she got all dolled up so she decided to go a little extra with her makeup routine applying a light foundation, a smoky eye, and a little highlighter on her cheekbones. She finished the look with a dark red lip paint from Rhianna's *Stunna Lipstick Collection*.

She'd wrapped her hair in a silk scarf before getting into the shower to preserve her Brazilian Silk Press and when she undid the scarf her tresses fell soft, and silky around her shoulders and down her back.

Remington padded barefoot to the closet, grabbed her dress, slipped it on then stepped into her stilettos. She closed the closet door to get a look at herself in the full length mirror fixed to the door. She was slightly in awe of the woman staring back at her. Gone was the down to earth, no nonsense writer in jeans and a t-shirt. The woman staring back at her was sophisticated and sexy. It was a different look for her and she liked it.

CHAPTER NINE

NATHAN

Nathan took a sip of his drink as he waited at the bar for Remington to come down. They were supposed to meet in the lobby but Nathan finished his work quicker than he thought and decided to get dressed and have a drink before they left for dinner. He could see the lobby from the bar and figured he'd head over when he saw Remington enter the lobby. Only problem was that Nathan was not ready for how stunning Remington looked. He nearly choked on his drink when he saw her enter the lobby dressed to kill in a fitted black dress that hugged her curves the way his roadster hugged the curves on the mountainside when he drove to his cabin.

Nathan had been trying to play it cool with Remington all day. His attraction to her was off the charts and he'd been doing his best to keep himself in check. And now to have her come down for dinner looking like that. Was she trying to drive him mad?

Nathan downed the rest of his drink then made his

way to the lobby.

Remington was standing near the entrance her back to him as Nathan walked up.

His eyes took in her backside; from her glossy mane that hung softly down her back to the delicate curve of her waist that tapered down to curvy hips and a plump little ass that sat nicely in her dress.

"Shit," Nathan breathed out. The woman was all sex and fire and he badly wanted to be consumed by her.

Remington turned just then and gave him a smile that hit him straight in the gut. If he thought her backside was amazing her front was devastating. She'd done a little more than normal with her make-up giving her a glamorous look. Nathan already thought Remington had a natural beauty so to enhance it like she had only made her that more beautiful.

Nathan was hooked and there was nothing he could do about it. He wanted to devour every inch of her. He was suddenly filled with a greed and possessiveness like he'd never known. His hands itched to trace a path along the soft curve of her waist. To tunnel his hand in the silky tresses at the nape of her neck and tilt her head back and devour her mouth.

"Hey," Remington greeted him. "You look nice."

"I'm a'ight but you…you look stunning," Nathan complimented.

He could see a light color stain her cheeks as she bit her lip and cast her whiskey colored eyes to the floor.

"Thank you," came her quiet reply.

Nathan watched her for a few seconds and the more he stared at her the more he wanted to ditch dinner and take Remington back to his room and fuck her senseless all night.

"Should we go?" Remington asked, tilting her head slightly as she looked up at him.

Nathan took a minute to get his head right. The woman had thrown him for a loop. "Yeah, of course," he said then placed his hand at the small of her back and escorted her to the door.

Remington drove the short distance to the restaurant and Nathan nearly jumped from the car before she barely had it in park. Being boxed in the small interior of the Superleggera with Remington's sweet jasmine scent floating around the car was driving him to the brink. He damn near had to sit on his hands to stop himself from reaching over and pressing his fingers into her thigh while she drove.

"So, who exactly are we meeting?" Remington asked as they walked into the restaurant.

"Two guys I went to college with. They're on the coaching staff for the Cowboys now."

"And what's the plan? Will you ask them to sign D'Mariyon to the team?"

"That's not really how it works. I'm sure they already know who D'Mariyon is being that he's highly sought after. I already know he's getting an invite to the combine-"

"Combine?"

"It's where college athletes are put through tests to showcase their ability. Coaches from every professional team are there watching and critiquing them and deciding who they want on their team."

"Wow! Sounds intimidating."

"It can be but it's tradition. College athletes are well aware of the process and prepare for it. The point of the dinner tonight is to see if the Cowboys are looking at

D'Mariyon at all. If they're not, hopefully I can convince my boys that they should be."

"Nathan P.D. Black!" A man called from behind Nathan and Remington.

Nathan spun around, an amused smile on his face. "Lance P.B. Anderson," Nathan hollered.

The two men clasped hands and gave each other the one arm hug that guys do when greeting each other.

"It's been a minute, man. How the hell are you?" Lance asked.

"I been good. Just working on building my sports agency. What about you? You look like you done gained a few LBs," Nathan laughed and tapped Lance on the stomach.

"Aw, c'mon now, Nate. Don't do me. Besides this is just a little more for the ladies to hold on to."

"Yeah, I bet," Nathan said then turned to Remington. "Lance, this is Remington English. The writer I mentioned. Remington, Lance Anderson."

"Nice to meet you," Remington said, extending her hand to Lance who gave her a good once over before taking it and giving it a gentle shake.

"Very nice to meet you, Remington."

Nathan noticed that Lance was still holding Remington's hand which annoyed him. "Damn, Lance! Can the woman have her hand back?"

"My bad," Lance said with a crooked grin. "I was stuck on stupid for a minute. She is gorgeous. Nate, you didn't mention that. You are gorgeous," he finished, smiling wickedly at Remington.

"Thank you, Lance. That's very sweet," Remington blushed.

"Well if it isn't Panty Dropper and Playboy," a deep

voice called from the doorway.

Nathan, Remington and Lance all looked towards the door.

Warren Stone, retired NFL running back turned coach for the Cowboys, was sauntering towards them. He hadn't aged a bit and was still just as fit as he was in college.

Remington looked over at Nathan, her eyes dancing with amusement. "Panty Dropper and Playboy?"

"Old college nicknames. Nobody goes by those names anymore," Nathan said, waving it off.

"Oh, no you don't. You're not getting out of explaining those names. I need to know who's who," Remington said, trying not to laugh.

"I can help you with that, darlin'. First let me introduce myself. I'm Warren Stone."

"Nice to meet you, Warren. Remington English."

Warren cocked his head giving Remington an appreciative once over before looking over at Nathan and Lance. "Remington, meet Panty Dropper and Playboy," he said pointing to Nathan then Lance.

Nathan dropped his head. Leave it to Warren to be an instigator. He was one in college and Nathan could see that nothing had changed. The man loved getting under people's skin. It was all in good fun so Nathan couldn't get mad if he wanted to.

"Nathan, I have to know the backstory behind these names," Remington said, a feigned look of innocence on her face.

Nathan could see the tipping of a smile at the corner of Remington's mouth and he wanted nothing more than to kiss that smile right off that pretty mouth of hers. It would certainly stall her curiosity about his college nickname. But since he couldn't do that he decided to dodge her curiosity. "I think our table is probably ready. We should go check."

Lance let out a riotous howl of laughter. "What's the matter, Nate? You earned that nickname outright. Can't be ashamed of it now. I know I'm proud of mine."

"Ain't nobody ashamed. I've just outgrown it is all."

"That's not what the headlines say," Warren smirked.

"Nathan Black scores again!" Lance hollered, calling out the latest headline about Nathan.

Both Lance and Warren burst into laughter.

Nathan was not amused. He looked over at Remington who was trying to hide a smile behind her hand.

"I'm going to check on the table," Nathan said and strode off towards the hostess stand.

Nathan forgot what asses his friends could be. Taking jabs at one another was a staple for them in college. One that Nathan participated in with no qualms so why was he trippin 'now? Playing the dozens was something they did. He looked over at Remington and immediately knew why. She already thought he was an arrogant ass and a playboy and Nathan didn't need his homeboys adding to that perspective.

"Hi, reservation for four for Nathan Black," Nathan said to the young woman at the hostess stand.

"Good evening, Mr. Black. We have your table ready. I'll take you to it."

Nathan motioned the others over and the hostess escorted them to a booth near the back of the restaurant.

Remington sat down first and Nathan made it a point to slide into the booth next to her before Lance or Warren could. Nathan was well aware of the two men's attraction towards her and he wasn't feeling it one bit.

"So you guys were tight in college?" Remington asked.

"Yep. The terrible three," Lance chuckled.

"Terrible three?" Remington asked, looking over at Nathan.

"Not terrible as in we got in a lot of trouble," Nathan started to explain but Warren cut him off.

"Terrible as in the ladies had a terrible time trying to choose between the three of us. We were the hottest athletes at the school. We drove the girls nuts," Warren said.

"Remember that Delta party that we had to book it out of because the sisters found out that we were messing with all of them?" Lance laughed.

"That was a crazy night. Nate's ass had to jump out the second story window. You remember that?" Warren asked, looking at Nathan.

Nathan nodded. "Man, we were some true jackasses in college."

"Yeah, but we sure had fun," Lance laughed.

"That we did. And as much as I'd love to sit and reminisce all night; that's not why I'm here. I know ya'll are in the process of looking at players for the draft and I was wondering if ya'll were looking at D'Mariyon Taylor."

"That kid's a badass running back, man. Any team would be better for having him but we got a running back. We need some defensive hittas. That's who we've been scouting for." Warren said.

"Why you asking, man? What's up?" Lance asked.

"He's a good kid. Talented as shit. I been meeting with him. Working on getting him signed to my agency."

"And what? He wants to play for the Cowboys?" Warren asked.

"Got his heart set on it," Nathan said.

The waiter came by the table stalling the conversation.

"Good evening," the young man said as he approached the table. He was all welcoming smiles and warmth when he asked, "Can I get you all some drinks to start?"

"Yeah, bring me a jack and coke," Lance said.

Warren held up a finger. "I'll have the same."

"For you, Miss?" The waiter asked, fixing his gaze on Remington.

"A glass of red wine. You pick the brand," Remington said.

"We have an amazing house wine that I think you'd like. It's very lively. It has intense aromas of ripe red fruit, berries, hibiscus tea, toasted brioche and a very nice sweet oak finish."

"Sounds great," Remington said.

"And for you, Sir?" the waiter asked, turning to Nathan.

"I'll take a bourbon. Henry McKenna if you got it."

"Sure thing. I'll just go grab your drinks and take your orders when I come back."

Lance leaned his elbows on the table and looked at Nathan. "Nate, man, we know the kid is bad. We've seen him play but like War said, we don't really need a running back."

Nathan sighed. "That's too bad. He's a good kid. Needs a good team around him and I know if he's on a team with you two he'll be looked out for."

"You're really invested in this kid, huh?" Warren asked.

"Yeah, man. Whether he signs with me or not I want him to go somewhere with people who'll genuinely care about his wellbeing and his future. And what two chumps better than you two for that," Nathan added with a laugh.

"Aww, fuck you, Black," Lance laughed. He looked at Warren. "This fool needs a favor from us and he's calling us chumps."

"Well you know Nate always was the least smart of the three of us," Warren said and the two men burst out laughing.

"Yeah, okay," Nathan said, shaking his head.

"So, does this mean you'll put in a good word for D'Mariyon?" Remington asked, her eyes hopeful.

Nathan looked over at her and his stomach tightened. Goddamn she was beautiful. She'd been quietly observing the conversation between him and his boys. Taking mental notes for the memoir, no doubt. Normally, he'd be annoyed with the thought of her gathering intel for the memoir but he didn't seem to mind much at all right now.

"You know the kid?" Warren asked.

"I do," Remington nodded. "He's a wonderful young man. Very talented, smart and quite devoted to his grandmother. He wants to stay close to her when he enters the league so he's hell bent on joining the Cowboys. It would be awesome if you could put in a word for him."

Warren considered her, his eyes roaming over her face and slowly darkening as he took in her beauty.

Nathan watched his friend and frowned. He knew that look. Warren liked what he saw and Nathan didn't like that at all. If he knew his old friend, dude was about to start flirting.

Luckily, the waiter returned with their drinks and took their food orders. Unfortunately, that only held Warren off for a bit.

"Smart man, Nate, bringing a beauty like this to help

plead your case," Warren joked.

"What can I say, War? Beautiful women have always been a weakness of yours."

"You got me there," Warren laughed. "I'll see what I can do about getting the team to take a look at the kid."

"Thanks, man," Nathan said.

The foursome spent the rest of the evening joking and laughing at old college stories. The whole time Nathan tried to keeps his eyes off Remington who took easily to the guys and the conversation. She was witty and was able to hang with the fellas when they started playing the dozens again. Nathan was impressed and becoming more turned on by her with every minute that passed. The softness of her mouth painted dark red drew him in and her dark hair fell like a silk curtain around her shoulders. It was so shiny and looked so soft. Nathan wanted to run his fingers through it and bunch it in his fist, messing it all up as he took her wildly from behind.

"So, you dating anyone, Remington?" Nathan heard Warren ask.

He shot a look at his friend but Warren just ignored him.

"Not right now," Remington replied. "I've just been kind of focusing on my career."

"I can dig that but you gotta have a little fun. All work and no play can drive a person crazy," Warren said.

"I play a little," Remington said, her eyes twinkling with mischief.

"There's a bar across the street with a pool table. How about you come play with me for a little bit," Warren said, turning up the charm.

"I don't know. I have to confess that I'm not that good at pool."

"Don't worry 'bout that. I'm a great teacher," Warren said, his voice thick with innuendo.

"Well in that case-,"

Nathan raged as he watched one of his oldest friends make a pass at the woman that he was becoming increasingly enamored with. Had it been anybody else, Nathan would have grabbed him by the collar, drug him out the restaurant and tossed his ass on the street.

"Sorry, Warren, but it's getting late and we have an early flight out in the morning," Nathan cut in, his voice a little gruffer than he intended.

Remington whipped her head in his direction, a questioning look in her eye.

Warren's look was one of amusement.

Nathan and Warren locked eyes in a silent challenge.

"Here we go," Lance mumbled as he stared from Nathan to Warren.

There was a quiet tension at the table now but Nathan didn't give one fuck about it. He was not about let Warren move in on Remington.

Nathan turned his gaze on Remington. "My plane will be at DFW at 8am tomorrow. It's already after ten so I figured we want to get back to the hotel and get a good night's sleep. Seeing how we've been on the move all day."

"I guess I could use some downtime," Remington agreed.

She looked over at Warren. "Raincheck on that game of pool?"

Warren leaned back against the booth and let out a small chuckle. "Absolutely."

"I'll just get the check," Nathan said, motioning for the waiter.

He paid the bill and the foursome headed for the door.

"Nate, man, it was good to see you," Lance said clasping hands with Nathan and pulling him in for a one-arm hug.

"You too, Lance. We'll have to really hang out next time I'm in town or better yet you boys need to come out to Cali."

"Oh, I'm there," Warren said, dapping Nathan up.

Lance turned to Remington. "It was great meeting you."

"You too," she replied.

Warren sidled up to Remington and took her hand. "It was such a pleasure meeting you, Remington. I'm going to hold you to that raincheck," he winked.

"I hope you do," Remington smiled sweetly at him.

Nathan cleared his throat causing both Warren and Remington to look over at him.

A devilish smile tipped the corners of Warren's mouth as he reached into his pocket and pulled out his wallet. He pulled a business card out and handed it to Remington. "Give me a call sometime. We can get to know each other better so that when you come back to Dallas we'll be well acquainted."

"You really are a big 'ole flirt," Remington said, taking the card.

"I think our car is here," Nathan said and grabbed Remington by the elbow. "Fellas, thanks for dinner and putting in a word for D'Mariyon. I'll be in touch."

Remington could barely say goodbye before Nathan was ushering her out the door.

Nathan grabbed the key from the valet. "I'll drive," he said.

Remington gave him a questioning look but didn't say

anything. She simply slid in the passenger's seat when he opened the car door.

Nathan bent down and pulled the seatbelt across her body fastening her in. Something he'd never done for any woman and he regretted it immediately because Remington's sweet scent smacked him right in the face. She smelled so good he could almost taste her on his tongue. Nathan swallowed loud and hard.

"You okay," Remington asked, her warm breath fanning the side of his face.

Nathan stilled but refused to look at her for fear that he would take her mouth right then and there. "I'm fine," he said then stepped back, closed the door and made his way to the driver's side.

Nathan took a deep inhale before getting into the car. His hormones were all over the place. He was agitated with the flirting that went on between Warren and Remington at dinner yet he was completely turned on right now. The shit was nerve wracking as hell.

Nathan gripped the steering wheel like his life depended on it as he drove the short distance to the hotel. The tension in the car was thick and he was on the verge of exploding with need for Remington.

Remington kept stealing glances at him but he was determined to keep his eyes on the road. One look at her would have him pulling over, settling her in his lap, pushing her panties to the side and fucking her right there in the front seat of the car.

Nathan was relieved when they pulled up to the Ritz. He was out of the car before the Valet guy came over.

Nathan hurried to the door, holding it open for Remington. They walked in silence to the elevator and waited quietly for the elevator car to descend and the doors to open.

Remington entered the car first. Nathan followed and moved to the far side of the elevator, his hands tucked securely in his pockets.

"Are you sure everything is okay, Nathan? I feel like your upset with me."

Nathan closed his eyes, trying to get his bearings together before responding to her. His body was tense when he turned to face her. "Definitely not upset," he said.

Remington took a step towards him. "Then what is it?"

Nathan bit his bottom lip as his eyes took in her delicious curves. "I'm trying to behave and keep my hands to myself but you're making it very difficult for me."

Remington's eyes rounded in shock and her mouth formed a little oh of surprise. Heat flushed her face and Nathan could see every emotion she was feeling – surprise, excitement, lust.

He was feeling all the same things. He knew he shouldn't act on any of them but he was at his wits end. All control was gone at this point.

Nathan took one stride, closing the distance between them. "I really want to taste you," he said, his voice low. He braced one hand on Remington's shoulder and pressed the other into her lower back. "Your hair. That dress. That mouth. You've been wreaking havoc on me all night and all I want to do is bury my face between your thighs."

Remington gasped.

"If that's not what you want just say so and I'll leave you as soon as these elevator doors open and we won't speak of this again. But, if you want me like I want you-"

Nathan couldn't even finish his sentence because Remington pressed her mouth to his showing him just what she wanted.

Desire, wild and hot coursed through Nathan. He took control of the kiss parting Remington's lips and driving his tongue inside. He backed her against the elevator wall, pressed his body to hers and kissed her with a fierceness that was wild, erratic and untamed.

Remington cried out as Nathan kissed a trail from her mouth down her throat and suckled the soft flesh between her neck and shoulder. He pressed his hips into hers and ground his dick into her. Nathan was hard as shit and he wanted her to feel just want she was doing to him.

"Nathan," Remington moaned.

"Mmmhmm," Nathan groaned against her skin. He skimmed his lips up her neck and found her mouth again."

"The elevator's not moving," Remington whispered against his lips.

Nathan laughed. "Too preoccupied I guess." Nathan kissed her again, hard and hot before moving away to hit the button for their floor.

The elevator started moving and Nathan made his way back over to Remington and took her mouth once again.

They barely made it inside the dark foyer of Remington's suite before they stripped each other with trembling fingers. Naked and heated, Nathan took a step back. He wanted to get a look at Remington and it was just as he thought. Her body was perfection. Her breast were round and full with chocolate nipples that sat hard and aroused and her tummy was flat and tapered down to softly, rounded hips.

Nathan reached out and slid his hand along her collar bone and down the center of her chest. The soft ripple of her abdomen under his touch turning him on even more. He stroked and caressed the contours of her body before pressing her to him and slinking them down to the cold marble floor.

Nathan wanted to be a gentleman. He wanted to take her to the bed but he couldn't wait. He needed to taste her now so he made a quick journey from her mouth to her thighs placing kisses along her flesh. He paused and hovered at the cute little strip of dark hair covering her pussy. He could smell the sweet heat of her sex and his heart pounded. He wanted her so badly. Nathan nudged her thighs apart and settled his mouth at her core.

"Look at me," he ordered, wanting her to watch as he devoured her.

Remington's breathing was thick and labored. She lifted her head and gazed down at him, her whiskey eyes glazed with need.

Nathan locked eyes with her and lowered his mouth. That first swipe of his tongue against her warm, wet clit was heaven. And Remington's reaction only amped up his need.

Remington let out a deep, guttural groan and lifted her hips to meet his mouth. Nathan loved it and dove right in kissing, licking and sucking at the tight little bud between her thighs.

Remington squirmed, bucked and tried to scramble away.

"Unh-unh. You ain't going nowhere," Nathan mumbled against her sopping wet pussy.

"Nathan, please," Remington begged.

"Nope," Nathan said, tightening his grip on her thighs.

He swirled his tongue around and up and down before thrusting it inside her quivering opening. This sent Remington wild and she bucked against his mouth while Nathan thrust his tongue in and out of her until her thighs quaked and warm honey dripped from her core into his mouth.

Nathan took in every drop, lapping eagerly at her juicy folds.

"Oh my God! Nathan, please," Remington begged again.

Nathan chuckled against her pussy then crawled up her body hovering over her.

"Damn, you taste good," he said then dipped his head and kissed her, letting her taste herself.

Remington wrapped her arms around him, gripping his ass with one hand and pushing down so his rock hard dick pressed against her. She started a slow grind against him and Nathan wanted nothing more than to drive his dick deep inside her but he didn't have on any protection and he didn't want to take her for the first time on the floor.

"Come on," he said lifting off her and pulling her up. "Let's go to the bed." He grabbed Remington's hand then stopped. "One sec." He moved over to his pants which were in a heap by the door and grabbed two condoms from his wallet. He made his way back over to where Remington was waiting and lifted her over his shoulder barbarian style.

"Nathan," she squealed.

Nathan ignored her protest and moved to the bedroom. He laid Remington on the bed then pressed a knee into the plushness to join her but she rolled away from him.

"My turn," Remington said with sexy confidence as she pressed him down into the mattress with on hand.

Nathan grinned up at her like a kid in a candy story. Lord knows he loved a sexually confident woman.

"Such a great view," Remington said with a wicked smile as she perused his body. Her eyes roaming over him. She ran her hands over the tattoos that covered his chest and torso. "So beautiful," she whispered.

"You a fan of tats?"

She nodded then trailed her eyes from his chest down to his waist.

The way she was looking at him, worshipping him with her eyes sent Nathan over the edge and his dick hardened even more if that was possible. His dick literally jumped and pointed straight at her. He wanted to grab her and shove himself deep inside of her but she was in charge for the moment so Nathan put his hands behind his head and stared up at her. Her pert breasts were the perfect handful and sat perky on her chest. Her brown skin was soft and smooth over the delicate but firm frame of her body. And don't get him started on that face of hers. Pure perfection. Fuck, she was stunning.

"You should see my view," Nathan teased.

Remington smiled as she leaned forward and wrapped her fingers around the base of his dick. She kept her eyes locked with his as she lowered her head and flicked her tongue over the tip of his dick.

Nathan shuttered. This woman would be the death of him.

"You like that?" Remington whispered then ran her tongue all around the tip before sliding it down the length of him and back up.

"Fuck yeah," Nathan groaned, watching her through

lust hazed eyes.

Remington smiled then took the entire length of him in her mouth. She moved her head up and down, squeezing her lips gently around his shaft.

She was all mouth and Nathan loved that. Her hands were busy sliding up and down his torso, her nails scraping gently against his skin while she worked his dick over with her mouth.

Nathan tried to contain himself but she was working him so good that he couldn't help but dig his fingers into her scalp. He watched as his dick, slick with her spit, disappeared between that lovely mouth of hers.

Nathan could feel a tightening in his balls and he knew he was on the verge of coming but he wasn't ready for that yet. He needed to feel the sweet heat of her pussy squeezing and milking him.

"Baby girl," he groaned and gently pushed her head back. His dick popped out of her mouth and bounced gently up and down. "Come here so I can fuck you," Nathan said and sat up.

Remington crawled up his body and Nathan wrapped his hand around the back of her neck and pulled her in for a kiss before pressing her back onto the bed. He lifted one of her legs over his shoulder opening her up wide. Nathan stared down at her as he positioned his dick at her opening then pushed inside.

Remington's back arched off the bed. "Fuck, you're big," she moaned.

"I'm barely halfway in," Nathan said, his brow lifting and his mouth tipped in a cocky grin.

"Well shit," Remington said and bit her bottom lip.

"I'll go slowly," Nathan said pushing himself in a little deeper. He watched her closely as he inched himself inside. He was eager to fill her up but he didn't want to hurt her.

"Gawtdamn, you're tight," he said.

"It's been a minute."

"You good? You want me to stop?"

"I'm great. You better not stop. Can you not feel how wet I am?"

Oh, he could feel it alright. She was a fucking waterfall. Nathan pushed himself all the way inside her until his balls rested against her ass cheeks then he stilled allowing her to adjust to the full girth of him.

He pressed kisses along her ankle and calve as he slowly began to move his hips back and forth.

Her pussy was a vice grip on his shaft, squeezing and releasing with every in and out thrust. He wanted to take it slow but she felt too good. Nathan couldn't stop himself from picking up the pace and slamming into her.

Remington took it like a champ, bucking against him and grabbing and clutching the sheets as she cried out. Her moans floating to the ceiling and filling the room.

Nathan watched her, fixated on the unadulterated ecstasy in her face. The sight of it revved him up even more.

"Shit!" Nathan roared and pumped his hips faster. Sweat coated his muscled frame as he looked down at his dick as it disappeared and then reappeared with each hot glide. He could feel her walls tightening around him as her climax was building. Nathan leaned forward taking the leg that was pressed against his shoulder with him. This exposed her pink core even more and Nathan couldn't look away even if he wanted to as his dick glistened with her juices.

"Oh fuck!" Remington screamed out in climax, juices gushing from her opening.

Nathan rode her hard pulling every last drop of that sweet nectar from her body before pulling out and turning her over on her stomach. He tapped his dick lightly against her butt cheeks before shoving it back inside her. He pounded into her for a few seconds before pulling her up on all fours, grabbing a handful of her hair and gently tugging her head back creating the perfect dip in her spine so her ass poked out just right.

"Fuuuuuck!" Nathan cried. "I thought about fucking you like this so many times. Fucking fantasies were never this good," Nathan growled then shoved his dick back inside her. Nathan fucked her hard, ramming his dick in and out of her, his thighs slapping loudly against her backside.

Remington moaned and worked her hips back against him driving Nathan crazy.

Nathan felt himself stiffen like iron and he deepened his thrusts pumping furiously into her. He was on the verge of cumming and there was nothing he could do about it.

"God, yes!" Remington hissed as her body began to shake violently with another orgasm.

Nathan lost all control slamming into her, his grip on her hip and hair tightened and his entire body went rigid as he climaxed releasing weeks of pent up lust and frustration.

Nathan stilled taking a moment to gather himself before releasing Remington's hair and gently pressing her down into the mattress. He followed her down laying lightly on top of her. He was still buried deep inside her, not ready to break the connection just yet.

Nathan placed soft kisses along the back of her neck and shoulders and Remington sighed out every time his lips touched her skin. The sound was music to his ears. These past few weeks of pent-up frustration had been laid bare in this hotel room and Nathan never felt more satisfied in his entire life.

CHAPTER TEN

REMINGTON

Remington lay nestled with her backside against Nathan, his arm draped lazily across her middle. She couldn't believe what happened. One minute she and Nathan were standing tense and awkward in the elevator and the next minute she was kissing him. This was not how she thought the trip to Dallas would go at all but she was happy it did. These past few weeks with Nathan had been a crazy, intense ride of anger, longing, annoyance and lust. It felt good to unleash all those pent up emotions. And unleash she did. Remington felt her body heat and flush as she thought about the deliciously dirty things they did. The naughty things *she* did. Taking Nathan in her mouth like that. She'd given head before but never so wantonly and so enthusiastically. The memory of his heavy length on her tongue had her wanting more. She shifted closer to Nathan pressing her bare ass deeper into his middle. Nathan's dick twitched and hardened just like she wanted. His hand shifted from her belly to cup her breast and Remington let out a low moan. He kneaded the fleshy mound and Remington covered his hand with hers. Their hands stayed there for a few minutes massaging her breast before Remington guided his hand down her belly to her pussy which was pulsing and already wet. Nathan played his fingers up and down her slit before slipping two fingers inside.

Remington opened her legs and arched into him. His fingers were magic as they strummed her into a quick, hot orgasm. She rolled over to face him. The room was dark but she could just make out the hard, beautiful contours of his face. The man was as gorgeous as all get out. She ran her fingers lightly across his lips before bringing her mouth to his and kissing him hard and deep.

"Mmmm, I like the way you wake me up," Nathan mumbled against her mouth. He pulled her on top of him and pressed his fingers into her fleshy bottom and ground up into her.

They kissed, their tongues dueling and lashing at each other hungrily.

Remington spread her thighs straddling Nathan's waist. She lifted her hips, grabbed Nathan's thick and weighty dick and guided her core down onto him. Her lips welcomed him; suckled him as she sank downward with deliberate slowness until she was so completely full of him that there was no telling where she began and he ended. They both tensed and the air in the room electrified heightening the intensity of their union.

Nathan's dick throbbed inside her and Remington closed her eyes, tossed her head back and reveled in the feel of it.

It wasn't until Nathan brought his hands up to lightly grasp her waist that she started moving. She moved slow and rhythmically riding him in a snakelike motion. Her inner walls tightened, gripping and releasing his hard rod as she slid up and down the length of him. She arched her back and braced her hands behind her on his thighs and popped her hips up and down and back and forth.

The shit felt so good that Remington thought she might drift away into oblivion from ecstasy. Moan after moan rang out deep from her gut as her heart raged and her body soared.

Nathan lowered his hand from her hip and ran his thumb across the tiny bud peeking out from her folds. The sensation was so intense that Remington bucked and sped up her pace grinding down on him harder and faster.

Remington was lost in pure pleasure. She'd had sex with other men and not one of them compared to what she was experiencing with Nathan. Being with Nathan was like staring at a Picasso for hours then finally being able to call it your own and take it home. Everything about the man was incredible. He crept into the very heart of her and ran rampant through her veins leaving his mark irrevocably etched in her soul.

"Come for me, baby girl," Nathan ordered, his voice gruff.

And that was all she wrote. Remington fell apart. Her mouth fell open on a throaty cry from deep in her belly. Her hips thundered down grinding on Nathan's dick and the wet, sticky noise of her orgasm bounced off the hotel walls.

"Shit, I'm gonna cum. You gotta get up," Nathan ground out through clenched teeth."

Nathan's words were lost on Remington as she rode the waves of orgasm, crashing; her hips still barreling down on him.

"Remington, I don't have on protection. I'm gonna cum in you if you don't get... aaah!" Whatever Nathan was about to say was lost as his balls tightened and his seed raced up his shaft and shot out the tip deep into Remington's womb.

Remington could feel the warm stream of cum filling her up and she relished in it. This was the first time a man had ever come inside her. Hell, this was the first time she'd ever had sex without a condom. She should feel some type of way about it but she didn't. All she felt was a delightful warmth permeating throughout her body. She released Nathan's thighs and fell forward landing softly on his chest which was heaving as he tried to catch his breath. Her own breathing was heavy like she'd just ran a marathon.

Remington stayed in that same position, laying on top of Nathan, covered in sweat, their bodies still connected at the waist until both of their breathing evened out.

"You're a very bad girl, Ms. English. You don't play fair." Nathan said, breaking into the quiet.

"I have no idea what you mean," Remington smiled into his smooth chest.

Nathan shifted up on his elbows forcing Remington to sit up. They were still joined at the waist and the movement caused Nathan's dick to twitch and thicken a bit inside her.

"I think you do."

Remington just grinned and shrugged coyly. She enjoyed sex just like the next person but she'd never been as aggressive as she was with Nathan. She normally let the guy take the lead but being with Nathan was different. He brought something primal out of her.

"I guess I got a little carried away," Remington admitted.

"A little?" Nathan tilted his head in mock indignation.

"Okay, maybe a lot. But, you should know that I'm on the pill and my last STD test came back with all negatives."

"That *is* good to know. And things are all good on my end as well. I get tested regularly and my last test, like all the rest, came back clean.

"Well there you go. Is my naughty behavior forgiven?" Remington asked, teasingly.

Nathan narrowed his eyes at her and before she knew what was happening he had flipped her on her back and pinned her arms above her head. His dick was on full rock again and Remington widened her legs opening herself up to him.

"Damn, girl! You got me so out of character right now," Nathan growled and pulled his hips back then rocketed into her. Nathan fucked her hard and fast, keeping her arms caged above her head and his eye locked with hers.

Remington felt utterly possessed by him. Her body, soul and heart surrendered to him completely with each punishing thrust he unleashed on her. She lifted her hips meeting him stroke for stroke until they both came again. This little dance happened all throughout the night; Remington on top, Nathan pounding her from behind with a fistful of her hair and so on until they finally drifted to sleep exhausted and utterly satisfied.

Remington groaned as she rolled over onto her back. Every muscle in her body ached. The way she and Nathan went at it like wild animals all night she would probably be sore for the next few days but she didn't mind at all.

She rolled onto to her side in search of Nathan only to find an empty bed. Concern creased her brow and she sat up wrapping the sheet around her naked body.

Panic started to set in. Had he hit it and skipped out? The man did have a reputation as the ultimate playboy. Scoring with any and every woman he laid eyes on.

Dread filled Remington and her heart sank into her belly. She should have known better. A playboy like Nathan Black wanted only one thing from a woman. Hell, he said it himself, long-term relationships and marriage was just not something he was interested in. Remington dropped her head in her hands and rubbed her temples.

"You good?"

Remington's head shot up to find Nathan standing in the bedroom door. He was leaning against the frame his chest bare and he wore a pair of dark grey pajama bottoms that hung low exposing the hard cut of muscle arrowing on either side of his hips. He looked like a Nubian God.

Remington held her breath choking down the moan that wanted so desperately to come out as she stared at him. The man was an entire snack. "I'm fine. Just woke up."

Nathan stood in the doorway watching her closely before the corner of his mouth tipped into a cocky grin. "So about last night..."

"About that," Remington said. She was confident as shit last night but suddenly, in the light of day, she was feeling completely exposed under his watchful gaze. She tugged the sheet tighter around her body.

"So you're back to being the modest, good little writer girl again," Nathan said, nodding towards the sheet.

Color flushed Remington's skin. "Very funny."

"I wasn't trying to be," Nathan said, pushing off the doorframe and moving towards the bed.

He pressed one knee into the mattress and leaned over on his hands. He was close enough to Remington that she could feel the heat of his body but far enough away that she'd have to lean over to touch him.

"Last night you were wild and completely uninhibited and now you're tucked away behind that sheet hiding from me. What's up?" Nathan asked, his dark eyes piercing through Remington like glass.

"Nothing," she replied, shifting her gaze away from him.

Nathan cocked his head to the side and studied her. "You can talk to me, Remington. Hell, after what we did last night there should be no shame between us at all."

Remington bit her lower lip. He was right. All barriers were down last night. Literally.

She brought her gaze up to meet his, "It's just that I woke up and you weren't here. I thought..."

Nathan pulled back and sat down on the edge of the bed. His dark eyes smoked over like a cloudy, grey sky as he stared at Remington and her heart clenched. She looked away unable to hold the intense disappointment in his gaze.

"Remington," he called then waited for her to look at

him but she couldn't.

He continued anyway. "You're different from other women I've been with. I've never been more frustrated, horny, angry or needy with any other woman. Shit, I've never in my life fucked a woman raw before. You do something to me. I can barely think straight when I'm around you. You know that?"

Remington closed her eyes against the force of feelings that moved through her at his words.

She felt the bed dip and knew he was moving over to where she sat.

"Baby girl," Nathan whispered. "You gotta tell me something."

"This scares me. You scare me. You have such a crazy reputation when it comes to women and you said yourself that you don't see yourself in a long term relationship. And me, I have all these feelings. And the way I lost control last night. The things I did. I turned into a complete floosy. And I'm not like that, Nathan. It's you and the way you make me feel. I just want to do anything and everything with you..." Remington rambled.

Nathan scooted closer to her spreading his legs out wide and pulling her over and settling her between his thighs. He tucked a finger under her chin and titled her head up.

Remington kept her gaze cast down, too embarrassed to look at him after all she'd just said.

"Baby girl," Nathan coaxed. "Did you hear anything I said? You got me completely open and fucking reckless over here. I don't fuck without a condom. I never have and never imagined I ever would. Then you come along and fuck my whole shit up. Now I'm a mess. You a mess. Hell, we're both just two hot fucking messes but I'm not even mad about it."

Remington's heart melted into a million pieces and she slowly lifted her gaze to meet his. "So what do we do?"

"We ride it out and see what happens."

"Jax is gonna be pissed. I know he warned you not to get involved with me."

"He did, but I'm a grown ass man and you're a full grown woman. What we do is none of his business," Nathan smirked.

"So we're not telling him then," Remington laughed.

"Nah," Nathan said then pulled her in for a kiss that Remington felt all the way to her toes.

Nathan's jet was waiting for them on one of the private runways at the Dallas Fort Worth Airport. This time they sat next to each other, Remington by the window and Nathan in the aisle seat. When Amber came by to ask if they wanted drinks or snacks they both declined and Nathan told her they would be good the entire flight and there was no need to check on them again.

Amber smiled politely and without instruction closed the little curtain shutting them off from the back of the plane creating their own little private section.

"Did you really just send her away for the rest of the flight?" Remington asked, cocking a brow at Nathan.

"If there's anything you need, I got you," Nathan replied sliding his hand over her thigh.

"Oh, so it's going to be that kind of flight home," Remington smirked.

Nathan didn't say anything. Instead, he reached over, unbuckled her seatbelt and slid her onto his lap so she was straddling him.

"You ever joined the mile high club?" He asked.

With her lip pulled between her teeth, Remington stared down at Nathan through hooded eyes and shook her head.

"We'll you're about to," he said licking his lips as his fingers tightened on her hips.

Remington stared down at his mouth, so full and thick. She flicked her tongue out and ran it across his bottom lip.

Nathan's eyes darkened, swallowed in lust so strong she could feel the depths of it all throughout her body.

"Fuck, you're sexy," Nathan breathed out. He reached down and tugged at the hem of Remington's t-shirt. "Take this off," he ordered.

Remington shifted and pulled the shirt over her head. She shivered as Nathan ran his fingers lightly up her back, over her shoulders and down the slope of her breast before running his thumb over her hardened nipple. She arched into his touch and bit down on her tongue suppressing the moan that was sure to come out if she opened her mouth even an inch.

"Shit, I wanna fuck you. Stand up," Nathan said.

Remington didn't hesitate. She was already his and would do anything he asked. It didn't matter that they were on a plane and that despite the curtain separating them from the rest of the plane, Amber could easily come back and catch them.

Remington eased off his lap and stood in the aisle.

Nathan went to work quickly unfastening her jeans and pushing them down her thighs. He traced his fingers along the lace trim of her panties then pulled them down too.

Remington watched with bated breath as he moved his face close to her sex, his breath fanning lightly across the tiny strip of hair covering it. Juices leaked from her core and slid down her inner thigh and he hadn't even touched her yet.

"Damn. I love how wet you get for me, girl," Nathan said then ran his tongue up her inner thigh slaving up the trail of wetness.

Remington groaned, thrusting her head back. "Nathan!" Her legs trembled as she stared down at his dark head.

"Hmmm?" He mumbled as he worked his mouth up her thigh to the apex of her sex. "Tell me what you want, Baby girl."

Remington was so worked up and ready for him that she couldn't find the words to speak.

Nathan tipped his head up and looked at her expectantly.

"Nathan, please," she begged.

He grinned then coasted his mouth over the tender folds hiding her tight little bud. He stayed there for a few seconds running his tongue up and down the seam before dipping into the silken wetness inside.

"Shit!" Remington gasped as she grabbed the back of his head and held on while he licked, sucked and devoured her.

After he had his fill, Nathan stood up, his mouth glistening with her juices.

It turned Remington on even more seeing his mouth saturated with her essence and she drove forward nipping and sucking at his lips.

Nathan let her have her fill for a few minutes before tangling his fingers in the hairs at base of her neck and pulling her head back.

Remington stared up at him, heart thumping, pussy throbbing. She wanted him so badly. Without a word she turned around and bent over bracing herself on the back of the seat and poked her ass out presenting herself to him like a prized stallion. She tossed her gaze over her shoulder welcoming him with her eyes.

A slow, menacing grin transformed Nathan's handsome face into something sinister and sexy. Remington held her breath as Nathan undid his pants and pulled out his dick. It was already thick and rock hard. He grabbed the base and slid it down the crack of her ass then between the slick folds of her sex. A new stream of juices flowed from her center coating Nathan's dick, lubing it with her arousal.

Sparks tickled Remington's belly as he teased the tip at her entrance.

"I don't think I've been this hard in my entire life," Nathan rasped before sliding inside her wet, tight cavern stretching her wide until he was buried balls deep.

Remington's head jerked back on a low moan and her fingers dug into the leather seat as she scrambled desperately for something grounding as her body and mind soared to heights they've never been before.

Nathan tangled his fingers in her hair, tugged sharply and went to town pounding into her.

His thrusts were savage and Remington loved every punishing stab and every hard slap of his thighs against her ass. The pleasure of having this amazingly virile, sexy and powerful man inside her body, taking her and owning her sent Remington up in flames. Her mouth slackened as a slow whine built in the base of her throat. She was so close to coming. The way his thick dick beat at the tender spots inside her.

Nathan pressed down on her spine pushing her hips higher in the air and opening her up even more.

Sensations exploded throughout Remington's body and she thought she might faint from the sheer pleasure rocking her. She could hear the wet slosh of her cum saturating his dick as she cried out for him to fuck her harder.

"That's right, baby girl, come all over this dick," Nathan coaxed as he rode out her climax.

Nathan's voice was gruff with pleasure and Remington loved the sound of it. It traveled across her body taking her to new heights and prolonging her climax.

Nathan continued riding her, his thrusts turning into a series of quick strokes as he moved both hands to her hips. He drove into her over and over before jerking and dumping his entire load into her.

The cabin was filled with quiet pants as they both came down.

Nathan leaned over and placed a sweet kiss on Remington's shoulder before pulling out of her. Thick, white semen dripped from her core and trickled slowly down her inner thigh.

"Seems we made a mess," Nathan said, running his finger up her thigh and wiping her off.

Remington turned on shaky legs. She looked at the thick, white stickiness on his fingers, then at him, then back at his fingers before grabbing his hand and pulling his fingers into her mouth. She took in the sweet and slightly tangy taste of his cum and decided that she liked the taste of him.

Remington licked his fingers dry then politely released them as if it was something she did for him all the time.

"Gawtdamn!" Nathan said biting his lip and staring at her like he wanted to take a bite of out of her.

Remington chuckled. "It's your fault. I can't seem to control myself when it comes to you. You've turned me into a little harlot."

Nathan slung his arm around her waist and pulled her to him. "*My* little harlot," he growled then kissed her full on the mouth.

CHAPTER ELEVEN

NATHAN

T he minute they touch down in Burbank, Nathan was filled with worry and apprehension at the thought of being away from Remington. He wanted what they started in Dallas to continue when they got home. He wasn't ready to be away from her yet which was crazy because he normally couldn't stand to be with any one woman longer than a few hours at a time outside of having sex.

He stole a glance at Remington who was busy gathering her things. But damn, she was gorgeous. He wanted to grab her, lock her securely in his arms and kiss the shit out of her. If he thought she drove him crazy before; after having her taste on his tongue and hearing her deep, guttural moans as he lay into her over and over again, he was completely insane behind her now.

"I think I've got everything," she said, turning to face him, her large overnight bag in hand.

Nathan swallowed the lump that had formed in his throat. "After you," he said sweeping his arm wide to allow her to move down the aisle before him.

They rode in silence to her place. The air in the car thick with sexual tension. Nathan could feel Remington's eyes on him as he drove. They roamed freely across his face and down his body several times before she reached over and placed her hand lightly on his thigh.

Nathan tensed and gripped the steering wheel as he tried to focus on the road. It was a hard thing to do with her hand so near his dick which was thickening by the second.

He let out a low hiss when she grazed her fingers along the side of it. "You trying to make me crash, girl?"

"Sorry," she said, snatching her hand back and pressing it between her thighs.

Nathan cut his eyes at her. She looked like a naughty school girl caught smoking under the bleachers.

"Don't apologize. There's nothing I want more then your hands on me but if you want us to get safely to your place you're gonna have to keep those naughty little fingers to yourself."

"Well you better hurry because I'm not sure how long I can keep my hands to myself," Remington said, her eyes teasing.

Nathan pressed on the gas and gunned it hoping there were no cops around.

They made it to Remington's place quickly, safely and without getting pulled over. Nathan grabbed her bag out of the car and carried it to her apartment.

"So Dallas was fun," Remington said, stopping in front of her apartment door.

"It was," Nathan nodded.

A sensual curl of longing floated in the air between them and Nathan leaned into Remington pressing her back against the door. "Come to my cabin with me," he said.

"Your cabin in Lake Almanor? Where you go to get away?"

"That's the one. You can pack some clothes and we'll head out there right now."

"What about work?"

"I'm the boss. I can work from anywhere and since your work is all about me right now, you go where I go."

Remington's lids lowered hiding her thoughts from him and Nathan worried that she would say no.

He put a finger under her chin and tipped her head up. "I'm not ready to leave you yet," he confessed.

Nathan watched as Remington's pretty face went from shock to delight before she reared up on her toes and kissed him lightly on the mouth.

"I'll just grab a few things then," she said, then turned and unlocked the door.

Nathan followed her inside and shut the door.

"I'll just be a minute. Have a seat. Do you want anything to drink while you wait?"

"I'm good. Just hurry your little ass up," Nathan said, slapping her playfully on the behind. He watched her hips sway slightly as she disappeared down the hall.

Nathan looked around her space while he waited. Her apartment smelled of that sweet vanilla scent that sometimes wafted off her body when she was near.

The living room was nice. It was spacious and decorated in vibrant reds and tans. A fireplace sat on one side of the room and the mantle was crowded with pictures of her with an older couple who he assumed where her parents. The older woman had the same light brown skin and cute little nose that Remington had. There were also several pictures of her with an attractive, young Latina woman about her same age. They were smiling and laughing in almost all of the pictures.

"Ready," Remington sang from behind him.

"Are these your parents?" Nathan asked, pointing to the pictures on the mantle.

Remington moved over to stand next to him. "Yeah, that's my mom and dad."

"Your mom is beautiful. You look just like her."

"Thank you," Remington said, heat coloring her cheeks.

Nathan liked how easily embarrassed she got when he complemented her.

"And who's that?" He asked, pointing to a picture of Remington and the young, Latina woman standing in Times Square arm and arm with big, cheesy grins.

"That's my best friend, Natalie."

"She lives in San Francisco, right?"

Remington's eyes lit up and her full lips split into a sweet smile. "You do listen when I talk," she joked, jabbing him lightly in the stomach.

"I hear everything you say and I remember everything you tell me. Even if it doesn't seem that way."

She blushed and looked away.

Nathan shook his head. She was so damn cute.

"C'mon," he said, grabbing the bag from her hand. "I can't wait to show you my cabin and take you fishing on the lake."

"I've never been fishing."

"I'll teach you," Nathan said then dipped his head and kissed her. "Let's go."

"Are we stopping at your place so you can pack a bag?" Remington asked as they got in the car.

"Nah, I keep clothes at the cabin. But, I better call Captain Matt and tell him to head back to the airport and get the plane ready."

"Wait, we're flying?"

"Yeah. We could drive but it's nine hours by car. It's only about an hour and a half flight."

"Got cha. Flying it is. I feel sort of bad for Captain Matt, though. He just finished a long flight from Texas. Is he going to be cool with jumping right back in and flying to Lake Almanor?"

"He'll be fine. I pay him very well to be my personal pilot."

Captain Matt greeted them warmly when they arrived on the tarmac. He explained that Amber wouldn't make the trip seeing how she had already made it home and had plans. Nathan told him that was fine and they settled in for the short flight to Lake Almanor.

Nathan was excited and a little anxious as he drove the winding roads that led to his cabin. His cabin was his sanctuary, his man cave. It was where he went to get away from the constant grind of building his sports agency. Where he went to hide from the annoying headlines about his love life. His cabin was a place of quiet and solitude. He'd never brought a woman there and he never thought he would, until now.

Nathan turned his car off the main highway onto a long side road that fed into a long driveway leading to his cabin. He heard a slight gasp escape Remington as the cabin came into view.

"What?" He asked, looking over at her.

"You said it was a cabin."

"It is."

"No, it's not. Nathan, it's a damn mini-mansion."

"No," Nathan rebuffed as he pulled the car into a spot in front of the three car garage.

"Yes," Remington countered as she opened the door and climbed out. "Look at this place. It's gorgeous. I love all the windows. I bet it gets really great natural light."

Nathan got out and moved around the car to stand next to her. He stared up at his cabin. Looking it at from her viewpoint he supposed that it was not just a regular cabin by normal standards. It was a 5,500 square foot wood and stone building that sat on the edge of Lake Almanor. He had it built with lots of windows so he could he take in the breathtaking view of the lake from nearly every room in the place.

"I can't wait to see what the inside looks like," Remington said, moving towards the house.

Nathan jogged ahead of her and unlocked the door.

Remington breezed past him. "Oh my God, Nathan. This is beautiful." She moved through the foyer into the open and spacious living area. "It's elegant but casual, you know?"

"Exactly what I was going for," he chuckled.

"Don't make fun. C'mon, show me the rest of the house." She grabbed his hand and tugged him along.

Nathan moved through the house taking her from the living room to the large kitchen with state of the art appliances, a nice sized countertop island and a large dining table.

"Wow, this kitchen is huge. And look at this stove and

fridge. It's like a kitchen in a restaurant. What are you a chef?"

"I dabble a little bit," Nathan grinned.

"Well I know who'll be doing all the cooking while we're here. I can barely boil water," Remington laughed then moved over to the oversized sliding glass doors that led to an expansive deck.

Remington slid open the doors and stepped onto the patio which was surrounded by tall pine trees and had a breathtaking view of the crystal blue water that was Lake Almanor.

Nathan watched as she wrapped her arms around her middle, inhaled deeply and closed her eyes. She made for a lovely picture against the backdrop of the lake.

Nathan moved quietly behind her and wrapped his arms around her pulling her back against him. "It's beautiful, isn't it?" He whispered against her ear.

"Almost too beautiful to look at."

"This view is one of the reasons I chose this spot to build the cabin. I love coming out here with a beer or some wine and just chillin'."

They stood out on the deck for a while, Remington locked snugly in Nathan's arms. Nathan rested his chin lightly on the top of her head and thought how much he liked being out there enjoying the view with her pressed tightly against him.

He dipped his head and pressed his lips to her ear. "C'mon, I'll show you the rest of the place."

"Okay," she said, turning to look up at him.

Nathan's heart clenched and tightened like a balled fist as she stared up at him with eyes that blazed a bright ember and were as open and welcoming as the sun on a cold winter's day. His mouth curled into a small smile and he pressed her soft body tight against his one good time then took her by the hand and led her back into the house.

Nathan finished off the tour showing her the game room, his office, the downstairs bathroom, the Jacuzzi that sat tucked away beneath a rock that overlooked the lake, two spare bedrooms and finally the master bedroom.

"Wow! That's a big, beautiful bed," Remington said, staring wide-eyed at the California King sitting against the wall.

"I'm a big boy," Nathan grinned and wiggled his eyebrows.

He watched as she moved around the bedroom, running her hands over the soft comforter, along the back of the comfy high-back chair sitting in the corner of the room over to the dresser where she paused to look at the pictures of him, Mamma D, Jax and his parents.

"I love how close you are with your family," she smiled then moved through the large archway leading to the connecting sitting room.

Nathan followed her but kept a short distance. He liked watching her move through his personal space.

"I know you're probably tired of hearing this from me but, Oh My God! This view is amazing," Remington said, referring to the back wall of the sitting room. It was made up of floor to ceiling windows overlooking lush green trees that were the fore drop to the lake where crystal blue waves crawled gently towards the shore.

"That's the great thing about this place. Amazing views everywhere," Nathan said, coming to stand in front of her.

"Does that include the present view?" She teased, her

expression sassy and sexy as hell.

"You tell me."

Remington's eyes narrowed as she brought her hand up to caress the soft hairs at the nape of Nathan's neck.

Nathan grabbed her wrist running his thumb across the tender skin. Her pulse took off in a sprint. A tremor moved through him and his breath hissed softly in response. Damn, this woman did something to him. No other woman he'd ever been with set him off the way Remington did.

Nathan stared down at her, his gaze homing in on her mouth. They only just got to the cabin. Perhaps he should let her settle in, unpack, eat something before he had her on her back writhing beneath him. He probably should but his need for her overshadowed everything.

Nathan released her wrist and caught her around the waist. He pulled her up against him molding their bodies together. Chest to breast, belly to belly, straining erection to aching sex. He slid his other hand to her ass, kneading each cheek.

Remington's jaw went slack and a low moan floated from her throat.

Next thing Nathan knew they were a tangle of arms and hands caressing and pulling at each other. Remington reared up on her toes and slammed her mouth against his, prying his lips apart and thrusting her sweet tongue in his mouth. Nathan gripped her ass and held her in place as he ground into her a few times before trailing his hand up from her waist to tangle in her hair. His breath was hot and serrated and he felt completely out of control as he moved them out of the sitting room and towards the bed, never breaking the connection of their mouths.

Nathan tugged at the button on her jeans unfastening it and pulling down so hard on the zipper he thought he might break it. At the same time Remington reached into the waistband of his joggers and slipped her hand inside and gripped his rigid dick.

"Take these off," Nathan mumbled against her mouth as he pulled at her jeans.

Remington pulled back from the kiss and quickly shoved her jeans down her thighs and kicked them to the side. She pulled her shirt over her head and tossed that as well.

Nathan rid himself of his own shirt and shoved his pants down his thighs. They barely hit the floor before Remington was on her knees taking his throbbing dick into her mouth.

Nathan nearly came on the spot. "Damn, girl," he moaned as he gripped the back of her head and guided her mouth up and down his dick.

The sounds coming from Remington as she took the entire length of him down her throat was music to Nathan's ears and his dick hardened to a level he'd never experienced. He needed to be inside her.

Nathan slid Remington's head back and held it in place. Her soft whiskey eyes, cloudy with lust, stared questioningly up at him.

"I need you in my mouth. Now!" he growled then bent down and pulled her up from the floor. He tossed her gently, playfully, on the bed and spread her thighs wide then proceeded to run his tongue up and down her slit. He licked, sucked and nibbled on her hard bud until Remington was scrambling to away from him.

"Unh, unh! Come here," Nathan growled, pulling her to him. He shoved his tongue deep in her pussy and she came instantly, drenching his mouth with her sweet honey taste.

After taking his fill, Nathan stood up and drove his dick deep into her body. He loved how Remington arched high off the bed and clutched at the comforter.

Nathan kept his eyes locked on her as he fucked her hard and fast. Pumping in and out and moving his hips in circles.

Remington's cries echoed off the walls as she came over and over again, lubricating his dick.

Nathan couldn't hold out any longer. He ran his hand up her flat belly, between the valley of her firm breasts to gently wrap his fingers around her throat as he pounded into her until he felt his entire body tighten and his seed come bursting down his shaft, pouring out the tip and filling her up.

He was breathless as he fell forward covering her body with his but careful not to put the full weight of himself on her.

"You good?" He breathed out.

"I'm perfect," came Remington's dazed and choppy reply.

Nathan pushed up off her and rolled over pulling her to him. They lay there wrapped around each other until they both drifted to sleep.

CHAPTER TWELVE

REMINGTON

Remington murmured groggily as her eyes fluttered trying to adjust to the dark. Her body was heavy and her muscles were tender as she shifted and sat up. For a second she forgot where she was until her eyes fully adjusted to the darkened room and she saw the expensive furnishings surrounding her. The lush sheets sliding smoothly against her naked flesh, the large plush bed swallowing her tiny body in comfort, the 70 inch flat screen hanging on the wall at the foot of the bed and the gorgeous view that made up the back wall of the sitting room. Earlier it had been bathed in light and the sun sparkled off the lake. Now the view was blanketed in darkness with the moon cutting a soft glow over it.

The spot in the bed next to her was empty and instead of dreading the worst like she had the last time she woke up alone, this time Remington got out of bed, pulled on Nathan's t-shirt that was lying on the floor and went to look for him.

Nathan's earthy-sweet scent wafted from his t-shirt and teased Remington's nostrils as she padded through the house. God, she loved his smell.

Remington stopped in front of a lovely circular, golden mirror with hundreds of golden wires reaching out from its edges. It reminded her of a sunburst. It was beautiful. Something not as lovely as the mirror was the reflection staring back at her. She looked like a woman completely worked over. Her lips were slightly swollen and her hair was a tangled mess. She ran her fingers across her lips. They were tender to the touch. She smiled a bit, not really able to help it as she thought about all the things she'd done that got her mouth that way.

Her hair was another story. Nothing to smile about at all. It was a hot mess. Remington combed her fingers through her hair then twisted it up in a knot on top of her head. Much better. Now she at least looked halfway descent.

Remington made her way down the stairs to the first level of the cabin. She checked the living room, game room and study but no Nathan. She finally found him in the kitchen. He was standing at the counter seasoning steaks. His back was to her and he didn't seem to hear her come in. Remington braced herself against the entryway and quietly watched him for a few minutes.

He was shirtless, his strong back muscles flexing and moving as he reached for different seasonings. His joggers hung low and sexy off his hips, he was barefoot and wore a fitted cap turned backwards. The man was sex personified and Remington had to lick at the corners of her mouth to catch the saliva gathering there. She was still in shock at everything they'd done over the past few days and every second she spent with him had her falling more and more for him. The Nathan she was getting to know was nothing like the gossip sites painted him. Her Nathan was considerate, affectionate and sweet. He was definitely not the lothario they made him out to be. Mr. Love 'em and leave 'em alone. No, that wasn't her Nathan at all.

Remington rested her head against the archway frame as thoughts of their lovemaking flooded her mind. Yes, things for her had quickly shifted from fucking to making love. Her feelings for Nathan had morphed into something deeper the minute she stood on the terrace overlooking the breathtaking view of the lake and he'd wrapped her in his arms and rested his chin on her head. She felt at home in his arms, in his space. She wasn't sure what his feelings were for her but she knew right then that Nathan Black had woven his way into her bones and intertwined himself in her heart.

"Hey sleepyhead," Nathan said turning to look at her, a half smile gracing his generous mouth.

His eyes took her in moving over her face, down her stomach where his gaze lingered on the hem of his t-shirt she wore, down her bare legs and back up again. He was looking at her like she was his next meal and the tiny bud between Remington's thighs quaked and she pressed her legs together trying to take control. The fact that this man could make her fall apart with a look was amazing. It was like there was some magnetic current between them.

"Hey," Remington said, moving into the kitchen. "What 'cha doing?"

Nathan moved to the sink and washed his hands. "Making dinner. I figured you'd be hungry when you woke up. Wanna help?"

Remington watched as he grabbed a towel, dried his hands then tossed it on the counter. The way the muscles in his arms flexed was damn ridiculous.

"Well?" Nathan prompted.

"Well what?"

"I asked you if you wanted to help me cook but you seem...distracted by something," he replied, his brow lifting and his mouth tipping teasingly at the corners.

God, he was sexy. Remington wanted to rush him. To crush her body to his. To run her tongue over every inch of him. But she stayed put. Her body was still tender from what they'd done earlier." I don't cook, remember?" She said.

"That's right," Nathan said, narrowing his gaze as he stalked towards her.

Remington watched him in awe. His smooth, dark skin pulled taunt across his perfect chest. The intricate tattoos seeming to darken and become more prominent against his brown skin. His abs rippled with every step he took. Remington's breathing quickened and there was nothing she could do about it. The man was absolutely sinful. And she wanted to commit dirty deeds with him over and over again.

Nathan snaked an arm around Remington's waist and drew her to him. He bent his neck and stared down at her, his dark gaze piercing through her.

An inferno burnt up the space between them, the flames licking at Remington's skin. Somehow she was sure her only relief was Nathan and without a thought she raised up on her toes and closed the distance that lingered between their mouths.

The second her mouth touched his, stars exploded behind her closed eyelids. She pressed into Nathan wanting to feel every part of him. Remington took control of the kiss exploring his mouth. Running her tongue over his teeth, cheeks and the roof of his mouth before capturing his tongue and sucking on it.

Nathan rewarded her by running his hands down her back and cupping her bottom one good time before lifting her and bracing her thighs on either side of his hips.

Remington locked her legs at the ankles and ground into him as he moved them towards the kitchen counter. Without breaking the kiss, Nathan set Remington on the counter. He caressed and squeezed her thighs before finding his way to her center which was already soaked.

"Shit," he breathed into her mouth. "You're so fucking wet."

Nathan slid his fingers up and down her slit a few times before slipping two fingers inside.

Remington's head fell back, mouth open as she arched into him. Nathan's fingers were masterful, stroking in and out and around and around. Remington moved her hips in time with him, riding his fingers. In no time she felt her body humming and sizzling as ecstasy raced through her.

"Fuck, Nathan. I'm about to come," she stuttered.

Nathan dug his fingers into the hairs at the base of Remington's neck pushing her head forward. "Open your eyes," he ordered. "Look at me. I want to see those beautiful ass whiskey eyes when you come."

His words were like hot iron stoking the fire burning between Remington's thighs and she rode Nathan's fingers like a jockey looking to win his first race.

Nathan pressed his forehead to hers, his parted lips feathered lightly across hers. Their breaths mingled. Their eyes locked. It was the most erotic thing Remington had yet to experience. And she came, hard.

Nathan slipped his fingers from between her thighs and presented them to her.

Remington was still trying to catch her breath as she stared at his fingers glistening with her juices. It was a beautiful sight. How he could make her come so hard just with his fingers was a wonder.

"I could play inside that sweet pussy of yours all day and night," he said before slipping his fingers in his mouth. "Fucking delicious," he praised after licking his fingers clean.

"You're so bad," Remington giggled.

"I'm bad? I was in here minding my own business cooking us a nice dinner and you came in looking all sexy and shit in my t-shirt, no panties, and seduce me."

Remington's head fell back as she laughed. "Okay, you're right. I'm clearly the naughty one here."

"You are but I like it," Nathan said and kissed her on the nose.

Remington's heart fluttered. Like, literally fluttered and she wondered if he could feel it. They were still so very close to each other. She searched his handsome face and saw lust, raw and pure. He was certainly as horny as she was but she couldn't tell if it was all physical with him or if perhaps he was starting to feel something deeper like she was.

"I should probably finish cooking," Nathan said and shifted back putting some space between them but kept his hands on her thighs.

"You do that. I'll sit right here and watch."

Nathan grinned, gave her a quick peck on the mouth then moved over to the counter where the steaks were.

Remington watched as he finished seasoning the steaks then seared them in butter and rosemary in a cast iron skillet before placing them in the oven. She hadn't even noticed the potatoes boiling on the stove until he removed the pot and drained them from the water.

Nathan looked over at her. "Come here little miss I don't cook. I'm going to teach you how to make mashed potatoes."

"Okay," Remington said, sliding off the counter.

"Grab the milk, butter and sour cream out of the fridge."

Remington did as he instructed and set the items on the counter next to him.

"First we mash the potatoes a bit," he said then pulled her to stand between him and the counter.

Remington bristled at the feel of his front pressed to her backside.

"Grab the masher," he whispered against her ear.

Remington grabbed the plastic handle and Nathan wrapped his fingers around hers and guided her hand up and down, smashing the potatoes.

"Now we add the milk, butter and sour cream."

Remington reached for the milk. "How do we know how much to put in? Don't we need a measuring cup?"

Nathan chucked. "Nah, Momma D taught me how to cook without a measuring cup in sight. She eyeballed everything so that's what I do."

"Okay, tell me when to stop," Remington said and slowly poured milk into the pot.

"I think that's good," Nathan said after a few seconds. He cut off a few pieces of butter and dropped them into the pot then scooped out a few heaping tablespoons of sour cream and dropped them in as well.

"Now for the seasonings," he said and reached over and grabbed salt, pepper and garlic powder. "You mix and I'll add in the seasonings."

Remington had never felt so good in a kitchen. She was never one to spend time there seeing how she didn't care for cooking but it was different with Nathan. She was enjoying herself. She was enjoying cooking and she knew it was because of him.

They finished the mashed potatoes and Nathan pulled the steaks and a pan of asparagus out of the oven.

"You made asparagus too?"

"We need some veggies with this meal, girl. And I know you don't like peas so…"

Remington smiled at his thoughtfulness. He'd made such a nice meal for them she wanted to do something other than smash a few potatoes.

"Let me make the plates. You already did the most important part. The least I can do is serve you."

Nathan's eyes blazed onyx as he stared back at Remington. His Adam's apple struggled up his throat and he swallowed hard. He lifted his hand and traced his fingers along her bottom lip. "Do you realize what you do to me when you say things like that?"

"Like what?" Remington asked, her eyes wide and feigning innocence.

Nathan bit into his lip as he gazed down at her. "Things like you want to serve me?"

"Well, I do," Remington said without shame.

Nathan growled, deep and feral as he grabbed the front of Remington's t-shirt and pulled him to her. "You can't say things like that and stand there half naked looking at me like you're ready to give me everything."

"I can't help it," Remington shrugged lightly. He was right. She did want to give him everything.

"Damn, girl! You know we'll never eat at this rate, right?" Nathan growled.

Remington chuckled and pushed lightly against his chest. "We're gonna eat right now. Go sit. I'll make the plates and be right over."

Nathan didn't release her. Instead, he wrapped his arms tighter around her.

"Nathan," she softly chastised.

"Fine," he pouted then released her, slowly, reluctantly, then made his way out of the kitchen.

Remington filled two plates with steak, potatoes and asparagus then made her way into the dining room. Nathan was seated at the head of the long rectangular table. Remington placed a plate in front of him then sat her own plate in front of the chair to his right then sat down.

"This looks amazing. I can't wait to taste it. I suppose you spent a lot of time in the kitchen with Momma D growing up," she remarked.

"Yeah, Momma D loves to cook and she made sure me and Jax knew how to cook too. She had our little butts in the kitchen at the age of six whipping up collard greens, yams, roasted chicken and all kinds of shit," Nathan smiled.

"I wish I knew how to cook. Growing up I was more interested in working on cars with my Dad then being in the kitchen cooking with my mom."

"Stick with me. I'll teach you a thing or two," Nathan winked.

Remington's heart fluttered.

"We should eat before it gets cold," Nathan said.

That first bite of steak was heaven. It was tender and creamy and all but melted on Remington's tongue. She closed her eyes and enjoyed the flavors as they danced across her tongue. Delicious.

"Like, you really don't want us to get through dinner, do you?" Nathan asked.

Remington's eyes popped open. "What?"

"The way you eating that steak. The sounds you're making got your boy on rock over here," Nathan said, glancing down at his lap then back at Remington.

"Nathan," Remington laughed.

"I'm serious."

"Well, we have to eat so maybe I'll just finish my meal over there," Remington nodded towards his lap.

Nathan pushed back from the table a bit and leaned back inviting her over.

Remington wasted no time straddling him. "You'll have to feed me since my back is to the table," she grinned.

Nathan smirked.

"I'd like some asparagus please," she purred.

Nathan kept his eyes on her as he reached behind her and grabbed one of the firm spears from his plate. He ran the vegetable across her lips before pressing it softly between them.

Remington opened up and bit down on the stem. "Umm, that's good." As she chewed she began to slowly move her hips, sliding back and forth along his dick which was hard and thick beneath her.

Nathan took a bite of the asparagus then sat it back on his plate.

"Potatoes please," Remington said, the words a moan from deep in her throat.

Nathan reached behind her and not bothering to use a fork scooped up some potatoes on his fingers and fed them to her. Remington licked his fingers clean.

"We made some great potatoes. You should try them," she said then turned and dug her own fingers into the potatoes. She held her potato covered fingers up and Nathan opened his mouth for her but Remington shook her head and smeared the potatoes along the side of her throat.

Nathan didn't wait for instruction. He knew what to do. He leaned forward and ran his tongue along her neck sopping up every bit of potato then dove one hand into Remington's hair pinning her in place so he could plunder her mouth.

Remington surrendered to him completely. Her need for him surged through her like a raging storm. She reached down and placed her hand inside his joggers and stroked his dick a few times before pulling it out. She lifted off his lap and positioned herself over his tip then slowly slid down until she was completely filled, her pussy lips pressed tightly to the base of him.

"Feed me while I fuck you," Remington whispered as she moved up and down on him.

Nathan did as she said, grunting and trying to keep it together as he fed her steak while she worked her hips down on him like a pro.

Remington stared down at him. His face was savage with desire. His dark brow knit tightly together, his mouth ridged as he stared into her eyes. She knew he was fighting his release and she didn't want that. She wanted to feel him shudder beneath her. She wanted to feel the warmth of his cum shooting deep into her body.

Remington braced his shoulders for support and rode

him like a prized bull at a rodeo. She clutched at him as a low moan built in her throat.

Dinner forgotten, Nathan braced her waist and bucked his hips up slamming into her over and over until he tensed and a deep, guttural growl surged from him. He held her in place as he unleashed everything he had into her.

Remington's own orgasm hit and she joined him over the edge and her own release rained down on him like a vicious storm.

CHAPTER THIRTEEN

REMINGTON

Darkness blanketed the sky and the only sliver of light from the moon shining through the window cast an exquisite glow over Nathan as he slept.

Remington lay on her side quietly watching him, her eyes traveling over his broad shoulders and thick chest. The rest of his gorgeous body was unfortunately hidden beneath the covers so she traveled her eyes back up to settle on his face which was perfectly serene. His brow was smooth and his mouth curled slightly at the ends in a satisfied smile.

"What are you looking at?" Nathan mumbled, opening one eye to look at her.

"Just watching you sleep. You're a very peaceful sleeper. You know that?"

Nathan didn't respond. Instead he reached out for her, rolling her against him so her backside was pressed to his hard chest. He buried his nose in the crook of her neck, inhaled then sighed, deep and satisfied as if there were nowhere else he'd rather be.

The mere act of it filled Remington with joy because there was definitely nowhere else she'd rather be then tucked securely in his arms. They'd made love too many times throughout the night to count and her limbs were pure jelly.

"Why aren't you sleep? As many times as we went at it, you should be as tired as I am," Nathan said.

He was right. She was tired in a deeply satisfied way. "I could sleep," she said then snuggled deep into Nathan's embrace and closed her eyes.

"Ready?" Nathan asked, a big grin on his face as he stood before Remington in a pair of black waders, tan undershirt, fisherman's hat, and black rubber boots. The man was dressed like the old man in the sea and yet he still managed to look sexy as shit.

"Ready as I'll ever be," Remington said, staring down at her own attire. Nathan had went out earlier and purchased her a pair of rubbers, a fishing vest and a bucket hat.

Nathan strode over, gripped her waist and pulled her to him. "I have to say, no other person in life has ever looked this good in a fisherman's outfit."

Heat burned Remington's cheeks under his gaze. The way his dark eyes smoldered sent a shiver up her spine.

"Thank you," she said and kissed his chin.

Remington inhaled the crisp morning air as they stepped out the back door and made their way down the wooden pier that led from the house to the lake. It was still very early, not even eight o'clock. Remington tilted her head to the sky. It was an ethereal light blue with billowy clouds scattered about. Absolutely gorgeous.

Nathan's boat was docked at the end of the pier and it was a thing of beauty – all white trimmed in gold and black. And it was big. Bigger than any boat Remington had ever seen in person. It reminded her more of a yacht. The name Janie was scrawled across the side in large black letters trimmed in gold. She was aware that boat owners named their boats and she was definitely going to be asking Nathan about it later.

"Wow! This is a big boat," Remington said.

"Eh. It's about average size," Nathan said as he climbed inside. "Hand me the bags, Skipper," he said with a wink.

"Sure thing, Captain," Remington replied with a salute. She handed him the couple of bags with food and drinks they'd packed.

"You ready to come onboard?" Nathan asked, holding his hand out to her.

"Absolutely," Remington took his hand. She felt all the things as their fingers touched. Tickly stomach, dry throat, pounding heart. Would the effect of this man ever wear thin on her?

"Let's get this stuff below deck," Nathan said as he released her hand and grabbed the bags.

"Below deck? This boat has a lower deck?"

"Yeah, c'mon," Nathan said as he moved towards the door at the back of the deck.

Remington's jaw nearly hit the floor when she stepped

inside. Yeah, this was no ordinary boat. The lower deck was outfitted for the Gods. On one side of the interior was a mini kitchen complete with marble countertops sitting above glossy, wood cabinets. A tan leather sofa lined the other side of the interior and the floor was covered in what looked like a deep brown luxury carpet.

"Wow, Nathan, this is amazing." Remington complemented.

"Thanks. Sometimes I spend days out on the water so I wanted to be comfortable."

He moved towards the entryway off the kitchen. "Let me give you the grand tour. Not sure how much you know about boats but this is the inside galley and through here," he motioned for her to follow him. "Through here is the bedroom and the bathroom is over there."

The bedroom was made up of a queen sized bed outfitted with a plush ivory comforter and fluffy pillows. Shiny wood cabinets lined both sides of the interior and circular track lights lined the ceiling. Remington could already see her and Nathan tangled in the sheets.

The bathroom was not at all the tiny little box with a hole for a toilet that she expected. It was spacious and had a full sized shower, toilet and sink with a nice sized mirror sitting above it.

"This is like a little apartment you have here," Remington smiled.

"Something like that," Nathan grinned. "So, you ready to do this?"

"As ready as I'll ever be."

"Well, let's go." Nathan grabbed Remington's hand and led her back to the upper deck.

Remington stood next to Nathan at the helm as he

guided the boat out onto the lake. The morning air was crisp but the sun beaming down through the clouds provided some warmth. Remington eyed Nathan. He was a natural at this boating thing easily steering the boat and smiling like a kid in a candy store.

"I'm going to take us out to my favorite spot, drop the anchor and then the real fun begins," he said.

Nathan maneuvered the boat far out into the lake passing several buoys and a few other early morning fisherman before finally dropping anchor.

"So, I've got your pole all set up and ready to go. We just need to add bate," he said, wiggling his eyebrows.

"Please tell me we're not using worms for bate," Remington frowned.

Nathan laughed. "Nah, I use shrimp. Here, I'll show you." He opened the cooler that was sitting near them and pulled out a large shrimp and slipped it on the hook at the end of fishing line. "Alright, we're ready. You ever cast out a line before?"

Remington shook her head.

"It's easy. Keep your fingers on this black button here while you pull the pole back and as you bring the pole forward to toss out the line you let it go. Like this."

Remington watched as Nathan drew back the pole and flung it out. The translucent wire travelled far before the hook fell into the lake and disappeared under water.

"Now you try," Nathan said as he reeled the line back in.

Images of Ben Stiller getting a fishing hook through the lip in *There's Something About Mary* came to mind and a deep furrow creased the skin between Remington's eyebrows. "Are you sure?"

"Yeah, don't be nervous. I'll help you," Nathan said,

handing her the fishing rod.

He moved behind her and pressed his front to her back.

Remington shivered from the contact. She couldn't help it.

Nathan placed his hand over hers on the fishing rod. "Alright, we're going to pull it back then fling it out."

With his hand over hers, Nathan guided her movements swinging the fishing pole back behind them then tossing it out. The line sailed for a good while before dropping into the lake.

"Nice!" Nathan said and kissed her on the side of the neck.

Remington's skin tingled and burned from the contact.

Nathan moved from behind her. "So, you can have a seat and hold onto the pole and wait for a bite or you can sit it in one of these holes here." He pointed to what looked to Remington like skinny cup holders.

"I think I'll hold onto it for a bit," Remington said and sat down in the seat closest to her.

"Cool. I'll toss my line out and join you," Nathan said.

The two sat next to each other, fishing poles in hand, enjoying the quiet lapping of waves against the boat. Remington rather enjoyed the gentle rocking of the boat as they waited for a fish to take their bait.

"So, how long before we get a bite?" Remington asked.

"Can never tell," Nathan shrugged lightly. "Sometimes I'm out here for hours and nothing."

"Really?"

"Yep."

"Doesn't it get boring?"

"Never. I mean just look around. It's beautiful out here.

And quiet. I love the peace of it all,"

"It is peaceful. I suppose it's a great escape for someone like you," Remington said.

"Someone like me?" Nathan asked, casting a sideways glance at her.

"Don't go getting all defensive on me. Like I tried to explain the other day at dinner, you have a lot on your plate. It must be great to have a place you can go to get away from everything."

"You're right. It really is nice having this place. In the city I got people pulling me in all directions. Wanting me to attend all kinds of functions and then there's the Paps following my every move. This place is my sanctuary."

"Did you ever imagine that this would be your life? Being one of world's best and hottest soccer players of our decade? Not being able to go out without being recognized? Having your face plastered across the gossip websites every week?"

Nathan didn't answer right away. His gaze was focused on the open water and Remington couldn't read his expression. When he finally did speak he kept his gaze focused forward.

"All I really wanted was to play soccer. I love the game. I have since before I can remember. My mom got me a soccer ball when I was just three. I used to run around everywhere with that ball under my arm. Mamma D use to have to make me put it away at mealtimes."

"Do you still have it?" Remington asked.

"Yeah. It's really old and worn now but I still have it. It's one of the few things my mom gave to me before she died. I mean she essentially set me on this path whether she knew it or not and I'm grateful to her for that. She played a part in introducing me to something that I love."

"That's really beautiful, Nathan," Remington said placing her hand on his thigh.

He turned to look at her then, his eyes were glossed over in happy remembrance of a mother long gone but one who left him with something to build a legacy on.

"*You're* beautiful," he whispered and leaned over and kissed her gently on the mouth.

One kiss from Nathan never seemed to be enough and Remington leaned in and pressed her mouth more firmly to his. She wanted to seal herself to him. To let him know through her kiss just how much she cared for him. Nathan, the millionaire playboy was so much more than that. He was gorgeous and cocky as all shit but that was all on the surface. Once he let you inside, he was so many other things. Thoughtful, caring, giving, protective. Nathan Black was everything any woman could want and he was here with her.

Remington slipped her tongue between Nathan's lips and just as she intertwined her tongue with his she felt an angry tug on her fishing pole. It was so strong it pulled her forward.

"I think I got something," she said, half panicked half excited.

"You sure do," Nathan said and got up. "Let's reel her in."

He helped Remington up and together they wrestled the rascally fish until they were able to reel it in.

Remington's eyes balked at the large, silver fish hanging on the end of her fishing line.

"Damn, girl! You caught a monster," Nathan said, grinning ear to ear.

"It's really big. What kind of fish is it?" Remington

asked.

"King salmon. We're eating good tonight all on you," he smiled, the dimple in his cheek making an appearance and tying Remington's stomach in knots.

"As long as you're cooking."

"I got you. Now, hold tight to that pole while I grab the pliers to cut him loose."

Remington gripped the fishing pole with both hands as she watched the fish flop around on the deck.

Nathan returned quickly and went to work freeing the fish of the hook then tossing it into an ice chest.

"You really are a natural at this fishing thing," he said with a smile.

"Beginner's luck."

"Maybe but there ain't nothing wrong with luck."

Remington and Nathan sat on the deck with their lines in the water, the sun cutting through the chill and warming them as they enjoyed each other's company. Remington told Nathan all about growing up as a Daddy's girl, reading books by Zora Neal Hurston, James Baldwin and Audre Lorde and wanting to be a writer. She talked about her time at Columbia University and her obsession with vintage sport cars.

Nathan opened up about his childhood and growing up without his parents but never going a day feeling alone or unloved. His grandmother made sure he knew every day how loved and wanted he was. He told her stories about his time at college and all the crazy things he and his friends got into and what it felt like being drafted to play soccer professionally.

"The day I was drafted was one of the best days of my life but nothing tops the first day I stepped onto that field with my new teammates. It was like breathing for the first time," Nathan said, a far away look in his eyes.

Remington sat quietly watching him talk, loving how his face lit with passion as he spoke. Her writer's cap had long turned on and although she didn't have a notepad or her laptop with her she knew she would remember every word he spoke. He was giving her everything she needed for his memoir, organically. They were well past the time when he was guarded and wanted to share absolutely nothing with her. Nathan now was relaxed and at ease talking about his life with her.

"I meant to ask. The name on the side of the boat. What's the story?" Remington asked.

"No real story. Janie was my mother's name. I thought it would be nice to name the boat after her."

"That's sweet, Nathan."

He didn't say anything more. Just fixed his gaze back out on the water.

Hours later Remington stared into the ice chest which was now filled with freshly caught fish. "We can't possibly eat all those."

"Not in one sitting. I'll clean and filet 'em then freeze whatever we don't eat tonight."

"Well that'll be a lot," Remington laughed.

Nathan grinned and pulled Remington to him. There was a devilish twinkle in his eyes. "It's your fault. You caught most of 'em," he said against her mouth.

Remington's entire body tingled as she stared up at him, seeing full on desire in his eyes. "I had a good teacher," she whispered then pressed her lips to his.

Nathan took control immediately prying her lips apart with his tongue and took possession of her mouth.

Remington's surrender was quick as she pressed closer to him and ran her hands over his body. Broad shoulders.

Strong back. Hard ass.

Nathan's own hands roamed Remington's body, caressing her back, skimming her thighs and squeezing her butt.

Remington's heart pounded and the little nub between her thighs throbbed. "Nathan," she moaned.

Nathan pulled back from the kiss, quickly swooped her up and tossed her over his shoulder.

"Nathan!" Remington squealed.

Nathan didn't respond. He moved quickly to the lower deck and into the bedroom before setting her on her feet.

"Don't move," he said then disappeared into the bathroom.

Remington heard the shower start and watched as Nathan came out of the bathroom and stalked towards her. He was completely naked by the time he reached her having removed his clothes as he made his way over to her.

Awareness skittered across her flesh wiggling underneath her skin and firing up the muscles underneath as her eyes roamed over his naked body. Hard, sinewy muscle rippled underneath tight dark, brown skin and Remington couldn't wait to get her hands on him.

"Too many clothes," Nathan growled as he reached her. He began undressing her, kissing her flesh with every article of clothing he removed. Remington's skin burned with need.

When she was fully undressed, Nathan took her hand and led her to the bathroom and into the running shower.

Remington shivered as hot water lightly pelted her back as Nathan moved her under the cascading droplets. Her natural locks softened under the water and sprang into vibrant corkscrew curls around her head and face.

Nathan grabbed her face between his hands and roamed his gaze over her. "So fucking beautiful," he breathed out as his eyes darkened with desire. He ran his fingers through her damp curls then dug his fingers into her scalp and tugged her head back so he could run his tongue along the side of her throat until he tipped her ear. "First, I'm gonna bathe you then I'm gonna fuck you," he whispered, his warm breath heating her ear.

Remington lost herself in the soft rumble of his words and a needy sigh bubbled up her throat.

She watched as he grabbed a bottle of soap and squeezed some of the liquid onto a washcloth. Lavender and sage filled the tiny space in the shower and Remington inhaled deeply loving the scent.

She held her breath as he took the washcloth and began running along her arms, shoulders and neck before moving down to gently wash her breasts. His movements were gentle yet erotic as hell. Remington could already feel a slippery wetness between her thighs and it wasn't from the shower.

She'd never taken a shower with a man before let alone had a man bathe her. It was a new and wildly sensual experience. Remington's head fell back and she closed her eyes and got lost in it as Nathan moved the washcloth down her belly and between her thighs.

"Look at me," Nathan whispered as he let the washcloth drop and his fingers moved back and forth against her clit.

Remington was so lost in the way he was making her feel it was hard for her to comprehend what he said.

"Babygirl," Nathan called as his fingers from his free hand founds it way to the back of her head and gently nudged it upright.

Remington's eyes fluttered open and she tried to focus on him but the way he was stoking the fire between her legs made it hard.

Nathan brought his forehead to hers and with his lips a whisper away from hers he said, "I need you to watch me. I'm about to eat the shit out of your pussy and I want your eyes on me the whole time."

His words sent a new flood of juices flowing from Remington's core. It covered his fingers and she watched as he brought those fingers to his mouth and sucked on them.

"So fuckin' good," he said then lowered to his knees.

Through hooded eyes Remington watched as Nathan kneeled before. Water splashed off his hard shoulders and back as he latched onto her sex. She couldn't stop her eyes from falling shut as all the cosmos exploded within her.

"Un-unh! Watch me," Nathan ordered in between licks.

Remington forced her eyes open and her mind was further blown as she watched him feast on her. His tongue darted in and out of her pussy then slowly ran over her clit before sucking on it. Her legs wobbled and she grabbed onto his shoulders for support, digging her nails into his flesh. Her hips ground against his mouth of their own volition and little mews of pleasure filtered from her mouth as an orgasm like no other crashed down on her. A tidal wave of earth shattering pleasure consumed her body and she happily drowned in it.

Remington was still shaky from orgasm when Nathan kissed his way up her body. His hands moving softly over her wet curves. His fingers found her fleshy bottom and squeezed before lifting her up. Remington wrapped her legs around his waist and pressed her mouth to his. The taste of her orgasm on his lips was sinful and she moaned into his mouth.

Nathan pressed her back to the shower wall. "Tell me you want it. Tell me you want this dick," he ordered with all the cock and grit that only turned Remington on even more.

Her heart was still beating fast from her orgasm and her walls throbbed to have him inside her. "I want it," she breathed out.

A delicious grin turned Nathan's generous mouth up at the corners as he guided his hard, heavy dick to her opening. But, he didn't breach her walls. He stilled, staring deeply into her brown eyes. "Say the words. Say you want me to fuck you."

"I want you to fuck me," Remington said without hesitation.

No sooner had she got the words out than Nathan plunged into her with one hard thrust.

Remington screamed at the intense and pleasurable intrusion. She felt her walls clamp down on him, tightening and milking him. The sensation of having him fill her so completely sent her spinning into a quick climax.

"Shit!" Nathan growled and bit down on the tender skin between her neck and shoulder as he slammed into her.

Remington loved the pressure his mouth put on the soft skin on her shoulder. He sucked on the tender flesh in unison with each pound into her saturated pussy. Her legs shook violently around his strong hips as she raked her nails down his back. Unbelievably, she was about to come again.

"Nathan," she gurgled, barely able to get his name out

through the haze of her climax.

"Say it baby. Tell me what you want," he said between thrust.

Remington was completely lost with the want and need to feel him cum deep inside her body. She craved the fusing of their essence on a level that she didn't even understand. All she knew was that she wanted it. "I want your cum."

There was a harsh growl from Nathan as he slammed once then twice more into her body before holding himself deep inside and unleashing a thick wave of cum into her womb.

CHAPTER FOURTEEN

NATHAN

Nathan groaned and rolled over to grab his cell phone off the nightstand. The damn thing had been vibrating incessantly for the past hour and he'd been ignoring it. The fact that he was wrapped around Remington's soft, warm body and knew he'd miss the feel her of against him the minute he moved away to check his phone had a lot to do with it.

Nathan peeked over at Remington who was still sleeping soundly on her side. It was no surprise that the annoying vibrations from his cell phone hadn't woke her up. After he'd worked her over in the shower, they'd fucked two more times when they got back to the cabin.

The woman was exhausted and rightfully so.

Nathan held his phone up to his face to unlock it and a plethora of messages covered his screen, all from Jazelle Banks.

Jazelle: *Nathan Black! You naughty boy! You touched down in Burbank and didn't call. You wound me.*

Jazelle: *I thought we were going to meet up when you got back from your trip??*

Jazelle: *You know I hate being ignored.*

Jazelle: *A lil birdie told me you're in Lake Almanor. I'm headed that way. Meet me at Cravings Bistro on Main Street in Chester at 10am or I'll just have to come invade that cute little cabin of yours.*

"Shit!" Nathan hissed under his breath. The last thing he needed was Jazelle Banks showing up at his cabin and especially with Remington being there. If it was anybody else he would ignore the threat of her showing up but he knew Jazelle meant it.

Nathan frowned. Who the hell told Jazelle where he was anyway? He didn't tell anyone he was going to his cabin. Did she hire someone to track him? He couldn't call it. How she found him didn't even matter at this point. She *had* found him and he knew that if he didn't meet her in Chester she'd show up at his door.

Nathan scrubbed his hand down his face. He should have ended things with Jazelle that last night they were together. Especially seeing how all he could think about was Remington while he was fucking her. Nathan made no bones about his entanglements with different women. He fucked with them until he didn't. He wasn't a dick about it when he ended things. He made a conscious effort to end things on a good note and he would try to do that with Jazelle.

He glanced at the time on his phone. It was just past 8a.m. and the neighboring town of Chester was only about a twenty minute drive from his cabin. If he got up now, he could shower and dress and still have plenty of time to get to Cravings Bistro.

Nathan sat up slowly, careful not to move too much so he wouldn't wake Remington. He thought he was in the clear as his feet touched the floor but that was not the case as he heard movement from the bed.

"It's too early to get up. Come back to me," Remington mumbled as she peeked at him through half-closed eyes.

An amused grin stretched Nathan's mouth wide as he stared down at her. She looked sexy as hell tangled up in the sheets. One of her long legs was kicked outside the sheet and Nathan was itching to climb back in bed and run his hand along the smooth skin.

"You're very tempting but I want to make my famous cheese omelet for you for breakfast."

"Mmmm, that sounds good."

"It's delicious. You'll love it. I'm missing a few ingredients though. I was gonna sneak off to the store and grab what I need while you slept."

"What did I do to deserve such special treatment?"

"Do you even have to ask? That pretty ass mouth of yours is deserving enough." Nathan leaned onto the bed and ran his thumb across her lips. "But if you need further explanation, I'd rather show you."

Nathan placed his hand on Remington's shoulder and pressed her back to the bed then used his knee to open her thighs so he could settle between them. The minute his pelvis came into contact with hers his dick throbbed and thickened. He brought his face close to hers. Her lovely whiskey eyes had taken on a dusky hue as she stared up at him.

Nathan dug his fingers into her unruly hair and tugged lightly, sending her chin tilting upward.

"Pretty ass mouth," he started and kissed her softly on the lips. "Lovely throat," he ran his mouth lightly down her neck and back up then settled his dark eyes against her light ones. "Beautiful eyes," he kissed each of her lids. "Gorgeous head of hair and the fact that you get my dick hard without even trying," he finished punctuating the last word with a slow grind against her. "With all this perfection, I'm not sure my famous omelet will do you justice."

Remington widened her thighs and joined Nathan in his slow grind. "I think they'll be perfect," she breathed out as she slipped her hand between them, wrapped her fingers around his shaft and guided his thick head to her opening. "I could use a little snack to hold me over while you're gone though."

"Say no more," Nathan said then thrust into her.

Nathan guided his car into an empty spot near the front of Cravings Bistro. His plan was to have a quick conversation with Jazelle then head out. He'd left Remington satiated and snoozing lightly in bed and he was eager to get back to her.

Nathan spotted Jazelle the moment he stepped into the restaurant. She was dressed in a white letter print knotted jumpsuit with clunky gold jewelry, her hair was blown out in long waves that cascaded around her shoulders and her full mouth was painted a sinful red. She looked gorgeous and glamorous in a sea of patrons wearing faded jeans and t-shirts.

She stood up and reached for him as soon as he got to the table. "Well don't you look delectable? I always did love you in joggers." Her greyish-blue eyes homed in on the bulge in his crotch.

Nathan just shook his head. That was Jazelle, forward as always. "Hello, Jazelle," Nathan said and kissed her on the cheek.

"Is that all I get? A mere kiss on the cheek? I haven't seen you in almost a week, Nathan," she pouted as she sat down.

Nathan ignored her hurt act and took the seat across from her. "So, this is a surprise. You being here. What are you doing way out here?"

"I thought my text was pretty clear. I wanted to see you. If I recall, the last time we were together you fucked the shit out of me and before you high-tailed it out of the hotel room you told me you'd hit me up when you came back from your trip. Yet, days have gone by and I haven't heard from you. What's going on? Have you tired of me already?"

Nathan stared at her, his eyes telling her everything she needed to know.

Jazelle's face went from playful to hurt in a matter of seconds. "You've got to be kidding me. Nathan Black, are you dumping me?"

Nathan shifted nervously in his seat. He didn't normally end things with women in public places. The risk of a scene was too high. He needed to tread lightly.

"I'm not dumping you, per se. I mean we were never official or anything. We were just having a good time, right?"

Jazelle pressed her lips in a tight line as she stared at him. The soft lines of her face hardened and her greyish-blue eyes had gone an angry silver. Nathan knew she wanted to lash out but appearances were important to Jazelle and Nathan was thankful for that. The last thing he needed was a story about him arguing with a woman in public.

Nathan sat quietly, his dark eyes watching her, waiting for her to speak. He thought it best to stay quiet and see what she'd do.

Jazelle tilted her chin, meeting Nathan's gaze head on. Her voice was calm and even when she spoke. "You know, I would be pissed if I didn't know exactly who I was getting involved with. I knew the type of man you were from jump and I chose to be with you anyway. Perhaps I thought you'd be different with me. I suppose I thought I could be the one to finally get Nathan Black to settle down but now I'm just one of the many women you've ran through."

"Don't say that."

"Why not? It's the truth, isn't it? Nathan, you were never serious about me. I guess I knew that all along. I mean, we rarely ever just hung out. I never met your family. Hell, most of our time together was spent in bed. Not that I minded that. Sex with us was always great but you know that."

Nathan wasn't about to touch that. Instead he focused on letting her down as gently as possible. "Look, Jazelle, you're an amazing woman. You're successful, smart, beautiful. Any guy would be lucky to have you."

"Just not you," came her quick counter.

Nathan felt terrible for the hurt and sadness he saw in Jazelle's eyes but she was right. He wasn't for her. Hell, he never really thought he was for any *one* woman. That is, until Remington English showed up. The woman had him all discombobulated. She's the first woman that he actually wanted to be around all the time. It blew his mind really.

"No, sweetheart, I'm not your guy but I'm sure there's a long line of fellas just waitin 'to step in and take my place."

"Of course there are, Nathan. But none of them are you," she countered.

"Well, we both know I'm one of a kind," Nathan teased.

"You are such a pompous ass," Jazelle laughed. "I should be mad at you, not over here laughing."

"Well, I'm glad you're not mad. For what it's worth, I had a lot of fun with you, Jazelle. You really kept a brotha' on his toes." He reached over and covered her hand with his. "I don't want us to part as enemies. Friends?"

Jazelle narrowed her eyes considering what he just said. "Nathan Black wants to remain friends with one of his ex-lovers? Really?"

Nathan leaned back in his chair and cocked his head a Jazelle. "What does that mean? I'm still friends with many of the women I use to mess around with."

Jazelle leaned forward. "But are you though?"

Nathan's brow furrowed as he thought hard about all the women he used to fuck with and couldn't think of one that he still spoke to other than a simple hello if he saw them out in public or at an event. He supposed they weren't friends but they weren't enemies either.

"Yeah, like I said. You don't stay friends with your ex-lovers," Jazelle said with a smug smile.

"Well, I'd like to change that now, with you."

"You're serious?" By the look on her face it was clear

she didn't believe him.

"Very. I want us to part amicably and have normal, decent conversations when we see each other out and about."

Jazelle pursed her lips and shook her head. "This is unexpected." She studied him for a few seconds. "What's going on with you, Nathan? There's something different about you."

"What do you mean?"

"I don't know. You're just...different. Your entire aura is lighter...softer." She cocked her head to the side studying him. Her eyes narrowed then widened as if she had an epiphany. "Holy shit! Are you already seeing someone else?"

Nathan cut his eyes away. He didn't normally cross women. He always made it a point to end things before he got involved with someone new. But, things with Remington were different. What happened with them, *was* happening with them, wasn't planned. Hell, he tried hard to get keep her at bay but it seemed like the more he tried, the more he wanted her.

"You don't have to say anything. Your face says it all. And now I *know* I should be pissed but I'm still not. Do you know why?"

Nathan shook his head.

"Because whoever she is, she has you wide open," Jazelle said with an amused grin.

"Yeah right! You have no idea what you're talking about," Nathan protested.

"Oh, yes I do. Like I said, it's written all over your face, Nathan. I don't know who this woman is but you got it bad. Props to her for doing what no other woman could do."

"And what is that?"

"She got Nathan Black to fall in love."

Love? A deep crease formed between Nathan's brows as he considered what Jazelle said. Love never crossed his mind. He could admit that he was damn near pussy whipped when it came to Remington but love? Being in love was such a foreign concept to him. He'd spent so much time avoiding it that he'd gone through his entire life never knowing what it felt like. Was that why he was so confused when it came to Remington? Why his chest tightened every time she smiled at him? Why he had an unquenchable need to be near her? Why his hackles went up when his boys were flirting with her? Why he relished it every time he unloaded his seed into her? Is that what love was? Maybe it was because he'd never felt that way about any other woman he'd dealt with.

"So, who is she?" Jazelle asked.

Nathan let out a small chuckle. "I'm not telling you that."

"Oh, come on. I thought you wanted to be friends."

"I do but that doesn't mean having you all up in my love life," Nathan countered.

Jazelle's brows lifted in shock. "Love life? Now I know I'm right. Nathan, we were a thing for a few months and I never heard you utter the word love."

"I don't know if you're right about this love shit but yes, I'm seeing someone and yes, things are different with her."

Never in a million years did Nathan think he would be talking to Jazelle about his relationship with another woman. Given her past behavior he thought she would throw a tantrum and storm out. Not sit down and have a conversation with him about his girl. *His girl?* Nathan swallowed hard at the thought. He'd never been one to define or label his affairs with women but he wanted to do that with Remington. This little chat with Jazelle was helping him see that.

Nathan sighed as he looked over at Jazelle. "Maybe you're right. I don't know. This is new territory for me. If I'm being honest it's really fucking confusing. You don't know how hard I tried to keep this woman at bay. I was a complete dick to her when we first met. Being near her made me angry. Being away from her made me angry. I was frustrated from wanting her and pissed for not acting on it. The shit was crazy. And now that we've hooked up, I have no idea what I'm doing. All I know is that I want her around all the time. And that's never happened."

"I think you should get out of that pretty head of yours and let your heart lead you. Talk to her. Tell her how you feel. Especially with your reputation. That's going to be very important."

"Yeah but it's a reputation built by the damn gossip sites."

"True but you're a public figure and let's be honest you blew through a gang of women, Nathan. And it's all been very publicly documented. I'm sure that's on her mind."

"You might be right but she hasn't said anything so I don't know."

"I'm totally right," Jazelle smirked then waved over the waiter. "Now that you've broken my heart and still managed to get me to give you advice on love, let's have breakfast."

Nathan checked the time on his phone. It was 10:30am. He'd been gone for over an hour and he should probably get back before Remington started to wonder where he was.

"I really should head out," Nathan said.

"Oh no, you don't. I came all the way to B.F.E. to see you. You're having breakfast with me."

The waiter walked up and smiled at the two of them. "Good morning! What can I get for you two?"

"I'll have the chorizo eggs benedict and a Mexican Mocha," Jazelle said.

"Very good. And for you, Sir?" The waiter asked turning to Nathan.

Nathan didn't want food. What he wanted was to get back to Remington but Jazelle had been so cool about things that he at least owed her a little bit more time. He glanced down at the menu. "Just bring me a coffee, black, and the breakfast burrito."

"Sure thing. I'll be back with your drinks in a few minutes," the waiter said then hurried away.

Nathan spent another hour at the bistro with Jazelle. They ate and talked about Jazelle's upcoming photo-shoots and travel. Nathan talked a little bit about his latest recruiting efforts but he didn't mention the memoir. It was happening. He knew that but he still had some reservations about it.

After they finished eating, Nathan paid the check and they walked out together.

"You know you didn't have to come all this way but I'm glad you did. I'm glad we talked," Nathan said.

"Me too. I had fun with you, Nathan Black," Jazelle grinned.

"Me too."

"Well, I guess I'll head out. One last kiss?" She offered, her greyish-blue eyes sparkling with mischief.

Nathan's mouth quirked in amusement. "Of course," he said then leaned down and placed a soft kiss on her lips. "See you around?"

"See you around, Nathan," Jazelle replied then walked over to a black sedan where a driver was waiting to open the back door for her.

Nathan watched as she got inside and they drove off before he got into his own car and headed out.

CHAPTER FIFTEEN

NATHAN

Nathan walked into the cabin to find Remington sitting out on the back deck. She was dressed in a black Nirvana graphic tee, her legs were bare and tucked under her bottom and her curly hair created a lovely halo around her head. Her laptop was on the table and she was typing away at the keyboard. She was completely focused and as much as Nathan wanted to walk over to her and run his hands along her bare thighs and kiss her senseless, he decided to leave her to her work.

Nathan made his way to the kitchen to prepare the cheese omelet he promised her. He had stopped at the market and grabbed some white pepper and shredded cheese on his way home. Nathan washed his hands and got to work.

Jax always told him he made the best cheese omelets.

He liked how airy and fluffy they were. The recipe was pretty standard; eggs, milk, salt, white pepper and a good brand of shredded cheese. Nathan swore the secret was the fact that he whisked his egg mixture until it was good and foamy. He was convinced that's what made the omelet so fluffy.

It took Nathan all of ten minutes to make his omelet. It was perfectly cooked with gooey cheese spilling out the sides. He put the omelet on a plate and garnished it with some spinach and tomatoes, grabbed a glass out the cabinet and filled it with orange juice then grabbed a knife and fork out the drawer. He pulled a wooden tray from one of the cabinets, set everything on it then made his way back out to the deck.

Remington was still clacking away on her keyboard.

"Breakfast is served," Nathan said as he set the tray on the table.

Remington looked up with a smile. Her eyes caught the sun and Nathan's breath hitched at the little gold flecks that danced around her pupils. "Damn, you're gorgeous," he breathed out and bent down and captured her mouth. She tasted like sunshine and honey. Nathan could drink from her lips all day and he would have if Remington hadn't pulled back from the kiss.

"Thank you. I'm glad you're back. I'm starving," she said, reaching for the tray of food. "This looks amazing."

"Dig in," Nathan said and sat down in the chair across from her. He watched as she tore into the omelet, liking the way she licked her lips after each bite.

"Oh, my gawd, Nathan! This is so good."

"Thanks. Glad you like it."

"I love it. It's so light and fluffy," she said bringing another bite to her mouth. She stopped and looked over at

195

him. "Hey, where's yours?"

"Oh, I'm good. I really just wanted to feed you," he winked.

"Well, I appreciate it. This is the best damn omelet I've ever had."

"Jax says the same thing every time he eats one."

"Well, he's not lying." Remington said then popped the last bite into her mouth before pushing the tray back. "I could be a total fatty and eat like two of those," she laughed.

"I can make you another," Nathan said and started to get up.

Remington placed her hand on his arm. "I'm kidding. Sort of. I could eat your cheese omelets all day but I'm actually quite full."

"Okay, but just say the word and Chef Boy R Nate is at your service."

Remington's smile deepened into laughter. "At my service, huh?"

"Oh, absolutely and not just for breakfast. I'll service you any way you want," Nathan said, his gaze falling to the creamy expanse of her neck.

Amusement laced in desire danced in Remington's eyes as she stared back at him. "I think I'll take you up on that."

Nathan watched as she got up and made her way over to him. He scooted his chair back from the table so she could straddle him. The minute her core pressed down onto his lap his dick jumped to life. He braced his hands on either side her hips and kneaded the soft flesh.

Remington moved her hips back and forth along his shaft and with each glide of her hips, his dick grew. He was hard as a rock in a matter of seconds.

"Damn, girl," he croaked out before nipping at her bottom lip then sucking it into his mouth.

Remington reached down and pulled his dick out of his joggers and ran her thumb over the tip, smearing his pre-cum all over it. She took that same thumb, brought it to her mouth and sucked.

Nathan thought he would come right then and there. His dick was aching to get inside her and he lifted her up, pushed her panties to the side and guided her down onto his bulging erection. His eyes rolled back and closed for a second as her warm, wet walls gripped him.

"Uh unh. Look at me while I ride this dick," she teased echoing his own words.

"Oh yeah? That's what we doin?" Nathan gritted out.

"Ummhmm," Remington moaned as she proceeded to roll her hips and ride him into one of the most powerful orgasms he'd ever had.

Later, after being fucked thoroughly, Nathan lay in the bed naked with the sheet pulled over his waist. He was raised on his elbow with his head resting in his hand staring at Remington who was laying across from him, hair wild from sex, with the bedsheet wrapped around her body. She looked like a fucking Goddess.

"So, what were you working on?" He asked already kind of knowing the answer.

"Your memoir," she replied. "You were gone for quite a while and I was feeling inspired. What took you so long anyway?"

Nathan tensed. He hadn't planned on telling her about meeting Jazelle. Especially since things ended well between them. He didn't want to drum up any unnecessary drama. "I wasn't gone that long. You were all engrossed in your writing and didn't hear me come in and I didn't want to interrupt you so I just went to work in the kitchen."

"Oh. I do have the tendency to zone out when I'm writing."

"So, how's the memoir going anyway?" He asked. As much as he loathed the topic, he'd rather talk about that if it moved the conversation away from how long he'd been gone.

"Really good actually. Whether you meant to or not, you've given me a lot of material to work with."

"Yay," he said and flopped onto his back.

Remington crawled over and laid on top of him. "Don't be like that. You're such an interesting person, Nathan. I think people are going to like getting to know the real you." She stared longingly into his eyes. "I know I have."

Nathan ran his hand up her back and rested it at the nape of her neck. "Is that right?"

She nodded. "You're a very complicated creature, Nathan Black. You're so guarded, yet with family you're open and loving. The way you are with your grandmother and Aunt and Uncle. One only has to watch you around them to know how important they are to you. And your work. Geez. You really care about the welfare of these young athletes. And God knows they need someone working for them that has only their best interest at heart. And then there's this thing between you and me. It was completely unexpected. I thought you couldn't stand me. But that night in the elevator changed everything. Being with you this past week has been...I don't even know. But the way you treat me, look at me. The way you touch me. Listen, I've had three boyfriends my entire life and none of them ever touched me the way you do."

Nathan's gut clenched at her words. He wanted to tell her that she was like no other woman he'd ever been with. That she was the only woman with the ability to make him angry, happy and horny all at the same time. That he wanted to fall asleep buried deep inside her every night just to wake up and feel her inner walls milking him. He wanted to tell her that thoughts of eternal bachelorhood were a thing of the past because of her. He wanted to tell her that he loved her but he didn't know how. He'd never in life told a woman how he felt and he just couldn't bring himself to say the words now. But he could show her.

"Come here," he whispered, titling his chin up silently ordering her to kiss him.

Remington wasted no time pressing her lips to his.

Nathan rolled her onto her back and devoured her mouth taking in all the sweetness she had to offer. He kissed her hard and long leaving her lips puffy and swollen before moving down her body to worship the lips between her thighs.

After three glorious days at the cabin it was time to head back to Burbank. Nathan was hard pressed to leave. He would stay in Lake Almanor with Remington fishing, fucking, cooking and talking for the rest of his life if he could but he had to get back to the city and back to work.

After packing up the car and locking up, Nathan drove to the airfield where Captain Matt and Amber were waiting for them.

"Good afternoon, Mr. Black. Ms. English," Amber greeted them as they boarded Nathan's jet.

"Hey Amber. Nice to see you," Nathan greeted her.

"Hello, Amber," Remington said.

"Can I get you something to drink?" She asked.

"Nothing for me, thanks," Remington declined.

"I'm good," Nathan said.

"Very well. I'll just go prepare for takeoff then. Enjoy the flight," she said then disappeared to the back of the plane.

"Why are you way over there?" Nathan asked.

Remington had taken the seat across from him.

"I don't know. This is where I sat the first time I flew on your plane."

"Yeah but that was before I came in you. *Repeatedly*," Nathan said, a devilish look in his eyes.

"Nathan," Remington blushed.

"What? It's true. Now get over here," he demanded.

Remington narrowed her gaze and shook her head but she got up and moved into the seat next to him.

Her familiar vanilla scent filled his nostrils and he was content. He rested his hand between her thighs and squeezed proprietarily. It wasn't long before they both dozed off.

Nathan was awakened by the sound of Captain Matt announcing the decent into Burbank airport. He looked over at Remington who was still asleep with her head resting on his shoulder. Soft snores filled the space which Nathan found utterly adorable. And not to mention how peaceful she looked, almost angelic. He hated to wake her. Nathan watched her for a few seconds then kissed her sweetly on the forehead.

Remington stirred, her lids fluttering a few times before opening. She stared up at him through sleep laden eyes. "Are we back home?" She asked.

"We're landing now."

"Mmmm," Remington moaned deep in her throat as she sat up and stretched. "I didn't even realize I fell asleep."

"Yeah, well you were snoring. Sounded like a mac truck," Nathan teased.

Remington swatted him on the shoulder. "I was not."

"Hey, it's okay. I like the sound of mac trucks in my ear," Nathan said and snagged a kiss.

Nathan was still teasing her as they got off the plane and headed to his car.

"I think I should drive," Remington smiled.

Nathan tossed her the keys with no hesitation. He liked watching her handle his roadster. Seeing her take control of all that horsepower turned him on.

They made it to Remington's place in no time and Nathan grabbed her bag and walked her to her door. He waited quietly while she fidgeted for her keys and unlocked the door. He knew this was where they parted even if only for a short time but there was an odd hollow feeling in his stomach. He didn't want to be away from her.

Nathan followed Remington inside and set her bag by the door. He moved behind her wrapping his big arms around her waist and pulling her against him. He pressed his nose into her hair and inhaled the sweet coconut fragrance before moving his mouth to the back of her neck and nibbling on the tender skin there.

"I had an amazing time with you," he breathed against her ear.

Remington spun around in his arms and stared up at him. "Me too," she smiled sweetly.

"So, will I see you at the office tomorrow?"

"Actually, I think I'll work from here tomorrow. I'm almost finished with the first draft of the memoir and I want to get it done. I think I can do that if I work on it this evening and all day tomorrow."

Nathan's face scrunched at the mention of the memoir. He couldn't help it. "Fine but I think you'd have a much better time at the office with me."

"Really?"

Nathan nodded then dipped his head so his mouth was against her ear. "Absolutely. I'd have you spread out over my desk while I eat your pussy then flip you over, grab a handful of that beautiful hair of yours and fuck the shit out of you."

Nathan could hear Remington's deep intake of breath as he whispered in her ear and his gut tightened. His blood boiled and his body hardened. Shit, he wanted her. He wanted her in every way a man could want a woman.

Nathan pulled back and stared down into her pretty face. "So, you'll come see me tomorrow?"

Remington's breathing was labored as she stared up at him. Her eyes were glossed over with lust. "It'll be late but I'll come by."

Nathan smiled, satisfied and already anticipating taking her on his desk. "Good. I'll see you tomorrow then." He slid his hands down her back, cupped her bottom and captured her mouth in a kiss so hot he was surprised they didn't burst into flames.

CHAPTER SIXTEEN

REMINGTON

Remington was still on a high from her time in Lake Almanor with Nathan. They'd spent three glorious days hanging out, talking, eating and sexing all over the place. Nathan had to be the sexiest, most virile made she'd ever been with. Sex with him was like diving straight into a pit of fire with no concern for being burned. In fact, she welcomed the stinging heat she felt when Nathan touched her. When he was inside of her. The man brought something out in her that she had no idea was there. She'd done things with him that she'd never done with any other man. Not only that, she'd gotten some great material for the memoir and was eager to get it all on paper and wrap up the first draft. But first she needed to hit up Natalie and fill her in on all everything that happened with Nathan.

Remington grabbed her phone.

Remington: *Guuurl! I have something to tell you!!!*

Natalie: *Oh shit! Spill it!!*

Remington: *I just spent 3 days in Lake Almanor with Nathan Black!!!*

Not a second passed before Remington's phone was vibrating and Natalie's pretty face appeared on her screen.

"Hello," Remington laughed.

"Bitch! What in the actual fuck? What do you mean you spent three days at some lake with Nathan Black? You better spill it and don't leave anything out."

Remington chuckled at her friend's candor. "Damn, Nat!"

"Whatever! I wanna hear everything. And now! Unless all ya'll did was work which I know is not the case or you wouldn't have texted me the way you did."

"I got some work done but we were definitely not there to work," Remington smiled into the phone.

"Okay, so tell me everything. How? Why? Did ya'll fuck? Is he as big as every woman in America thinks?"

Remington giggled at her friend's enthusiasm. "Those are a lot of questions. Where do you want me to start?"

"At the beginning, fool! I want to know everything."

"Okay, okay. It all started in Dallas-"

"Dallas?" Natalie hollered, cutting her off.

"Would you hush and let me tell you what happened."

"My bad."

"So, we went to College Station to check in on one of the prospects he's trying to sign to his agency. His name is D'Mariyon Taylor and he really wants to play for the Cowboys so after our visit with him we headed to Dallas to meet with some of Nathan's friends who work for the team. We all went to dinner. BTDubs, his friends are great. They had some great college stories about Nathan and really just loved fucking with him. It was fun for me to watch. Nathan, on the other hand seemed totally agitated throughout the entire dinner and when we got back to our hotel we were in the elevator and things were awkward as shit. I thought he was upset with me so I asked him what was going on and that's when he totally pushed up on me."

"Wait, Nathan Black pushed up on you? How? What did he do exactly?"

"He told me that he'd been trying to behave all night and that he really wanted to kiss me but if I wasn't interested he'd get off the elevator and not mention it again."

"Oh, bitch! I know you jumped his ass. Tell me you were all over that," Natalie squealed.

"Nat, girl! I didn't hesitate. I kissed him."

"Oh, shit! *You* kissed him? That's what I'm talking about. How was it? Is he a good kisser? He's a good kisser, isn't he?"

"Nat, girl! You have no idea. He's *the best* kisser." Remington's eyes closed as she went back to that first kiss in the elevator. "I initiated that kiss but he just sort of took control and devoured me. Nat! That first kiss...how do I even explain it? It infiltrated every fiber of my being and left a permanent stamp. I'm pretty sure I've never been kissed by anyone the way Nathan kissed me in that elevator."

"Daaamn! What happened after the kiss? Did ya'll fuck? I know ya'll fucked. It's Nathan Black. Of course ya'll fucked."

Prickles of remembrance trickled down Remington's

back and raised the hairs on her skin as she remembered all the times and ways they'd had sex.

"Remington?" Natalie called into the phone.

"Sorry. I was having a flashback."

"Thinking about the dick, huh?" Natalie teased.

Remington let out a wistful sigh. "Girl, you have no idea. Being with him that first time was…"

"What?" Natalie prodded her.

"I don't know. It almost defies description. It was like heaven and hell all wrapped into one. His touch was fire and my body was just consumed with flames from every kiss, every touch. And his dick. Oh, my God!"

"What, girl? What about the dick? Tell me," Natalie pleaded into the phone sounding just as lost in the sauce as Remington was.

"It's hard to explain but I guess it was like stepping out into the sun after being shut in the house all day. You know, like when the warm rays hit your face and you stand there for a minute basking in it. And for that moment the entire world stops and you're at perfect peace."

"Fuuuuuck! It was like that?"

Remington shivered at the memory. "Like that and then some. Nat, the man is a beast in bed. A master. The way he handled me. He was gentle but dominant. And the dirty talk. Girl! I'm low key feeling like I might like to be dominated in bed. At least by him anyway."

"Well, shit! I need a drink," Natalie laughed. "So, how did ya'll get from Dallas to Lake Almanor?"

"Well, when we got back to Burbank he said he wasn't ready for us to part and asked me to go with him to his cabin for a few days and I said yes."

"And I take it ya'll fucked all over that damn cabin."

"You know we did and it was fucking amazing but it

wasn't just all about sex. Nat, he taught me how to fish and he cooked for me. And we talked. He's nothing like the gossip sites make him out to be. Not really. The more time I spent with him I started to see who he really was. He's not some hard ass playboy with no feelings just running around banging every woman he sees. The Nathan I've come to know is deep. He cares about people. He lost a lot early in life but he was lucky enough to be raised by a strong grandmother who instilled good values in him. A grandmother he loves deeply. He has too much respect for her to treat women the way the tabloids report. That's not him."

"You really like him, don't you?"

Butterflies kicked around in Remington's stomach as she thought about just how much. She knew she was way past like. She was in love with him.

"I do," she replied.

A thoughtful silence passed between them then Natalie spoke. "I've known you for a long time. Been with you through three relationships and you've never spoken so passionately about any of those guys. I get the feeling it's more than just you liking him. Am I wrong?"

Remington couldn't lie to Natalie if she wanted to. They'd been friends for a very long time. Natalie knew her better than anyone. "You're not wrong."

"I just hope he's deserving of you. You're one of the best people I know and I will cut him if he hurts you."

They both burst out laughing at Natalie's momma bear-like protectiveness.

"So, what happens now?" Natalie asked.

"Now, I unpack, shower and get some writing done."

Natalie's annoyed tsk sounded loudly over the phone. "Bitch, you know what I mean."

Remington laughed. "What? I *am* about to unpack and shower but if you're referring to what happens with me and Nathan, meeting up with him tomorrow."

"So, are ya'll like dating now?"

"I don't know. We haven't DTR'd. I feel like it may be too soon for that. Things happened so fast. We've sort of just been going with the flow. Enjoying each other."

"Oh, bitch! I am so jealous."

"Jealous? Why?"

"Ummm! You're fucking Nathan Black. Fine as hell, rich as fuck, Nathan Black. Who cares about defining the relationship! Just keep fucking him!"

Remington laughed. "You are a mess."

"What? You said yourself that you don't know if you're dating and until you do, ya'll fuckin."

"You know what...I can't with you. I gotta go. Love you, bye," Remington sang and hung up.

Remington shook her head as she made her way over to her bag sitting by the door. Natalie was crazy as hell and she loved her for it. She wouldn't trade her for anything in the world.

One thing Natalie said did hit a nerve though. What *was* her relationship with Nathan?

Were they just messing around? Did he have real feelings for her? The whole time they were together he was attentive and made her feel like she was the most important person in his world. But was that him just being in the moment with her? He was good at expressing himself with his body and hands but not once did he verbalize his feelings for her or offer any insight into where things were heading with them.

Remington knew Nathan had a reputation for hopping from woman to woman as he saw fit. Hell, he was just on the blog sites not too long ago for his involvement with supermodel Jazelle Banks. And before her it was some high-profile CEO.

Remington frowned. Was she just another notch on his belt? She could obsess over this all day but she refused to do that. It would only serve to distract her all day and she wouldn't get any writing done. So, she pushed it from her mind.

After unpacking and showering, Remington sat down at her desk and got to work on the memoir. She was neck deep in it when her phone went off. A smile as big as a crater spread across her face when she saw Nathan's name flash across the screen. He'd sent her a text. It was a picture of an empty bed with the words "*Wish your pretty ass was here*" typed underneath.

Remington double-tapped the messaging leaving a little red heart to let him know she wished the same thing. She did that instead of texting back because she knew that would only lead to them exchanging flirty messages which would no doubt lead to her *actually* being in his bed and she needed to get this memoir done.

Remington set the phone down and refocused. She worked well into the night only stopping to make a turkey sandwich which she ate at her desk so she could continue working. She was pleased with what she'd written so far. She felt like she was really capturing who Nathan was at the core. She wanted to shifts people's view of him as a womanizing playboy to one of a man who was committed to his family and dedicated to building a sports agency that will work in the best interest of the athlete's and their families.

It was 3a.m. when Remington finally called it quits.

She had gotten so much done and honestly didn't have much more to go so she figured she could get in a few hours of sleep then get right back at it. And that's what she did. Remington woke up at eight, washed her face, brushed her teeth, made some coffee and got to work. It was just passed noon when she typed the last line into the document.

Remington leaned back and smiled triumphantly. She couldn't believe she was done with the first draft. This was huge. Her first gig. And for a high-profile athlete and business man. She felt so accomplished, like she'd just scaled Mount Kilimanjaro. She couldn't wait to get the draft over to Jax.

Remington pulled up her work email and with a quick note that said, *Done!*, she sent it over to him.

Remington felt *all* the things after hitting that send button. Excitement, anxiety, fear, relief. All of it was buzzing around in her belly like a firefly caught in a jar. Jax had put a lot of faith in her with this assignment and she wanted to make him proud. This was only the first draft and she knew revisions would be needed but none the less, she felt good about what she'd wrote.

Feeling good and on a high, Remington stood up and stretched. Now that the first draft was done it was time to go see Nathan. Thoughts of their last conversation flooded her mind. His mouth had been pressed to her ear, his warm breath tickling her earlobe as he told her what he was going to do to her in his office. Just the thought made her skin flush. She couldn't wait to get to N. Black Sports Agency and see him. She was more than ready for him to make good on his promise to spread her over his desk and have his way with her.

Remington's cell phone buzzed as she was making her

way to the bathroom to shower. Her brows scrunched together at seeing Natalie's face across the screen. Their communication normally started with a text so it was odd that she was calling.

"Hey, Nat, what's up?" Remington said into the phone.

"Where are you?" Natalie asked.

"At home. Why?"

"Go to your computer."

"What? Why?" Remington frowned.

"Have you been on the internet today?"

"No. I've been holed up finishing the first draft of the memoir. Which I got done by the way," she said proudly.

"That's awesome. Very happy for you, Friend. Now get to your computer."

"You're being weird. What's going on, Nat?" Remington asked her brows knitting together. Something wasn't right. She could hear it in Natalie's voice.

"It's better if you see for yourself. Just go to your pc," Natalie urged.

Worry knotted Remington's insides as she made her way back to her desk. "Okay, I'm at my pc."

Remington heard a heavy sigh on the other end of the phone and a major wave of apprehension swept through her. Natalie was dramatic by nature but this seemed different and that made her nervous. "Nat?" she whispered.

"Open the internet and go to The Rag's website," Natalie instructed.

"Nat, what's going on? Why you can't just tell me?"

"Because I love you and I can't bring myself to say words that will cause you pain."

Icy fear twisted around Remington's heart. The Rag gossip site constantly reported on Nathan's love life. Had they somehow found about her and Nathan? Was she about to see her and Nathan hugged up under some salacious headline? She didn't see how that could be the case. They were pretty low key. They hadn't ventured out to eat or shop while in in Lake Almanor so there was no way the Paps could have gotten any pictures of them together. And besides, Natalie said she didn't want to be the one to cause her pain and a headline about her and Nathan, no matter how embarrassing, wouldn't do that. She'd be embarrassed but in pain, no.

Remington typed in the URL for The Rag and all her bodily functions stalled at what she saw. Her breath lodged in her chest as she stared at a picture of Nathan in an intimate embrace with none other than Jazelle Banks. His hand was on the small of Jazelle's back and they were kissing.

Panicked, Remington's eyes quickly perused the page looking for the date hoping it was an old picture. But she knew right away that it wasn't because the picture was taken outside a bistro in Chester and Nathan was wearing the exact same outfit he was wearing the day he went into town to buy ingredients for his famous cheese omelet. It would be too much of a coincidence to think this picture was from some date before her and Nathan hooked up. And besides she'd never seen him in the same outfit twice.

Remington's eyes landed on the date underneath the picture and she crumbled. It was a blow to the gut. All the air that had been trapped in her chest came rushing out. Her lungs heaved, struggling to pull in air like she'd just run a marathon. For a second she could faintly hear Natalie calling to her through the phone but suddenly her entire word went silent, hallow. The only sound she heard was the jagged tearing of her heart. She clutched at her chest trying to stop the searing pain but it was no use. Nathan had played her. He was still seeing Jazelle Banks. Not only that, he had spent the morning with Jazelle in Chester while she was still in his bed at Lake Almanor. How could he do that to her?

"Remington? Momma? You okay?" Natalie's voice broke though the silence.

Remington blinked trying to stave off the burn at the back of her eyes. She would not cry. Not for a man who was a complete fraud. "I'm fine," she choked out.

"Are you sure? You don't sound fine. We should talk about this."

"I gotta go. I'll call you later," Remington said and hung up the phone.

Remington looked back at her pc, staring at the image of Nathan and Jazelle wondering how she could allow herself to get caught up in Nathan Black and his playboy ways. Was he really what the tabloids made him out to be? She didn't want to believe it even though the picture was right there in front of her face. The man she had come to know was generous and caring. Yes, he was a bit cocky and could be a total ass when he wanted to but everything about the time they'd spent together seemed genuine. The way he touched her and kissed her. The way they talked and made love. There was no way he was playing her. Or was he?

Remington was a zombie as she made her way to the bathroom. All her movements were mechanical as she showered and dressed. She felt nothing except for the nonstop ache in her chest and no matter how much she rubbed it, it wouldn't go away.

Several days passed since Remington saw the picture of Nathan and Jazelle and she was still holed up in her apartment. Nathan texted and called her several times but she ignored each and every one of his attempts to reach her. She just wasn't ready to face him. He'd made such a fool of her. She was embarrassed and extremely hurt.

In fact, she didn't want to see or speak to anyone. Her only human interaction was with Jax who had emailed saying he'd finished reading the memoir and he loved it. He told her he'd given it over to his best editor to work on and said editor would be in touch soon to give her notes. He ended the email saying how proud of her he was and that he knew all along that she was the perfect person for the job. Remington replied thanking him and telling him that she was going to take a few days off.

Other than responding to Jax's email, she'd cut off all communication, even with Natalie.

Now three days had gone by and Remington hadn't left her apartment once. She'd stayed curled up on the couch under her favorite blanket staring absently at the television. The only time she got up was to pee and grab something to eat. She was still reeling from the pain of seeing Nathan with Jazelle. It hurt her to know that after spending all night fucking her, he left her to be with someone else. Was she not enough for him? Did she not please him the way Jazelle could? Just the thought of it made her stomach ache. How could she be so stupid to think that she'd be enough for someone like Nathan Black who'd been with more women than she cared to count?

A loud knock on Remington's door plucked her out of her sad reverie. She sat up and stared at the door, panic creeping up her spine. She had refused to answer the numerous texts and calls from Nathan and she was hoping he hadn't finally decided to show up at her door.

Remington got up and tip-toed to the door. She pressed her eye to the peephole, careful not to touch the door.

"Remington Elise English! Open this door!" Natalie shouted.

Remington frowned and snatched open the door. One look at her friend standing there, worry etched into her pretty face and Remington crumbled. Fat tears tipped her eyelids and rolled down her cheeks as she threw herself into Natalie's embrace.

Natalie hugged her tight. She didn't say a word. She just rubbed her back and allowed her to get it all out.

They stood in the doorway for a long time. Remington bawling and Natalie comforting her, until finally Remington's cries turned to light sniffles.

Natalie pulled back and stared into her friend's face. "I was worried about you. You weren't answering my texts or calls. I know you, friend. I knew you were hurt when you saw that picture."

"I was. I still am but you didn't have to come all the way out here. I just need some time and I'll be fine," Remington sniffled.

"I know but you're my best friend and you've been totally fucked over. There's no way in hell I'd let you go through this alone."

"Thanks, Nat. You really are a good friend."

"Duh," Natalie smiled and guided her and Remington inside the condo and closed the door. "I know you probably don't feel like talking or anything but we need an old-school girl's night. I'm talking wine, junk food the whole nine. We'll get into our PJs," she eyed Remington who was already in her PJs. "Okay, I'll change into *my* PJs and we'll gorge on junk food and trash men all night. How does that sound?"

Remington smiled. The first one in days. She had wanted to be alone to process her feelings but she was actually happy Natalie showed up.

"That sounds good," Remington replied doing her best to sound at least a little upbeat.

"Great! Order us a pizza. I'll go change real quick," Natalie said and headed for the guest bedroom.

Remington ordered a pepperoni and black olive pizza, grabbed chips, cookies and a couple bottles of wine and set everything up on the coffee table while Natalie changed.

Remington was sitting on the couch nibbling on a chip when Natalie enter the room.

"Oooh! You got the good shit," Natalie said and made her way over.

Natalie made a beeline for the wine and filled both glasses on the table to the brim. She handed one to Remington and took the other one with her as she sat down on the other end of the couch. She tucked her legs under her bottom and faced Remington. "So, have you heard from him?" she asked.

Remington cast her eyes down and studied her wineglass. "He's been texting and calling but I haven't answered."

"Why not? Don't you want to know what he's going to say? How he's going to explain that picture?"

"Not really. I knew who he was before I got involved with him. I was on the gossip sites just like everyone else reading about all of his sexploits. He's nothing but a player, Nat. I just wish I didn't allow myself to get caught up in him. I feel so stupid."

"You're not stupid. You fell for a guy who was not what you thought he was. You're not the first woman to be duped by a man and you won't be the last. Don't be too hard on yourself."

"That's easier said than done," Remington said then took a big swig of her wine.

"I feel you on that but I have a question. Before picture-gate, when you were describing him to me, you said he was nothing like the tabloids painted him out to be so let me play devil's advocate for a sec. What if he's *not* what the tabloids say he is? What if there's a good explanation for that picture?"

Remington took another swig of her wine, the spicy, sweet liquid going straight to her head. "What explanation could there be? That photo was taken while we were in Lake Almanor. Nat, he had another bitch in the next town over. He was going back and forth between the two of us." Anger, cold and putrid washed over Remington. "He's the absolute worst kind of man. He gets women to fall for him by pretending to be something he's not. It's fucked up," she added then downed the remaining wine in her glass.

Natalie refilled Remington's glass then said, "Look, if in fact he had you and Jazelle up there at the same time, he's a whole different kind of ass. I'm talkin 'next level. But, I still think that you should talk to him and see what he says."

"I'll pass," Remington frowned then chugged her newly filled glass until it was empty. She wipe her mouth with the back of her hand then reached for the bottle of wine. Instead of refilling her glass, she took it straight to the head.

"Alright now!" Natalie said, giving her friend an air toast. "It's finna be *that* kind of night."

"It is! And you know why?" Remington asked, her speech slurring a bit.

"Why girl?" Natalie smiled, knowing her friend was full on wine but she was indulging her because she needed it.

"Because I'm a nice fucking person. A great fucking catch. And I'm smart " –

"So smart!" Natalie added.

"And I don't deserve to be treated the way Nathan Black treated me."

"Nobody does. Especially not you," Natalie egged her on.

"I'm just so mad at myself." Remington flopped back against the couch and stared numbly at the bottle of wine in her hand. Anger and hurt bubbled deep in her belly traveling up to the base of her throat then settling like acid on the back of her tongue. She'd never been more hurt in her life. "I should have known better, Nat," Remington whispered.

Natalie set her wine glass on the table and motioned Remington over. "Come here," she said patting her lap.

Remington scooched over and laid her head in her friend's lap.

"I know you're hurting right now but it won't last forever. Nathan Black could easily just be a blip on your radar. One that you had a great time with for a short period of time -"

"A blip that deceived and hurt me like no other," Remington spat.

"Yes, but it's really just one of many life experiences. You'll learn from this, grow and move past it."

Remington wasn't so sure about that. Everything in her felt deeply for Nathan. Somehow in such a short amount of time he'd woven himself around her heart and she didn't know how she was going to untangle that mess.

An hour later, the melodic sound of Jhene 'Aiko's *A&B* was blaring throughout the apartment. Remington and Natalie, more than tipsy, were singing along.

Remington felt the lyrics to her core and she was bleeding it out, putting her feelings into every word she sang.

The doorbell sounded interrupting their mini concert.

"That's probably the pizza. I paid online," Remington sang.

"Ooh, I'll get it," Natalie sang as she headed towards the door.

Sure enough, standing on the other side was a lanky young man holding a large pizza with an amused grin on his face. "Delivery for Remington English," he said.

"I'll take that," Natalie said.

Remington slid her arm around Natalie and shoved a ten-dollar bill at the delivery guy. "Your tip," she said, the words coming out slurred.

"Thanks," he smiled. "Seems like ya'll are having a good night."

"If drinking too much wine and cursing the guy who broke your heart sounds like fun, then I guess we are. Good night, pizza guy," Remington sang then flung the door closed.

"Okay, drunkie. Let's get some food in you," Natalie laughed. She set the pizza on the coffee table then grabbed a slice for Remington and one for herself.

Remington took a bite and her eyes rolled back in her head. "This is so good," she moaned.

"It really is," Natalie said as she flopped down on the couch. She looked over at Remington, her eyes serious. "You're gonna be okay, you know that, right?"

Remington squeezed her eyes shut. "Eventually. I know..."

CHAPTER SEVENTEEN

NATHAN

Nathan fumed as he stared down at his phone. He was on The Rag's website for the umpteenth time looking at the picture of him and Jazelle saying their last goodbye in Chester. Only the headline above the picture painted a very different scene.

"*Things Heat Up with Ex-Soccer Phenom and The Supermodel!*" That's what the headline said and it couldn't be more wrong. What he and Jazelle were doing was just the opposite. The problem was that nobody in the world, looking at that picture and reading that headline, would believe that. But he didn't care about what the world thought. He only cared about what Remington thought.

And given the fact that he'd called and texted her at least twenty times with no response made him think that she believed what everyone else in the world believed.

What must she think of him? As if the picture of him with Jazelle wasn't bad enough but it was taken while he and Remington were together in Lake Almanor. She had to have put that together which probably infuriated her. She must think he's a real fuck-boy. A no-good player who couldn't care less about anyone other than himself.

"Fuck!" Nathan ground out and tossed his phone on his desk. He was used to The Rag reporting on his love life but this was different. Normally they weren't too far off on the pictures and headlines they touted even though they sensationalized things a lot. This time they were dead wrong and their post was fucking up his shit with Remington.

"Everything alright, cuz?" Jax asked as he breezed through Nathan's office door.

Leanne was on his heels, her face tense. "Sorry, Mr. Black. I would have rang you but-"

"It's alright, Leanne. I knew he was coming," Nathan said.

Leanne relaxed a bit but shot a reprimanding look at Jax who just chuckled and laid a wide, boyish grin on her. Leanne couldn't help but smile as she left the office, closing the door behind her.

"So, what's going on? You look a little tense," Jax said, studying Nathan.

"Same 'ole shit," Nathan replied, his jaw tight as he looked at his cousin.

Jax crossed his arms and raised an eyebrow as he stared back at Nathan. "Does this have anything to do with the latest blog post on The Rag's website?"

"It has everything to do with that headline, man."

Jax sat down in one of the chairs in front of Nathan's desk. "I don't see what the problem is. So you got caught on a lil getaway with your girl. So what?"

"For one, she's not my girl," Nathan damn near growled.

"She's not?" Jax raised an eyebrow at him. "Bro, you just told me about a month ago that ya'll were seeing each other. And didn't ya'll just hook up a couple of weeks ago? I know you weren't shopping for rings or anything but you *were* seeing her. Is that not the case anymore?"

"No, it's not. In fact, I didn't see Jazelle at all after you and I had that conversation in my office. It wasn't until you were talking shit at Sunday dinner that I saw her again." Nathan pointed at his cousin accusingly.

"So, this is my fault?"

Nathan pinched the bridge of his nose. "It's not your fault. You were right. I was tense as hell and I needed a release. I just hooked up with the wrong person that night is all..."

Jax cocked his head to the side and stared amusingly at his cousin. "Wrong person, huh?"

"Don't start, Jax. The point is that picture on The Rag's website is misleading."

"How? It looks pretty clear to me. Ya'll were kissing."

"It was a goodbye kiss."

"A goodbye kiss?" Jax lifted a brow in doubt.

Nathan glared at his cousin. "Yes, a goodbye kiss."

"So, ya'll went all the way to Chester for a goodbye kiss? Sorry, cuz, but you know that sounds like straight bullshit, right?"

Nathan released a heavy sigh as he stood up and

started pacing back and forth behind his desk. "I know but I'm telling you. It's not what it looks like."

"Then enlighten me," Jax said, folding his arms across his chest.

Nathan stopped pacing and looked at his cousin. "Fine. I was out at my cabin and Jazelle was blowing me up because I ghosted her. Somehow, she found out where I was and showed up in Chester and asked me to meet her there. We had breakfast, I broke things off, she understood and before we parted ways she asked for a goodbye kiss. That was it."

"Okay, I get it but why are you so mad about the headline? It shouldn't even matter."

"Because The Rag is reporting it like me and her were on some getaway trip together and we weren't."

"So?" Jax replied, still not understanding what the issue was.

"So, everyone will see that and think that it's true," Nathan explained.

"Since when do you care what everyone thinks? The Rag is always posting something about you, Nate. You never paid it any mind before."

Jax was right. The blog posts and articles never bothered him like this. He used to laugh it off or just ignore it altogether but that was before Remington. Before her he'd never cared enough about any one woman to be bothered with what the gossip sites wrote about him. If a woman had an issue with it she could push on and he'd do the same. Not this time though. He cared more than anything what Remington thought and that nagged at his gut because it meant that she meant something to him. She wasn't just a fling. All those feelings he'd been having since she showed up were making him crazy and to finally be able to act on those feelings and have her recip-rocate was like exhaling after holding his breath for too long. He wanted to be with her. Like really be with her and this post on The Rag's website may have fucked that up for good.

Nathan knew his cousin wasn't going to be thrilled that he'd hooked up with Remington but there was no other person on earth other than Momma D that he could talk to about this. Besides, he had a feeling his cousin was already hip to his attraction to her.

Nathan sat down on the edge of his desk and stared down at his black, leather Gucci dress shoes. "I don't care what everyone thinks, Jax. I care what *one* person thinks," he confessed.

"And who might that be?" Jax asked, a hint of a smile tugging at the corners of his mouth.

"Oh, you think this is funny? You know good and well who I'm talking about."

"Do I? The last woman you told me about was Jaz-elle. Are you seeing someone new, Nathan?" Jax leaned forward in his chair, rested his elbows on his knees and clasped his hands together in front of his mouth attempt-ing to hide his smile.

Nathan took in the feigned seriousness on his cousin's face and it annoyed the fuck out of him. "Do you always have to be such a dick?"

"Why am I a dick? You're the one over here pissed off and pussy-footin' around. What's really bothering you?"

Nathan signed deep and heavy. Jax was right. He needed to spit it out but man it was hard for him to ver-balize what he was feeling when he'd never felt this way about a woman before.

"You're right, man. It's just that this all so new for me.

As long as you've known me, I've never been really into a woman as far as catching feelings."

"True."

"Well, it seems that I've caught some feelings...for Remington..."

Jax was quiet for quite some time as he stared at Nathan, his face pensive.

"Say something, man!" Nathan grumbled, needing desperately to know what his cousin thought about what he'd just revealed.

"Well, I can't say I'm surprised. Remington is a beautiful woman and so smart. And kind. And talented. You've been spending an enormous amount of time with her. I could see how you could catch feelings for her. It's not like with other women who you go on a date with here and there, not really taking the time to get to know them or really caring to. You didn't really have a choice with Remington. You two were stuck together. You had to get to know her and to know her is to like her. She's an amazing young woman."

"So, you're cool with this?"

Jax shrugged. "What can I say? Ya'll are adults. Don't get me wrong, I would have preferred that you *not* fuck with her given your reputation with the ladies-"

"What the hell does that mean?"

"Oh, c'mon, Nate. You know you. You fuck women until you're bored then you move on. You don't make real connections with them-"

"Neither do you," Nathan challenged.

"We're not talking about me though. We're talking about you." Jax stood up. "Look, man, you've bagged many women and I been right there doing the same thing. So, you get no judgement from me. It's just that Remington's a good girl. She deserves to be with someone who wants to settle down one day and that's not you which is why I didn't want you getting involved with her."

Nathan shoved his hands in his pockets. "What if I tell you that it's different with her? That I really like her."

"Nate, you *like* women in general," Jax retorted.

Nathan flinched a bit at the truth in his cousin's words. For years, he ran around from woman to woman enjoying their company but making no real commitments. But things with Remington are different. She brought out feelings in him that he'd never experienced with any other woman.

"I know that, Jax. But this is different. She's different and I'm afraid that blog post is going to ruin everything."

"How serious are things with you two?"

"I took her to my cabin."

Jax's brows flew up. "You took her to Lake Almanor?"

Nathan nodded.

"Well shit, Nate! This is serious. You've never taken any woman to that cabin."

"I know which is why I'm telling you that what I have with her is different. It's real."

"Wait, when did you take her to Lake Almanor?" Jax asked.

"We were up there last week."

"Last week? When the photo of you and Jazelle was taken in the town over?" Jax asked, confusion clear on his face.

"Yeah, man. Thus, my dilemma."

Nathan watched as his cousin's face went from confused to comical as he burst out laughing.

"Fuck you, Jax," Nathan said and stood up. He moved back around his desk and dropped down heavy into his seat.

"I'm sorry, man. It's just...damn, Nate! Leave it you to you fuck this up so severely."

"Tell me about it. I have no idea how to fix this."

"Have you talked to her?"

"I called. I texted. She won't talk to me."

"Well she's clearly seen the blog post."

"No shit!" Nathan glowered. "Have you heard from her?"

"She emailed me the other day," Jax said.

Nathan leaned forward in his chair. "What'd she say?"

"She sent over the first draft of the memoir. It's really good, Nate."

"That's great," Nathan said dismissively. "Did she say anything about me?"

"Nope. She turned in the first draft of the memoir and said she was taking a few days off but that was it." Jax stood up. "Listen, maybe you should just give her some space. I'm sure she's pissed after seeing that photo. Maybe she'll reach out when she calms down."

"So, what am I supposed to do in the meantime?" Nathan asked, feeling completely helpless. A new feeling for a man who never in life pined after a woman.

"For starters, you can get your ass up so we can make it to the football game before kickoff."

"Shit! I damn near forgot about that." Nathan was so preoccupied with what to do about Remington that he'd completely forgotten that he and Jax were going to see the Rams play the Cowboys then meet Lance and Warren at a sports bar after.

"Let's go," Jax said, heading for the door.

Nathan grabbed his phone off the desk and followed his cousin out.

A week had passed and Nathan still hadn't heard from Remington. He was tempted to drive over to her place and bang on the door until she agreed to speak with him. But he tossed that idea out thinking that he would probably look like some crazy stalker and her neighbors would end up calling the police. So, instead he threw himself into his work.

He'd learned from Warren and Lance that the Cowboys were now taking a look at D'Mariyon based on his recommendation which was great news. He decided to head to College Station to tell the kid in person and hopefully finally close the deal on signing him.

Nathan pulled up to the same coffee shop he'd met D'Mariyon at before. D'Mariyon was already there seated at a table near the back when Nathan arrived. He stood upon and motioned Nathan over.

"What's up D?" Nathan greeted, extending his hand.

D'Mariyon clasped his hand and Nathan pulled him in for a half hug.

"What's up Nathan," D'Mariyon replied.

"I'm good. Came out to check on you and to give you some good news," Nathan grinned.

"Oh yeah?" D'Mariyon said.

Nathan studied D'Mariyon for a second. Something was off. The kid was usually open and friendly. Not that he was being unfriendly but he was certainly closed off. His face was tense and there was a sadness to him.

"Should we sit?" Nathan asked.

D'Mariyon sat down and Nathan followed suit.

"So, how've you been? How's your grandmother?" Nathan asked.

D'Mariyon's eyes shifted downward. "Not so good, man."

"What's going on?"

"My granny's in the hospital. She got real sick and has been in ICU for the past week." D'Mariyon's shoulders slouched forward, heavy with grief.

"Damn, man. I'm sorry to hear that. How are you holding up?"

"I've been better. It's been a little hard to focus. She's the only family I got. You know?"

Nathan nodded. He could only imagine what the kid was feeling. He would be devastated if something happened to Momma D.

"It's hard when someone close to you is in pain. You gotta stay focused though because you know that's what she'd want."

"Yeah, I guess."

"Well, if it's any constellation I have some good news regarding the Cowboys," Nathan said, hoping to spark some kid of joy in the kid but D'Mariyon's head remained low as he stared blankly at the table.

"I talked to my contacts on the team and The Cowboys are taking a serious look at you based on my recommendation.

D'Mariyon let out a heavy sigh and shook his head.

Not the reaction Nathan expected.

"D'Mariyon, is there anything else going on? I know you're upset about your granny and I was hoping the good news about the Cowboys would bring you a little bit of joy."

"My bad, Nate. The Cowboys giving me a look is great it's just…"

"What? You worried about the combine? Don't even

sweat that. I think I can get The Cowboys to sign you. We have to finalize your deal with N. Black Sports Agency first but I'm sure we'll come to an agreement you'll be good with," Nathan smiled.

D'Mariyon looked at him, that grim look still on his face. "You're a good dude, Nathan. I know that signing with you would be the best thing for me and I had every intention of doing that but..."

Nathan was filled with dread as he stared at D'Mariyon. Whatever the kid was about to say wasn't going to be good.

"What happened?" Nathan asked.

"The hospital bills for my granny. I can't afford to pay them. She's in a private facility now but they sayin' they'll have to move her to one of the county hospitals which are shit. More people die than survive at those places. I couldn't send my granny there."

"What did you do, D'Mariyon?" Nathan asked, concern wrinkling his brow.

"Sy McIntyre from McIntyre and Welch has been trying to sign me but I never really entertained him because I knew I wanted to sign with you."

Nathan knew there was more to it and it was going to be bad – very bad. Not just for him but for D'Mariyon as well. Sy McIntyre was a money hungry snake. "What did you do?"

"Sy offered to pay for my granny's medical bills if I signed with his agency..."

Nathan didn't need to hear more. This was bad. NCAA rules forbade college athletes from accepting money of any kind. Sy knew that yet he chose to put the kid's future in jeopardy. Sure, it wouldn't matter if no one found out but if someone did, things would get ugly real quick.

Nathan scrubbed his hand down his face and let out a heavy sigh. "I'm really sorry about your granny but you know that accepting money can get you in a lot of trouble, right. You could be barred from participating in the draft."

"I know but it's my granny, man. What was I supposed to do?"

"You should have called me and let me know what was going on. Taking money from Sy was not the way the go."

"Well, what can I do about it now? I signed with Sy yesterday and he said he'll have my granny's hospital bills paid by the end of the week"

"I guess there's nothing to do," Nathan said in resignation. "I wish things worked out differently. My agency would have looked out for you way better than Sy McIntyre."

D'Mariyon said nothing but Nathan could see the disappointment and sadness in the kid.

"I should get going but you watch your back with Sy. He's not known for doing what's best for his clients. Don't allow him to get you into anything you're not comfortable with, okay."

"I won't."

"Alright. Take care, kid," Nathan said then stood to leave.

"Hey Nate," D'Mariyon called.

"What's up?"

"I'm really sorry."

"Yeah, me too," Nathan replied then turned and left.

How things got so fucked so quickly Nathan would never know. First, he lost Remington now he lost the one kid he really wanted to sign. What else could go wrong?

Nathan boarded his jet with a heavy head and heart. For the first in his life he felt completely out of control of his life.

CHAPTER EIGHTEEN

REMINGTON

It had been over a week since Remington ventured out of her apartment. Natalie had stayed and kept her company for a few days which really helped her through the initial pain of being hurt so badly by Nathan. She still couldn't believe the audacity of him to have her at his cabin and another woman on standby in the town over. Like, who does that? It's cruel and of all the things she'd ever thought about Nathan Black, cruelty wasn't one of them. Yeah, they got off to a rocky start but each day that passed revealed a side to him that was caring and genuine. She wasn't naïve. She knew he had a healthy sex life but all the tabloid stories about his affairs never reported on any doggish behavior towards the women he dealt with. And on top of that, all his past lovers, as many as there were, all gushed about him.

Remington was so confused. Could it be that Nathan really was a big 'ole dog and that those other women were fine with it as long as they got to be with him? Well, she wasn't like that. Sharing her man or turning a blind eye to his Casanova ways was not something she'd ever do. She just wished she hadn't fallen so hard for Nathan. She was in love with him and it sucked because the only thing she had now was a gaping hole in her chest and the man she loved was to blame.

Remington wanted to hideaway in her apartment a bit longer but she knew she couldn't do that. She had a life to tend to. Goals she wanted to reach. One of which centered on the memoir. Things had to go perfectly with this book. The launch of her writing career depended on it.

She'd been going back and forth via email on re-writes with, Angela Anderson, the editor Jax assigned to work with her on the memoir. Things were going well with Angela but Remington missed collaborating in person so she scheduled a meeting with her at Black Publishing House to go over the last set of notes Angela had sent over.

Not sure if she was ready to face the world yet but for-cing herself to do so anyway, Remington showered and dressed simply in a pair of skinny jeans and a flowy top. She put some leave-in conditioner and Jamaican castor oil in her wet locks and headed to the office.

It took her no time to get to the office and she was sur-prised to see Jax waiting at her cubicle when she arrived. He was leaning casually against the cubicle wall staring down at his phone.

"Hey, Jax," Remington said as she moved past him into her cubicle and set her bag down.

Jax looked up with a smile. "There she is. My favorite memoir writer has returned to the office. How've you been?"

"I've been alright. Just working with Angela on the edits. In fact, that's why I came in today. I'm meeting with her so we can go over the last set of notes she sent me."

"I'm aware which is why I'm hanging out by your desk. I wanted to chat with you before your meeting."

"Okay."

"Let's go to my office," Jax suggested.

Remington followed Jax to his office and sat down in one of the chairs in front of his desk. She watched as Jax moved behind his desk but didn't sit down. Instead, he stood behind his chair, planted his hands on the back of it and stared at her.

"I haven't seen you since Sunday dinner at Momma D's house. How've you been?" He asked.

"I've been good," Remington replied. *Clearly a lie.*

"Good. I'm glad you're working so well with Angela. She's a great editor."

"Yeah, she's awesome."

"So, I know I've already said this but you did a phenomenal job on the memoir. I know Nathan was and is probably still opposed to it but I think he'll change his tune when he reads it. You really did him justice. You showed a side to him that not a lot of people get to see."

Remington's chest tightened at the mention of Nathan. She held her face in neutral, determined not to show any emotion. Guess she didn't do a good enough job because Jax's eyes narrowed in concern.

"You alright?" He asked.

"Yeah, I'm fine," she lied again.

Jax cocked his head to the side and studied her for a few seconds. "I know I'm your boss but you can talk to me if something's bothering you."

Remington swallowed hard as tears stung the back of her eyes. Spilling the beans to Jax about her unprofessional relationship with his cousin was not a good idea. But then again, he probably already knew. He and Nathan were super close. And while she was fond of Jax and was very comfortable with him there was no way she was about to spill her guts to him about Nathan.

"No pressure," Jax smiled when she didn't say anything. "I just want you to know that I'm here if you wanna talk."

"Thanks," Remington said, giving him a weak smile.

"So, have you talked to Nathan this week?" Jax asked.

"Nope. I already have everything I need for the memoir. I figured I didn't need to intrude on him any longer."

"Right..." Jax nodded. "Well, I talked to him the other day and he wasn't doing so well. Things fell through with a kid he was trying to sign."

Remington's brows flew up. "D'Mariyon Taylor?"

"Yeah, you know him?"

Remington nodded. "I met him when I flew out to Dallas with Nathan. D'Mariyon's a good kid. Nathan really wanted to sign him."

"Yeah, well, it didn't happen," Jax said.

Jax looked as disappointed as Remington felt. And as mad as she was at Nathan, Remington still thought he was a great sports agent and would take good care of D'Mariyon and his career.

"Do you know what happened?" Remington asked.

"Apparently, D'Mariyon's grandmother got sick and the hospital bills were outrageous and they couldn't afford them. The hospital was threatening to have his grandmother moved to another hospital that wasn't as good since he couldn't pay. Another sports agency swooped in and offered to pay for the medical bills if he signed with them and he did."

"Really? I don't know much about the draft but I do know that student athletes aren't allowed to take money or gifts. Won't he get in trouble if the league or the NCAA finds out?"

"He'll be in big trouble."

"Is there nothing Nathan can do?" Remington asked, already wracking her brain for a solution.

"He's looking into it. The good thing is that no money has passed hands yet and D'Mariyon has a thirty day out in the contract he signed so if something is done quickly, he may be able to save his future."

Remington's cell phone buzzed. Angela was messaging asking if she was ready to meet. "I've gotta head to my meeting with Angela but I really hope things work out with D'Mariyon."

Remington swung by her Dad's office after her meeting with Angela. She wanted to talk to him about what happened with D'Mariyon to see if he could offer up some advice.

"Hey Daddy," Remington smiled as she walked into her father's office.

He smiled warmly and stood up as she came in. "Hey there, baby girl. Come give your old man a hug," he said opening his arms.

Remington flew into them and hugged him tight. She

was truly a daddy's girl. Growing up, one hug from her father would set everything right in her life. She wished that would work now. She wished a simple hug from her father could fill the empty cavern in her chest caused by Nathan but as it stood right now, nothing was able to temper the pain in her chest.

"What brings you by?" Her father asked, leaning back and staring down at her.

"I wanted to talk to you about something. A friend of mine is in a bit of a dilemma and I wanted to see if you could offer some advice."

"Well come on over and sit down and tell me what's going on. I'll do what I can to help."

Remington sat down and wasted no time telling her father about the situation with D'Mariyon. While her father agreed that what he did was very problematic he did offer her a way out for the kid.

He told her that if she could get a charity organization to pay for the grandmother's hospital bills before Sy McIntyre did, it would absolve D'Mariyon from having to move forward with his contract and ensure he wouldn't get in trouble for accepting money.

CHAPTER NINETEEN

NATHAN

Nathan tied his boat to the cleat at the end of the pier leading to his cabin. After fucking things up so royally with Remington and losing the opportunity to sign D'Mariyon, he'd disappeared to his cabin for some alone time. He'd left his cell phone at the cabin and spent the past few days out on the water. Things were peaceful on the water. No gossip sites, no woman problems, no work bullshit. It was just him, his fishing gear and lots of beer.

Nathan's cell phone was buzzing like crazy when he got back to the cabin. He grabbed it off the counter and checked his messages. Leanne had called him a dozen times saying that D'Mariyon Taylor was trying to get in touch with him. Jax had sent a few messages and even Momma D called once.

He was most curious about the messages from Leanne regarding D'Mariyon so he called him first. "D'Mariyon, it's Nathan Black," he said as soon as the kid answered. "You've been trying to reach me?"

"Yeah, man. Good news. I ended my contract with McIntyre and Welsh."

"What? How? What about your granny's hospital bills?" Nathan asked.

"It's all taken care of. Your girl Remington came through for the kid."

"She did? How?"

"She found a charity to pay for my granny's hospital bills and they paid it before Sy could so I was able to get out of the contract with no issue. He was pissed but what could he do?"

Nathan was floored. Remington refused to answer his calls or texts yet she helped D'Mariyon knowing that helping the kid would also help him. And how did she even find out what was going on?

"D'Mariyon, this is really good news," Nathan told him.

"I know, right? So, what's up on signing with your agency, man?"

"Shit, let me get with my team to start putting together some contract options. Once that's done, I'll fly back out to College Station so we can meet and go over them. I want us both to be happy with the contract. This is a partnership."

"That sounds good, Nate. I look forward to meeting with you. Look, I gotta jet but tell Remington thanks again. She's a good lady, man. If you ain't tappin 'that send her this young boy's way," he laughed.

Nathan frowned, not finding it funny at all. "Back up young'n she's already taken."

"Oh, my bad. You better be glad cuz she's fine and smart. That's the kind of girl I'm looking to have on my team."

"Well look somewhere else cuz she's mine," Nathan let him know in no uncertain terms.

"I see you, Nate. I'mma quit messin' with you about Remington," D'Mariyon laughed.

"Yeah, you better," Nathan half joked. "I'll be in touch, D," Nathan said then hung up.

Nathan dialed Leanne right away.

"Hi, Mr. Black. How can I help you?" Leanne answered on the first ring.

"I just got off a call with D'Mariyon Taylor. I need you to get with legal and have them start working on a couple contract options for him. They should have all of my notes already on what I want."

"I'll get right on it. Are you coming back to the city today?"

"I need to. Get in touch with Captain Matt and have him fly the jet out to scoop me up."

"Sure thing. I'll text you and let you know what time he'll have the jet there."

"Thanks, Leanne."

Nathan landed in Burbank a little after seven and went straight to Momma D's house. Things were looking up professionally but his love life was still in the shitter and he needed some sound advice from the one person that was dearer to him than anyone.

"Momma D," Nathan called as he entered the house.

Momma D's voice floated down the hallway. "In the kitchen."

Nathan made his way to the kitchen and found Momma D at the stove cooking up some gumbo. The rich and earthy spices of the roux infiltrated his nostrils, swarmed around his brain and settled in his belly. Nathan loved his grandmother's gumbo.

Momma D looked up from the pot and smiled warmly at him. "Well aren't you a sight. I didn't expect to see you until Sunday but this is a nice surprise."

Nathan planted a soft kiss on her cheek. "Yeah, I just got back in town and wanted to stop by and check on you. That gumbo spells amazing by the way."

Momma D studied him for a minute her eagle eyes assessing him. "Well as you can see, I'm fine. You on the other hand, don't look so good."

Nathan sighed, his broad shoulders rising and falling heavily. "I'm not, Momma D. I'm not."

"Well, come on and sit down and tell me what's going on."

Nathan slid into one of the chairs at the island counter. The last thing he ever thought he would be doing was talking to his grandmother about a woman.

Momma D stood on the other side of the counter waiting for him to speak but Nathan wasn't even sure where to begin. He was sure his grandmother knew a little bit about his dealings with the opposite sex but she never said anything to him about it.

"Momma D, I messed up," Nathan started, casting his eyes down and shaking his head.

"What'd you do?"

"I hurt someone that I really care about. I didn't mean to and really it's all just a misunderstanding but the optics are so bad that she won't even talk to me so I can't even explain."

"Is this someone Remington?" Momma D asked but seemly already knew the answer.

Nathan nodded. "I never thought I would fall for someone this hard. Especially not her. We did nothing but butt heads from the moment we met."

"Yeah but you two have a certain chemistry. Reminds me of Deborah Kerr and Cary Grant in *An Affair to Remember*." I noticed it that Sunday ya'll were here for dinner. How annoyed you were that she was here yet you couldn't take your eyes off her. I knew my grandbaby was smitten even if he didn't," she chuckled.

Momma D was right. The chemistry between him and Remington was next level. It was hot, angry, wild and all consuming. Nathan needed this woman like he needed his next breath. She had woven her way into his very soul and he couldn't, *he wouldn't* spend his life without her.

"Not sure how much that chemistry can help me now," Nathan lamented.

"Look, son, I don't need to know all the details of what happened but if you say it's a misunderstanding, I believe you. I know you're not innocent when it comes to women but you're respectable. I know cuz I raised you to be that way. You're just gon' have to convince Remington that what happened is not what it seems."

"Easier said than done. She won't talk to me. I've called and texted so many times."

"Sometimes a woman needs space to process her feelings. I'm sure she's hurting right now. She'll talk to you when she's ready."

Momma D reached over and patted Nathan on the hand and while it was comforting, Nathan still felt like shit.

"It's been two weeks. I don't know how much longer I can wait. I know I've never brought any women around you but that's because I've never felt anything beyond physical attraction for them but it's not like that with Remington. I want *everything* from her, Momma D. Is that crazy?"

Momma D let out a small laugh. "It's not crazy, son. It's love."

"What up, boy?" Jax said, strolling into Nathan's office the next day.

Nathan looked up from the contract he was reviewing and scowled at his cousin. "Did you bully your way past Leanne again?"

"Nope. She's not even at her desk," Jax smirked.

"Oh, so you snuck in while she stepped away," Nathan accused.

"I didn't sneak in nowhere. I walked my ass in here like I always do. Now stop being an ass."

"Whatever, man. What do you want?" Nathan grumbled. He was busy and didn't have time to deal with his cousin's shenanigans.

"I came to bring you this," Jax said and slapped an invitation on his desk.

"What's this?" Nathan asked, reaching for it.

"It's your invite to this year's gala for Black Publishing."

Nathan slid the invite back across his desk at Jax. "I think I'll skip this year. I got a lot going on with work. No time for parties."

"You sure?"

"Yeah, why?"

"I don't know. Remington will be there and I figured you'd want to see her," Jax threw out casually.

Nathan set the contract on his desk giving his cousin his full attention. He still hadn't seen or heard from Remington and he was itching for any kind of contact with her. Any opportunity to explain what happened and get her back in his life.

"Hell yeah I want to see her. I haven't talked to her in weeks."

"Well come to the gala next weekend and you'll have your chance."

"Guess I'll be there then," Nathan said, motioning for Jax to slide the invitation back to him.

"Yeah, that's what I thought," Jax laughed and pushed the invite back across the desk.

"Question for ya," Nathan said.

"What's up?"

"Did you tell Remington about what was going on with D'Mariyon?"

Jax shifted his eyes away guiltily. "I may have. Why?"

"Because she got a charity organization to pay for his grandmother's hospital bills which allowed him to get out of his contract with McIntyre and Welsh. He wants to go with my agency. We're working on contract options right now."

"That's good news. Congrats, Nate. I know you really wanted to sign that kid."

"I really did and thanks to Remington I get to."

"Yeah, she's a smart cookie to think of that charity option. And the fact that she's pissed at you yet she still helped you out..."

Nathan shot his cousin a look. "You been talking to her?" He growled.

"I haven't talked to her since she came into the office a week ago to work on edits for your memoir which by the way I emailed you a copy this morning. Did you get it?"

Nathan had seen the email from Jax but he didn't open it. The memoir was the last thing on his mind right now.

"I saw it. Haven't opened it yet," Nathan replied.

"You need to read it, Nate. It's really good."

"I'll get to it when I have time," Nathan muttered and grabbed the contract documents off his desk and started reviewing them again.

"So, does that mean you're done with me?" Jax grinned.

"Yep," Nathan replied without looking up.

Jax chuckled and shook his head. "Alright, cuz. Just make sure you read that damn memoir."

Nathan said nothing and he didn't look up. Even though he knew ignoring Jax did nothing to thwart his cousin, he ignored him anyway.

"I'll holla," Jax said and made his way out of the office.

As soon as Jax was gone Nathan tossed the contract onto his desk and pulled up his email. He found the email from Jax and opened the PDF doc attached to it. His mouth dropped at the first line. It personified who he was to the core and everything he wanted people to know about him.

The true measure of man can only be counted by his actions and every move I've made in my life and career have been dictated by the values instilled in me by a Grandmother who took me in and raised me like her own when my parents died.

Nathan was intrigued and continued reading. Before he knew it an entire hour had passed and he was still reading. He didn't know how Remington managed to capture the essence of who he was in words but she did. And the entire thing was written from his perspective which blew his mind. If he had an inkling of writing talent he would have written this memoir exactly as she had. He felt like a world class ass for giving her such a hard time about it.

At the gala he would explain what really happened in Chester with Jazelle, thank her for what she did for D'Mariyon and give her much deserved props for what she did with the memoir.

CHAPTER TWENTY

REMINGTON

Remington stared at her reflection. The floor length black gown she wore was stunning. The sweetheart neckline showcased the swell of her breast perfectly, the cinched waist made her look curvier then normal and the crystal embellishment throughout the dress gave her that high fashion, glamorous look. Her hair was blown straight and pulled tight in a low ponytail that hung over her shoulder and her makeup was an earthy color palate that highlighted her natural skin tone. Remington knew she looked great. If only she felt as good on the inside as she looked on the outside.

"Well shit, girl! You look amazing," Natalie complimented as she came to stand behind her.

Remington stared at her friend through the mirror and smiled. "Thanks. You look gorgeous yourself. That deep v-neck is gonna be a problem. You bout to have boys drooling all over the place."

Natalie was wearing a stunning red maxi dress with a plunging neckline that stopped just above her navel revealing the creamy fawn colored flesh between her size c-cup boobies. The top of the dress was held up by two thin straps and was covered in intricate gold leafs.

"You know I had to come with it, right? I wasn't blessed with these jugs for nothing," Natalie winked and ran her fingers across her ample boobs.

Remington laughed. She was happy that Natalie was there. The minute she got the gala invite from Jax she'd phoned Natalie and told her that she had to come down and be her date. Natalie agreed with no hesitation and showed up a day ago.

"You're nuts, Nat. Let's go. I bet the car's here."

Remington's cell phone buzzed. It was the car service letting her know their driver was outside.

Remington sat quietly staring out the window as the car drove to the hotel where the gala was being held. Her stomach was in knots. She knew Nathan would be there and she still wasn't ready to face him. The man had literally torn her heart from her chest leaving an abyss of searing pain that tore at her insides every time she thought of him. How one person could have such a profound impact on another was beyond her. All she knew was the connection she shared with Nathan went beyond everything rational to her. Deep in her bones she felt that he was meant for her and her for him which was why his betrayal hurt so much.

Natalie pressed a hand to her shoulder. "You alright?"

Desperate to keep her emotions in check, Remington stiffened her shoulders, swallowed hard then turned to her friend hoping her tragic feelings wouldn't show in her eyes. "I'm good. Looking forward to tonight actually. I've been cooped up too long. I need a night out."

Natalie narrowed her gaze. "It's okay to still be sad about what happened, you know."

"I know," Remington whispered.

"And it's okay to be nervous about seeing Nathan for the first time in weeks."

"I've just been sort of hoping he won't show up tonight. These past few weeks have been so hard for me. And it's crazy because I go back and forth between not wanting to see him and wanting to see him so badly. But then my mind goes back to that picture of him and Jazelle Banks and I get so furious. I sit around thinking about how fast and hard I fell for him and I wonder if I'll ever have that deep connection with anyone else."

Natalie grabbed Remington's hand and squeezed. "I'm sorry that you're hurting, friend. But, I have to say this."

Remington leaned back and fixed her gazed on Natalie. She had a feeling she wasn't going to like what she had to say.

"Maybe you're not supposed to find it with someone else. Maybe you've already found your person. Maybe that's why it hurts so badly."

"So, my person is supposed to lie to me and leave me in bed while he goes off and fucks other women?" Remington hurled.

"That's not what I'm saying and you know it. It's just..."

"What?"

"You haven't spoken to him at all, Remi. You have no idea what his side of the story is."

"Do I need to know his story? What can he tell me that that picture didn't show me?" Remington pulled her hand back from Natalie's and folded it in her lap.

"Don't be mad. It just hurts me to see you so sad and if there is some explanation for that picture that will make things right between you two, wouldn't you want to know?"

"Of course I would," Remington sighed. She looked at her friend who was staring back at her with love etched in concern. She knew that Natalie only wanted the best for her and she appreciated the support but her heart had a crater-sized wound so she really didn't care to hear what Nathan had to say.

The car pulled up to the front of the hotel and the driver came around and opened the door for Remington to get out.

"Enjoy your evening, ma'am," he smiled.

Remington smiled back then joined Natalie who was already out of the car and waiting for her. They made their way into the hotel and were directed to the large ballroom. Remington could hear music and chatter floating down the hall as they neared the ballroom. Butterflies, mean and agitated, thundered around her stomach. She was nervous about seeing Nathan for the first time in weeks.

"I got you, friend," Natalie leaned over and whispered as they walked through the ballroom door.

Remington smiled, happy to have her BFF at her side.

The ballroom was modeled in the Gothic architecture of old Flemish buildings. It was enormous with a beautifully arched ceiling lined in gold trimmings, the walls were made up of lovely archways and dozens of gold chandeliers hung throughout the space. Tables were situated strategically around the room, there were several bars, a DJ and waiters were roaming around offering extravagant hors d'oeuvres to guests.

"Well this is some fancy shit," Natalie said as her eyes roamed around the room.

"I would expect nothing less from Jaxson Black," Remington smiled. "Let's get a drink."

As they made their way over to one of the many bars, several co-workers stopped Remington to say hi and compliment her on her dress and overall look. She made an effort to be upbeat and conversational. Just because she was not in a good headspace didn't mean she needed to unleash her dour mood on others.

"Can we get two vodka tonics please," Natalie ordered when they finally got to the bar.

Remington leaned her back against the bar and stared out into the space, her eyes roving purposefully around the room.

"You spot him yet?" Natalie asked.

Remington cocked an eye at her. "Who?"

"You know who. You been checking for him since we walked through that door."

Remington let out an exasperated sigh. "If he's here I haven't seen him yet."

"Your drinks, ladies," the bartender said, placing their drinks on the counter.

"Thanks," Natalie said grabbing them. She handed one to Remington. "Let's not stand around looking for trouble. C'mon, we're hitting the dance floor."

The dance floor was in the middle of the room and was fairly packed. Remington followed Natalie to a spot on the outer edges.

The DJ was playing all the hits and they danced straight through three songs. Remington had chilled out a bit and was enjoying her drink and the music. Nathan was far from her mind and for a little while she was at peace.

"Who knew you could move like that, English," Jax joked from behind her.

Remington whipped around, flushed and a little overheated from all the dancing. "Hey Jax," she smiled.

"Hey yourself. Glad to see you're having a good time."

"I am," she nodded. "The DJ is great."

Natalie cleared her throat and nudged Remington in the back.

"Jax, this is my best friend, Natalie Gutierrez. Natalie, this is my boss, Jaxson Black," Remington introduced the two of them.

Jax extended his hand. "Very nice to meet you, Natalie."

"Likewise," Natalie smiled, her eyes roving appreciatively over Jax.

"You live in Burbank?" He asked.

"No, San Francisco."

"Nice. I get out that way from time to time for business."

Natalie leaned forward causing the sides of her breast to peek out a bit more from her dress. "Hopefully you can come out for a pleasure trip soon."

Remington nearly choked on her vodka tonic. Natalie was an incurable flirt but Jax was her boss and she in no way wanted to be a part of any entanglement with him and Natalie. One of them embroiled in drama with the Black cousins was enough.

Remington stared hard at her friend trying to silently signal for her stop with all the flirting but Natalie wasn't paying her any mind. "Ladies room," Remington blurted out then turned to Jax. "We'll catch up with you later, Jax."

Remington grabbed Natalie by the wrist and damn near dragged her off the dance floor.

"I was just being friendly," Natalie laughed.

"Yeah, well your kind of friendly's gonna leave me in an awkward position with my boss."

"Oh, calm down. I was just flirting. You have enough work drama going on. I for sure ain't about to add to it."

"Thank God for that," Remington snapped and headed towards the bathroom door.

"It's been a good night so far," Natalie commented as they were leaving the bathroom.

"Yeah but we've only been here about an hour," Remington added.

"Still, no sign of you know who *and* you're having fun. The night's off to a great start."

"Yeah, I guess..." Remington started but the next word died on her tongue as she looked towards the entrance to the ballroom and saw Nathan walking in with none other than Jazelle Banks.

It was like someone had ripped through her chest and took a vice grip to her heart. Pain, tight and unbearable took hold of her, paralyzing her.

"Remi?" Natalie called. "What's wrong?" She followed her friend's gaze. "Shit! C'mon."

Natalie grabbed Remington by the hand and dragged her back down the hall past the bathroom to a secluded enclosure at the end of the hallway. She pressed Remington to the wall and braced her hands on her shoulders.

"Breathe. Just breathe," she soothed.

Remington wanted to breathe but she couldn't seem to find her breath. Seeing Nathan after all these weeks and with Jazelle Banks, tore her to shreds. She tried to find her breath, her voice, but her tongue seemed too heavy to move and her mouth too dry. "I can't..." she sputtered.

"Look at me. I know you're upset and hurting and probably in shock at the nerve of that ass showing up with Jazelle Banks but you're strong, Remington. And I got your back. Just take a beat and breathe."

Remington gulped in air, closed her eyes and pressed her head against the wall. The back of her eyes stung like crazy and she felt as if she would vomit. How could he show up with Jazelle? He had to know she would be there. Did he really just give zero fucks about her? Hurt slowly transformed into rage and angry tears tipped her eyelids and rolled down her cheeks.

Natalie gently wiped them away. "Don't cry, doll. I was rooting for him but all that's out the window now. He doesn't deserve your tears."

"You're right. He doesn't. But these aren't pathetic tears of sadness. These are angry tears. The fucking audacity of him to show up with her. He had to know I would be here. He clearly doesn't give a damn about me so that's it. I refuse to waste another second in pain because of him."

Remington smoothed her hands over her hair and squared her shoulders. "How do I look? Is my make-up still good?"

Natalie traced her finger under Remington's right eye clearing away the little bit of eyeliner that had run. "You're gorgeous," she smiled.

"Let's go," Remington barked. She stepped around Natalie and started down the hall.

Natalie jogged after her. "Wait, are we leaving?"

"Hell no! We're going back in to eat, drink, dance and enjoy the party." Remington said, her face stark with determination.

"Alright, alright, alright," Natalie sang as she locked in step with her. "That's my girl."

Head held high, Remington marched into the ballroom and made a beeline for the bar. She ordered two shots of tequila and two vodka tonics.

"Oh yes, it's about to be poppin'," Natalie grinned.

Remington grabbed her shot and lifted it in the air. "Fuck men," she spit.

Natalie clinked her glass against Remington's. "Hear, hear."

They both slammed their shot, grabbed their drinks and headed for the dance floor.

CHAPTER TWENTY ONE

NATHAN

For the first time in his life, Nathan was nervous. Like legitimately nervous and he didn't know what to do with that feeling. Confidence was something he had in abundance and it served him when going into new, odd or highly charged situations and it definitely never failed him when it came to dealing with women. Yet, he knew the unease he was feeling now was because of Remington. He was about to see her for the first time in weeks and he wasn't sure how she would receive him. He wanted desperately to talk to her and explain what happened. He needed her to know that he didn't play her, that he respected her and that there was no other woman in the entire world that he wanted to be with other than her.

"Well hello there, friend," Jazelle called from behind Nathan as he was entering the hotel.

Nathan turned to see Jazelle walking towards him looking stunning in a glimmering, silver evening gown. Her presence was a surprise seeing how she didn't know his cousin. "Hello, Jazelle," Nathan greeted her.

"Surprised to see me?" She grinned.

"Yes, actually. What are you doing here?" Nathan asked, the question coming out a bit gruff.

Jazelle's smile only widened. "I was invited." She held up the same invite that Jax had given him.

"I didn't know you were acquainted with my cousin."

"I'm not. I was just as surprised as you that I got an invite but I thought, why not. He's your cousin, we've never met but I heard he's a real looker and a great lay."

Nathan shook his head. "Geez, Jazelle."

"What? You and I are just friends now. There's no conflict there." She moved past him then stopped. "Come, let's walk in together."

Thoughts of Remington immediately came to mind. "Not sure that's a good idea."

"Oh, come on. You said we could be friends. Friends attend parties together. Now come on," Jazelle coaxed and waved Nathan over.

Against his better judgement Nathan joined Jazelle and they headed to the ballroom. Jazelle slipped her arm through Nathan's just as they neared the entrance.

Nathan tensed, worried that Remington would see them. His eyes searched the room looking for her but he didn't see her.

"Well this is a nice little shindig," Jazelle commented. "Let's get a drink." She tugged Nathan towards the closest bar.

"You made it," Jax greeted as he walked up.

"What's up, Jax," Nathan said.

The two men clapped hands and pulled each other in for a half-hug.

"Nice turn out this year. This is a great space and it looks like everybody's having a good time," Nathan observed.

"Yeah, the party planner did an amazing job. I like this venue much better than last year's," Nathan said.

Jazelle who had been standing by quietly ogling Jax, cleared her throat.

Both Nathan and Jax looked at her.

"Jax, this is Jazelle Banks, who you've never met but invited anyway," Nathan added that last bit as a dig.

Jax let out a quiet chuckle then fixed his gaze on Jazelle. His smile widened as his eyes roamed appreciatively over her. "There's a lot of people here that I've never met, Nathan. But they're important people and it's my pleasure having them here. It's great publicity for Black Publishing." He turned to Jazelle. "It's very nice to finally meet you." Jax said, extending his hand to her.

Jazelle unleashed a wicked smile on him as she lifted her arm and took his hand. "Oh, the pleasure is all mine. You and I are definitely going to get to know each other."

"I'd like that," Jax said and wrapped her arm around his. "How 'bout we get a drink."

"Jax," Nathan called before he and Jazelle moved towards the bar. "Let me holla' at you real quick."

Jax bowed his head and whispered into Jazelle's ear. "Give me a minute." He disentangled himself from Jazelle.

The men moved a few feet away from Jazelle for privacy.

"You're cool with this, right?" Jax asked.

"Yeah, man. Me and Jazelle are way over. We're just friends now."

"Cool. So what's up?"

"Did Remington show up tonight? Have you seen her?" Nathan asked.

Jax slid his hands in his pockets. "This is a nice evening, Nate. You're not going to make a scene are you?"

Nathan frowned at his cousin. "I think you know me better than that. I just want to know if she's here because if she's not, I'm leaving."

"Why would you leave?"

"It's been too long and I really need to resolve this shit between us. If she's not here I'm going to her place."

"So you're just gonna show up at her house and what? Bang on her door until she lets you in?" Jax asked.

"I guess so if it'll get her to talk to me."

Nathan scrubbed his hand down his face. All he wanted was for his cousin to tell him if Remington was there. He wasn't in the mood for Jax's shenanigans.

"And if she is here, what are you going to do?"

"I'll pull her aside and talk to her. Look man, I won't make a scene in here. I respect you too much for that."

"I know you do but, Nate, I've never seen you this messed up over a woman. I want you to work things out with her and I know I dangled the fact that she would be here in your face in order to get you to come tonight but seeing you now, maybe that wasn't such a good idea."

"Like I said, I won't make a scene. I'm just gonna ask her to step outside and talk to me. If she refuses I'll leave it alone for now."

Jax slanted his head at his cousin as he considered his words. "Fine. She's here. Been here for about an hour although I haven't seen her in a while."

Nathan's face lit with anticipation.

Jax held up a hand. "Be gentle and patient with her, Nate. She may not be ready to talk to you and if she is, you're gonna have to do a helluva lot of explaining about that picture."

"I know."

Jax held out his hand and Nathan clapped it and pulled him in for a hug. "Stay close to Jazelle. I really don't want Remington seeing her. Things could get heated."

"Oh, don't worry about that. I'll keep Jazelle occupied."

"Good. Can I ask you something though?"

"What's up?"

"Why'd you invite her?" Nathan asked.

Jax slipped his hands into this pockets. "I have my reasons."

"Jax," Nathan frowned.

"Don't worry. I know what I'm doing. Go find Remington," Jax said then headed back over to Jazelle.

Nathan shook his head as he watched his cousin and Jazelle make their way to the bar.

Nathan was on a mission as he weaved his way through the groups of people gathered around the ballroom. He'd checked all of the six bars and most of the tables and hadn't found Remington. He was headed to the far end of the ballroom when he finally spotted her. His heart skipped on sight. She was on the far outer edge of the dance floor, drink in hand, eyes closed, swaying seductively to the music. The dress she wore clung to her in all the right places and revealed just enough skin to set his blood on fire. Nathan made a beeline for her. Just as he was within reach a pretty Latina with a beautiful face and defiant eyes stepped in front of him. Nathan's brow bunched as he stared at her. She looked familiar but he wasn't sure where he'd seen her before.

"Excuse me," he said, attempting to move around her.

She moved with him blocking his path.

"I'm sorry, do I know you?" He asked an agitated edge to his voice.

"No, but I know you," came her sassy reply.

Nathan frowned. "I'm sorry but I really need to speak to someone." He attempted to go around her again but she moved blocking his path again.

"Look lady, I don't have time for this. I don't know you and there's someone that I really need to speak to and you're blocking my path."

The woman popped out her hip, placed her hand against it and braced up to him. "Yeah, that's on purpose. The name's Natalie Gutierrez and the person you're try-ing to get to is my best friend and she doesn't want speak to you."

Nathan's eyes widened in recognition. He knew she looked familiar. It was the woman in the pictures he'd seen at Remington's place. She must have come down to attend the gala with Remington. He didn't want drama of any kind, especially not with Remington's best friend.

Nathan stretched his hand out to Natalie. "Hi, Natalie. It's very nice to meet you."

Natalie cocked her brow and stared at his hand. "Wish I could say the same."

Nathan dropped his hand and his head at the same time. Remington's best friend. What she must think of him.

"You should go. I have nothing to say to you."

Nathan looked up to see Remington standing next to

her friend. Her eyes were hard as glass as she glared at him. Something in him buckled at the way she looked at him. So much hurt and anger.

"Remington, please, if you'll just give me a few minutes-"

"Nah, I'm good. In fact, why don't you go spend those few minutes with Jazelle Banks? You two came together, right?" She spat.

Nathan pinched the bridge of his nose. She was not going to make this easy but he knew that. He also knew that he didn't want to make a scene at Jax's party. His voice was low, gentle, when he said, "Remington, baby-girl, please. Just come outside and talk to me. I'll explain everything."

Remington braced up to him, her nostrils flared, her chest heaving. "I don't care to hear anything from you. You're nothing but a lying, no good, fuckboy, Nathan Black. What you did was despicable. I can't believe I thought you were a decent guy. I should have known better. I knew who you were. You run through women like underwear. You don't care about the women you get involved with. All you care about is getting your dick wet. You don't give a fuck about the destruction you leave in your wake."

Her words were a viper's sting straight to Nathan's heart. "Remington-"

"No!" she croaked and stepped back. "Stay away from me. I don't ever want to speak to you again."

Nathan watched as she turned and hurried towards the exit. He made a move to go after her but Natalie placed a hand on his arm.

There was a modicum of sympathy in her eyes when she said, "Just let her go. You've hurt her enough."

Nathan's heart sank into his belly. Maybe he *should* let her go. Maybe this was his karma for all the women he messed around with and moved on from when he'd tired of them. To lose the one woman on earth he loved and would ever love was one helluva punishment. One that he just couldn't stand for. He had to make this right. He needed to talk to her. He needed her to understand that he wasn't what she said he was. He needed her to know that he cared desperately for her. He needed her to know that he loved her.

"I can't do that," Nathan whispered, the words tortured sounds.

"After what you did to her, it shouldn't be hard."

He stared at Natalie. "I know what you must think of me. I have the worst reputation for jumping from woman to woman but I've never mistreated a woman in my entire life. And I've never messed around with more than one woman at a time."

Natalie pursed her lips in disbelief.

"Okay maybe back in my college days but I was young and dumb back then. Look, I know you saw that photograph of me and Jazelle Banks but I promise you, it's not what it looked like."

"It looked like you were kissing her outside of a restaurant. Is that *not* what you were doing?" Natalie asked, eyeing him skeptically.

"We did kiss-"

"See! Boy bye," Natalie barked and turned to leave.

Nathan grabbed her arm. "Please just hear me out."

Natalie's face scrunched and her mouth twisted as she stared down at his hand on her arm.

"Please," Nathan pleaded.

Natalie narrowed her eyes at him. "You got five

minutes. Over here." She motioned for him to follow her off the dance floor.

Nathan followed her over to one of the empty tables. Natalie didn't sit. She turned on him, folded her arms across her chest and stared expectantly at him.

"It's really all a big misunderstanding. I met Jazelle in Chester to officially let her know that we were over. We met, talked and parted as friends."

"Okay, if that's true, why the kiss?"

"It was a goodbye kiss. Jazelle asked for one last good-bye kiss and I obliged."

Natalie shook her head disappointedly at him.

"I know. Not my best move. But I promise you that's all it was."

"So, you didn't have Jazelle holed up in Chester while you had my girl at your cabin?"

"No, that's ridiculous. I would never do something like that."

Natalie chewed her bottom lip as she considered what he said.

"Natalie, if it helps you get a clearer picture on things, I have to let you know that I'm in love with your friend. Love is something new for me. I've spent most of my life jumping from woman to woman never spending enough time with just one to even broker a chance at love. I didn't want to be in love...not until I met Remington. And even then I pushed against it but no matter how hard I tried to not fall in lover with her, it happened anyway. I just want a chance to explain that picture to her and tell her how I feel."

Nathan could see Natalie's resolve breaking as a semblance of a smile tugged at the corners of her mouth.

"Fine! You've won me over. I believe you. Let's go get

your girl." She grabbed Nathan by the hand and pulled him toward the ballroom exit.

CHAPTER
TWENTY TWO

REMINGTON

The entire world was spinning precariously in front of Remington's eyes as she fled the ballroom and Nathan. She knew she'd eventually run into him at the gala and she wanted to be tough. She wanted to hurt him the way he'd hurt her but even hurling those terrible insults at him hadn't dulled the pain in her chest. In fact, she was hurting even more now. The tears she'd been holding back broke through and came crashing down like a tsunami as soon as she entered the ladies room. Luckily, it was empty but it wouldn't have mattered if it wasn't. There was no way she could stop the outpouring of agony she felt.

Remington stood at the sink, head bowed, quietly sobbing. Her knuckles were pale from how hard she was gripping the counter.

After a few minutes her sobs settled into quiet sniffles.

"It can't be all *that* bad," a soft, honeyed voice said from behind her.

Remington turned to find Jazelle Banks standing before her. *Fucking great! I'm sure I look a hot mess and here she is looking like a goddamned rock star.* Remington thought. She quickly straightened and wiped at her eyes and cheeks. "Sorry if I'm in the way. Do you need the sink?" She asked.

Jazelle moved closer to her. "No, actually I came to find you."

"Me? Why?" Remington stiffened as she stared at Jazelle. Was this a confrontation? Was Jazelle gonna twist the knife that Nathan had already stabbed her with?

Jazelle braced a slender hip against the counter and fixed her eyes on Remington. "I want to talk to you about Nathan-"

"Yeah, no," Remington said then made a move towards the door.

Jazelle grabbed her arm. "Please. I'm not here to instigate or cause trouble. Nathan's a friend and he's actually a really good guy and since you won't speak to him I figured I'd give it a go at explaining that photo that's got you so pissed off."

"What do you know about me and Nathan?"

"I know a lot of things, honey," Jazelle smirked.

Remington folded her arms across her chest. "Say what you have to say so I can get out of here."

"You're a feisty little thing, aren't you?"

Remington's mouth tightened to a flat line as she stared defiantly at Jazelle.

Jazelle didn't seem bothered at all. The corners of her

mouth tipped in amusement. "That picture of me and Nathan in Chester is not at all what it seems. Yes, we kissed but it was a goodbye kiss. He and I are over. Hell, we were over before I flew out to Chester. In fact, I forced him to meet me at that restaurant. And when he did he officially broke things off."

"So ya'll *were* still together?"

"Not really. I mean he hadn't officially broke it off but we hadn't been in contact in a while so I knew something was going on with him." She looked Remington up and down. "Apparently that something was you. And when we met that morning in Chester and he told me about you I couldn't even be mad at him. You know why?"

Remington shook her head.

"Because he's in love with you. I could see it all over him the moment he sat down. And it amazed me because, honey, you did what no other woman has been able to do."

"And what's that?" Remington asked.

"You got Nathan Black, self-proclaimed bachelor for life, to fall in love with you."

Remington was floored. This was not what she expected Jazelle to say. "Did he tell you that? That he loved me."

"Not exactly. He wasn't really sure what he was feeling. Men never do at first. He was quite confused actually. What he did know was that he wanted you like he'd never wanted any other woman before. And not just physically. He told me he wanted you around all the time which is nuts because for all the fun me and Nathan had, he could only stand to be around *me* for a few hours."

"Wow, this is a lot," Remington confessed. The pain in her chest was still there but it was a lot less agonizing.

Nathan hadn't played her and according to Jazelle, he was in love with her. Little bubbles of excitement bounced around her belly.

Jazelle faced the mirror and checked herself out moving her head from side to side and pursing her lips. She eyed Remington through the mirror. "Yeah, well ,what are you going to do now that you know the truth?"

"I'm going to go find Nathan," Remington replied already headed for the door.

"Hold it!" Jazelle called out. "Let's get you cleaned up first. You've got tear stains streaking those lovely cheekbones."

Remington laughed and moved back over the sink. She let Jazelle clean her face and reapply her make-up. "Why are you being so nice to me? I basically stole your man."

Jazelle cocked an amused brow at her. "Honey, if he was truly mine, he couldn't be stolen. Besides, I low key like you. I can tell you've got gumption. And us women need to stick together. I know what the tabloids say about me but contrary to the exaggerated stories and all out lies they print, I *do* get along with other women. I don't make it a habit of competing with other women even though I work in one of *the* most shallow and competitive industries. A lot of us models are actually really good friends. We support each other."

Jazelle leaned back, taking in her handiwork. "Perfect!"

Remington looked at herself in the mirror. She looked better than she did when she showed up. "Wow! You're masterful with that makeup bag."

A light chuckle floated up Jazelle's throat. "Thanks. Now get out here."

Remington headed for the exit. Before leaving she

turned to Jazelle. "Thank you."

Jazelle smiled warmly and nodded.

Remington made her way towards the ballroom to find Nathan. She barely made it down the hall when she spotted him with Natalie. Their backs were to her and they were talking. She walked up behind them.

"Looking for me?"

They spun around simultaneously.

"Yes. Are you okay?" Natalie asked pulling Remington in for a hug.

"I'm fine. I need to talk to Nathan."

Natalie stared her in the eyes. "I think that's a good idea. I'll just head back to the ballroom. All these shenanigans got me hungry. Shoot me a text if you need me," she winked then turned to Nathan. "Don't fuck this up."

"I got you," Nathan grinned.

"You better," Natalie said as she backed away.

Remington and Nathan watched her until she disappeared into the ballroom.

Remington shifted her gaze towards Nathan. The way he was looking at her sent her heart, which seemed to barely beat these past few weeks, into a full court sprint. He was looking at her as if she was a blue moon, something so rare that he didn't dare blink for fear of missing it.

"Remington-"

"I talked to Jazelle. She told me everything. I know you didn't secretly have her in Chester while I was at your cabin."

Nathan nodded. "I would never do that. Not to you or any woman."

It was Remington's turn to nod.

"Look, I know I handled this shit all wrong. I should

have told you about Jazelle. The text messages she sent me. The fact that I hadn't officially broken things off with her. I shouldn't have snuck off to go meet her at that restaurant. It was a stupid decision. I don't know why I did it." Nathan scrubbed his hand down his face then shook his head. "That's bullshit. I do know why. I was scared. I didn't know how you would react. I was nervous I would lose you when we just barely got together."

Nathan moved in close, lifting a hand as if he wanted to caress her face but he dropped it as if he was unsure. "You had me, *have me* feeling things I've never felt about any woman in my entire life. I didn't know how to handle it. The shit was confusing and oddly enough Jazelle helped me realize what I guess I knew deep down but couldn't fathom."

Remington watched the flashes of emotion cross Nathan's face. Confusion. Embarrassment. Realization. Love. She reached her hand out and placed her palm over his heart. Her eyes locked with his, staring into their dark depths and she saw her entire future.

Nathan latched onto her gaze and stared as he lifted his own hand and gently ran his knuckles down her cheek then trailed his fingers along her neck, his thumb gliding back and forth across the thrumming pulse at its base.

"I'm in love with you, Remington English," he started, his voice raw with emotion. "I think I knew it that first moment you walked into my office and I said hello and you said bathroom."

A soft chuckle trickled from Remington's throat.

"I can't say I know much about love but I know that you're the only woman who makes my heart beat fast and slow at the same damn time. It's a foreign feeling for me but it's one I've come accustomed to. One I can't see myself doing without...*ever.*"

Remington smiled a heavy-lidded sensuous smile, the kind that spoke of steamy nights in the dark, the slide of skin against skin but more importantly, that of futures, children and family.

Her heartbeat galloped as she tilted her face up bringing her mouth just inches from his. "I'm in love with you too," she breathed out.

Nathan inhaled sharply, grabbed her face and kissed her over and over again. Hot, wet, deep kisses that left Remington dizzy and breathless.

After having his fill, Nathan smiled down at her. His fingers played possessively at the soft hairs at the nape of her neck. "Thank you what you did for D'Mariyon. What you did helped me sign him. I'll be forever grateful to you for that."

"You're very welcome."

"I read the memoir, by the way."

Remington's breath hitched as her nerves kicked up sending a firestorm of butterflies in her belly. Even now after reconciling and being wrapped in his embrace she was nervous about how he received what she wrote.

"You know I wasn't a fan of it. Pushed back and thwarted you at every turn. I was determined to hate it but what you wrote was exactly me. That memoir encapsulates everything I am and everything I wish people would see and focus on if they have to be all up in my business," he added with a laugh.

Remington let out a huge sigh of relief. "You mean that? You really liked?"

"I loved it. Just about as much as I love you," Nathan said then pressed his lips to hers sealing his words with a kiss.

274

EPILOGUE

One year later

N athan sat at his desk looking over the files of prospective athlete's he wanted to sign. Business at N. Black Sports Agency was booming. His reputation for putting his athlete's first had spread across the globe and his agency was named Top New Sports Agency of the Year. He no longer had to chase after top athletes. They were all clamoring to be represented by his agency and it felt damn good to see his dream of creating a sports agency that put the interests of the athlete before profits doing so well.

His memior had also tuned out to be a mega hit. It topped every bestseller list and sold millions around the world. Once everyone found out that Remington was the ghostwriter, her career took off like lightening. She snagged a lucrative writing deal with Black Publishing and started her own blog that boasted over half a million subscribers.

Not only was everything going great professionally but Nathan's relationship with Remington had flourished over the past year. Things hadn't been perfect but they stuck together and worked through every issue as a team. Nathan was more in love with her than ever.

Nathan continued flipping through the files and was

jotting down notes on one of the hottest basketball players in the game when the doors to his office burst open. Startled, he looked up to see Remington barreling through the doors her pretty face marred in a deep frown. She was charging towards him holding her cell phone up.

"Have you seen this? Another headline on The Rag's website," she raged.

Nathan stood up, his face scrunching in confusion. "Baby girl, what are you talking about?"

Remington stopped in front of his desk, her feet planted apart in a battle stance. She thrust her phone forward. "There's a picture of you on The Rag's website hugged up with some woman-"

"Whoa, whoa, whoa," Nathan said as he made his way around his desk. "That's bullshit. You know I haven't been with anyone else."

"Is it? How do I know you're not hooking up with random women when you fly out to those scouting trips all over the country? For all I know you have a different woman in every city."

Nathan was thoroughly confused. He hadn't been with anyone else since that first time he and Remington made love. She knew that. He knew she knew that so he had no idea what was driving this craziness. He reached for her but she reared back.

"Don't touch me. I want an explanation, Nathan."

"I really don't know what to tell you. You know I haven't been with anyone but you. Hell, you accompany me on most of my scouting trips. When the hell would I have time to cheat on you?"

"You were able to sneak off and meet Jazelle..." Remington hit back, her eyes accusing.

Nathan scrubbed his hand down his face. Did she really

just bring that up? They'd been together for a year now but had kept their romance low-key and off the radar and from time to time the gossip sites ran a salacious, untrue story about him and some woman. The women in their stories were usually business associates that they labeled as love interests. Remington knew the truth and those headlines never bothered her so why was she so worked up about this new headline?

"Are you really bringing up the Jazelle thing? That was ages ago and besides we both know nothing happened there. Remington, you know I love you. I would never do anything to jeopardize what we have."

"Really? Well, explain this," Remington snapped and shoved her phone in his face.

Frustrated and in a panic, Nathan grabbed the phone to see what lies The Rag had put on their site that had his woman so heated.

Nathan Black Scores His Last Goal As He Announces His Engagement to Writer Remington English

"Got 'cha!" Remington laughed.

Nathan pressed his lips together in mock anger before pulling her to him. "You little ass. That shit is not funny."

"*I* thought it was very funny. You should have seen your face," she said and lifted up on her toes and kissed him on the chin. "I thought you were going to burst a blood vessel."

"I just might have. The thought of you being that upset at me took me back to last year at the gala when I tried to talk to you. I don't want to relive that mess."

Remington smiled sheepishly at him.

"You're terrible, woman. You know that? I could spank you right now."

Remington's whiskey eyes darkened and need roughened her voice. "It *was* a dirty, little trick I played on you. I probably should be punished."

Nathan grinned, sexy and wicked as he locked his hands onto her hips, lifted her up and fixed her legs around his waist. He kissed her hard and deep as he walked them to his desk and planted her on top of it. She was wearing a cute little blue dress that stopped mid-thigh and gave him easy access to her honeypot. As he ravished her mouth with biting kisses his hands ran all over her body before sliding under the fluttery hem of her dress. His fingers trailed softly up her thigh to brush lightly against the silky fabric of her panties.

Remington let out a low moan and opened her legs wider urging him on.

"You wear this dress for me?" Nathan breathed out.

Remington nodded. "Easy access."

Nathan grinned as he slid his fingers under her panties and curled them inside her, pressing hard against her front wall. "Damn, you're wet," he murmured.

Remington nearly came undone as a wave of juices poured from her center coating his fingers. Her sex was throbbing with need. "Nathan," his name floated from her lips filling the room.

"You ready for your punishment?" he asked sliding her off the desk and spinning her around.

Remington nodded. It was all she could do. Her tongue was thick with need and her throat was dry, all the moisture in her body seemed to be pooling between her legs and running down her thighs.

"Palms on the desk," Nathan ordered.

Remington did as he said and jutted her bottom out and leaned forward. She was more than ready to be *pun-*

ished by him.

"Goddamn that ass looks good," Nathan groaned and hooked his fingers in her panties and shoved them down her legs.

Remington watched him over her shoulder as he quickly undid his pants and pulled out his dick. It was thick, heavy and throbbing. As if she couldn't get any wetter, a whole new gush of honey flowed out of her. "Nathan, please," she begged.

He ran his hand up and down his shaft as he stared at her round ass lifted high in the air, her swollen lips glistening. He tapped the tip of his dick against her left cheek then the right before sliding it down the crease of her ass to her pussy.

Remington moaned and wiggled against him. She was aching to feel him inside of her but he didn't enter her. Instead, he unleashed a hard smack to her right cheek. Remington bucked forward as pain and pleasure ripped through her body. She bit down on her arm and groaned.

"Such a naughty girl," Nathan growled and proceeded to smack each cheek in turn over and over again while stroking his dick.

Remington's ass was on fire and she loved every blistering sting so much that she was on the verge of begging him to fuck her when he impaled her, thrusting his dick so deep she felt his thick tip tap her womb.

"Fuck!" she cried as her body locked and stiffened around him.

Nathan gripped her hips and pounded into her, his thighs slapping against the back of hers. He raised one hand and with each punching thrust he slapped her ass over and over again, going from cheek to cheek.

"Oh my God, harder. Please," Remington begged.

Nathan slammed into her, smacking her harder and faster. "Come for me, baby," he hissed.

Remington fell apart at his words and came hard all over his thick rod, her legs shaking and pussy clenching him like a vise.

"Goddamn, baby! That's what I'm talkin 'bout. Come all over that dick," Nathan goaded as he slammed into her one last time before erupting with his own climax.

Remington collapsed on the desk, laying helpless as she tried to catch her breath.

Nathan pressed soft kisses along the back of her neck before righting himself then gently pulling her up by the shoulders and turning her to face him. "God, I love you and I cannot wait to make you my wife." he whispered.

Remington threw her arms around his neck crushing her breasts against his chest and her mouth to his. She never imagined that her first writing assignment would lead her to the man she was going to spend the rest of her life with but she was so happy it did.

THANKS YA'LL!

The idea for Remington and Nathan's story came to me in the shower. It was the scene of the two of them hugged up on the deck overlooking the lake at Nathan's cabin. It was such an enchanting vision of them standing against the backdrop of a beautiful lake with the sun beaming down casting a magical glow over them. They seemed so content. So in love. Just the picture of them made me want to explore thier story. To discover how they got to that moment on the deck overlooking the lake.

The minute I started writing this story, I knew this was going to be a fun journey. Nathan Black is raw and real and represents different facets of men I know and have known. He's such an interesting, difficult, charming and sexy character. And his family unit was so important to this story. I really enjoyed writing scenes with him and Jax and him and Momma D.

Remington is my every woman character. She's smart, gorgeous, ambitious, steadfast, and just a wonderful human being. Her love of fast cars was so fun to write and her relationship with bestie, Natalie, was just errrthang!

Anyway, I really hope you enjoyed Remington and Nathan's story. Thank you so much for indulging me and spending some time getting lost in this little world I created.

If you feel so inclined, please head over to Amazon and leave a review. Reviews are so important for authors. Especially, Indie Authors as they help us connect with readers, craft and improve our writing, spread the word to other readers and really help us with building community.

I love chopping it up with fellow writers, creators and readers. Supporting each other is so important. Hit me up on Instagram @AuthorRowdyRooksy.

For updates on upcoming books, events and etc. check out my website at ww.authorrowdyrooksy.com.

Thanks again for allowing me to entertain you for a bit!

OTHER BOOKS BY ROWDY ROOKSY

Turned Out: A Collection of Erotic Shorts

Dare: A Bradford Academy Novel

ABOUT THE AUTHOR

Rowdy Rooksy

 Rowdy Rooksy is a writer, filmmaker and podcaster who has a love for all things creative. She graduated from college with a degree in International Business but her love for storytelling was too strong to deny so she made the exciting leap into screenwriting and filmmaking. Rowdy has been recognized several times for her screenplays and short films and the natural next step was to venture into writing books and become an author. She loves to read and write erotica, contemporary romance, sci-fi/fantasy and YA.

Made in the USA
Columbia, SC
09 December 2024

48437022R00161